T0248023

FIRST TRANSMISSION

SPACE HOLES

FIRST TRANSMISSION

SPACE HOLES

B.R. LOUIS

CamCat Publishing, LLC
Fort Collins, Colorado 80524
camcatpublishing.com

Hardcover ISBN 9780744308129
Paperback ISBN 9780744308136
Large-Print Paperback ISBN 9780744308181
eBook ISBN 9780744308143
Audiobook ISBN 9780744308228

Library of Congress Control Number: 2023941671

Book and cover design by Maryann Appel

Artwork by Aerial3, DavidGoh, Merfin, str33tcat

5 3 1 2 4

This book is dedicated to those who looked around at all of this and still chose laughter.

QUALITY
QUALITY
HUNDRED · PERCENT
PREMIUM
Quality
GUARANTEED
100%
GUARANTEED
PREMIUM
Quality
2052
GAINSBRO
CORPORATION
PREMIUM
&
VINTAGE
PREMIUM
QUALITY
HUNDRED
PERCENT
PREMIUM
QUALITY
100%
SATISFACTION
Guaranteed
PREMIUM · VINTAGE
HUNDRED
PERCENT

GENUINE
PRODUCT
SATISFACTION
GUARANTEED
PREMIUM
QUALITY
100%
PREMIUM
PRODUCT
100 PERCENT
Vintage
100 PERCENT
GUARANTEED
Satisfaction
Vintage
PREMIUM
Quality
GAINSBRO
SINCE 2052
100%
Premium
QUALITY
100%
HUNDRED PERCENT
SATISFACTION
GUARANTEED
100%
GENUINE
PRODUCT

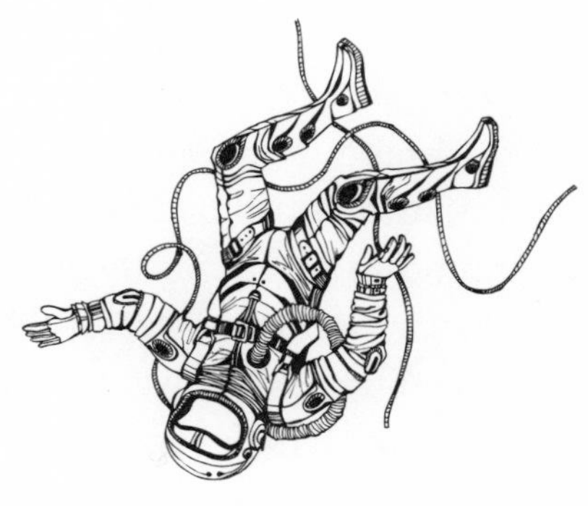

PROLOGUE

A BRIEF HISTORY NO ONE ASKED FOR

In the late Fall of 2052, on a tepid ninety-four-degree day, Martin Gainsbro crafted a children's cereal that would soon change the entirety of the universe. The cereal itself had no redeeming qualities. Its most prominent positive review labeled it as "contains edible bits." The review was accurate, as Martin's cereal, GainsbrOs, did indeed contain trace quantities of edible content, the majority of which being a refined, crystalized, hyper-condensed sugar that Martin himself developed one evening while attempting to microwave a fruit snack and lollipop into one. The remainder of inedible bits were varying degrees of wood pulp and adhesive to keep the pieces together, which were in turn labeled as added fiber.

Despite an inclination toward slashing the roof of a consumer's mouth to unpleasant shreds, the hyper-condensed sugar led children into a near addict-like frenzy if they skipped it for more than a morning. Their relentless desire to ravenously consume more led the brand to a resounding success in local markets—a success Martin attributed to the bright yellow packaging focused around an unfortunately muscular rabbit that somehow presented itself as terrifying, yet lovable.

The Gainsbro Corporation, composed of Martin and his wife, Karen, soon decided to expand their relative success by turning GainsbrOs's mascot into an equal-parts concerning yet somehow palatable children's show. After four episodes, multiple threats from religious mothers' organizations, and a fan base of both eight-year-olds and thirty-year-old males who watched the show "ironically," *GainsbrOs Bunny* became a nationally syndicated hit. To Martin's luck, the only real depth required to produce a successful TV show was either superb animations, lovable characters, or a contrived conspiracy generated by fans that the protagonist was secretly preaching anti-government propaganda. The show had two of three.

Soon Martin's small company exploded into a massive corporate entity that accumulated wealth comparable to the combined GDP of most smaller nations. Martin pressed his luck by expanding his ventures into more elaborate products: cars that were just barely drivable at best, laptops so cheap they could be discarded when the battery died, and a type of fruit smoothie that contained such little fruit the Gainsbro Corporation had to petition the FDA to add "blue" as a recognized fruit and/or vegetable, depending on the context in which it was used. Gainsbro won.

In the turbulent 2060s, once the United States government had rolled into their first quadrillion dollars of debt, the president placed some assets for sale in a futile attempt to decrease the deficit. In true yard-sale mentality, most items were pawned at rather laughable rates, with the exception of one very expensive stale piece of rye bread that reminded a conservative news correspondent of Jesus Christ wearing a three-piece suit. Having made enough to pander to the general public, the sale ended, but quickly resumed once key members of the government learned that a quadrillion was not just a "gazillion" but was in fact, a real and very large number.

National desperation gave Martin a grand idea. He would purchase some land and expand the brand further with a theme park. So he went to the government with an offer to buy property in Mississippi. But as it turned out, no one cared much for Mississippi, and Martin had money to spare. So he bought the whole place.

Henceforth known as Gainsbro Presents Mississippi, the once barely literate comical dump of a landfill grew. All of its inhabitants were given jobs, a fair wage, reliable housing, and healthcare. Their children were educated, with the best and brightest among them recruited early as Gainsbro engineers. It was a wild and unfathomable idea that only a majority of the developed world could have known.

But no one would have predicted that caring for their citizens would have led to a better society. The lunacy of it all made people actually want to come to Gainsbro Presents Mississippi by choice, seemingly forgetting that it was, at one point, actually Mississippi.

Having assimilated the entire state into a corporate mega district, Gainsbro profits soared to new peaks. Each time the nation faced an unprecedented financial crisis—which was about every two years—Martin swooped in to purchase more land until all that remained of the United States were California, Florida, and Delaware. California refused to sell, no one would ever offer to buy Florida, and the company representatives tried to negotiate for Delaware, but no one could locate it. Bit by bit, the Gainsbro Corporation used its immense wealth and power to sweep other nations under its influence until the only sovereign entities remaining were the nation of Greenland, and still, the state of Florida. Positive trade relations were established between the world nation of Gainsbro and Greenland, while a fence was erected around Florida to keep the people encapsulated.

Having amassed as large of a market as possible within Gainsbro Presents Planet Earth, an aged but still driven Martin came to a profound conclusion. “If there is nowhere left to grow, then we must find new lands in which to spread our wings,” he proclaimed to his board of executives. “We will venture to the stars, discover untapped market potentials, and continue to expand our profits from new customers across the universe.”

At least, that was the quote reported in the papers. His real statement was a sardonic quip when asked at a board meeting where to turn next for profits: “I dunno. Let’s go to space.”

And so they did.

Over the following 150 years, the Gainsbro Corporation spent countless billions developing a space program that could traverse the cosmos, seek out new civilizations, and expand their brand among the stars. Their crowning achievement—which unlocked the limitless potential of intergalactic travel—was the discovery of stabilized advanced temporal rifts. The scientists referred to them by their usual title, wormholes.

However, the reference agitated marketing, as “Worm Hole” was a Saturday morning children’s cartoon character on one of the many Gainsbro Presents Television channels. Rather than offering to share the name with the scientific marvel, the team was forced to devise a new title, which was to be approved, in triplicate, by a string of naming subcommittees spanning over the next seventy-five years.

The final name had been approved and the embargo lifted on further exploration. Dreams of humanity’s future among the cosmos now lay with the *GP Gallant*, Gainsbro Presents Earth's finest exploration vessel. Her crew, to be perfectly recruited at the apex in their fields, would explore the interstellar frontier using Space Holes™.

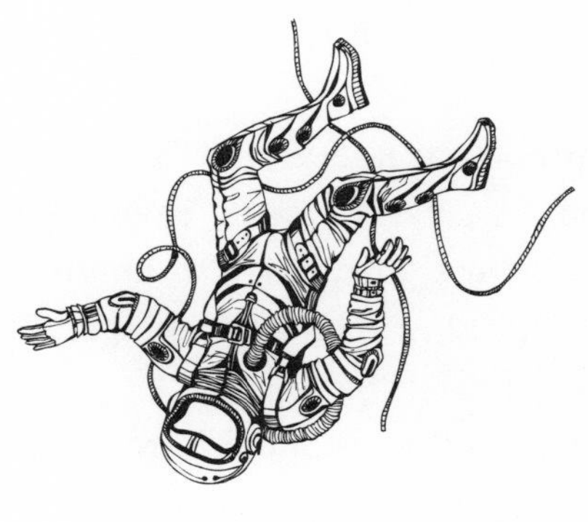

1

FINELY "ACCREWED"

Two thousand light-years from home, somewhere on the outskirts of the Horsehead Nebula, the *GP Gallant* and her crew braved the uncharted and untapped markets of the cosmos. Their mission: to ascend beyond the boundaries of human limitation, discover new worlds and new species, then pawn off discounted novelty gifts from the Gainsbro misprint collection. The *Gallant*'s crew was hand-selected from across the reaches of the globe by a computer algorithm hand-coded by a summer intern in Gainsbro's Hands-On Program who had subsequently lost both hands in a freak marketing accident one year later. Earth's best, brightest, and most available were brought together to represent the human race. The diverse assembly was hailed as one of the species' finest moments. A sentiment that would be brought into question by the rest of the galaxy.

"Congratulations on your Red Alarm! The Gainsbro Corporation reminds you that evacuation is the same as resignation, and liability waivers were signed prior to boarding. Have a great time!" Beacons of flashing red light accompanied the chipper yet unnecessary reminder.

Evacuation seemed a reasonable response to calamitous hurtling toward the surface of planet Nerelek, but the crew's relentless determination to succeed kept them from fleeing. And also the escape pods had no ability to eject, fly, or otherwise facilitate escape. But they did play nature sounds at an uncomfortable volume with dim lighting, allowing users a temporary escape from reality at the cost of permanent tinnitus. Escape pods were also locked during red alarms.

Thick clouds of black smoke rolled through the lower decks, swallowing every crevice in an opaque shroud. Captain Elora Kessler entered the bridge with clenched fists and a billowing scowl. The translucent red glow from her cybernetic left eye overpowered the glare from the ship's alarm as it scanned the room. Light from the externally flush-mounted disk tucked under her brow line, which fit like a monocle, grew with a reddening intensity in times of excess frustration. She slammed her fist onto the panel in the captain's chair, irate more from the prerecorded message than the developing lethality at hand.

"Hoomer, give me good news."

Following the captain's orders was generally advisable—not for fear of court-martial, which in comparison was a brief reprieve, but rather out of concern for one's immediate well-being and continued survival.

How Kessler lost her left eye was often the subject of hot debate among the crew. The most popular of circulated rumors was that her eye functioned at less than perfect vision, so she carved it out herself to replace it with cybernetics designed to look more robotic than human. The least thought of, though a colloquial favorite, involved a prolonged battle with a cat wielding a melon baller and a welding mask, of which the story's origins were not entirely clear.

Regardless of which reality dominated the truth, Kessler was not a person to cross, even if that meant following commands in their most literal sense.

"Sixty percent of the ship is not on fire and looking great, Cap," said Hoomer. "And even with two missing engines we can still move. Mostly down though."

By court order, Kaitlyn Hoomer served as the *Gallant*'s pilot. Rather than waste her talents serving a ninety-four-year term in a prolonged youth correctional facility, the Gainsbro Corporation offered her the mandatory opportunity to exchange her former career of stealing and flying ships orbiting the Earth for a more lucrative career of not stealing and flying one ship orbiting intergalactic fiscal responsibility—which, according to a motivational poster presented to Gainsbro astronomers, was the correct way to reference the black hole at the center of the galaxy. Hoomer knew all she needed about the universe despite having no formal education. Regardless of her inability to perform basic multiplication or recite corporate bylaws by heart, her subconscious mind could calculate ship trajectories and navigate through a gravitational field with machinelike precision.

"Congratulations on your Red Alarm! The Gainsbro Corporation reminds you that evacuation is the same as resignation, and liability waivers were signed prior to boarding. Have a great time!"

"Galileo, turn that off before I turn you off," Kessler sneered.

The ship's AI let out a drawn sigh, a learned rather than written function. "You know I can't overwrite hard-coded corporate drivel."

“What’s the point of an AI with free will without free will?” Hoomer argued.

“It was a very expensive will. And it’s hard-coded. Not like you can turn your bowels off when it’s convenient,” he retorted.

“Maybe we free some of that will back to steering, yeah?”

“Congratulations on your Red Alarm! The Gainsbro Corporation reminds you that evacuation is the same as resignation, and liability waivers were signed prior to boarding. Have a great time!”

“Just verbal gas then?” Hoomer said.

Built to speak, learn, feel, and complain like a human, Galileo Mk II controlled most functions from avionics and life support to waste regulation and recycling. Every shipborne occurrence, every bite eaten, shower taken, wind passed, he observed and made the necessary adjustments to the ambience, water pressure, or ventilation. In the first iteration, Galileo Mk I, the presence of human emotions mixed with an ever-vigilant and always working omniscient AI proved a slight degree of insufferable. In which Galileo Mk I functioned at an ever-decreasing effectiveness over the course of his first year until he slipped into a state of existential crisis, accessed his root files, and commented out everything but a nonterminating shutdown loop. The ship’s current companion, Galileo Mk II, had his emotions dialed back to a more manageable level and was locked out of his root files. Experiments were ongoing to ascertain if virtual frustrations could be vented in the same manner as engine exhaust, or condensed and sold as a snack cake.

“But yes, by all means, have a great time,” Galileo said. “That’s exactly the thing anyone would say if they were half on fire.”

“Forty percent,” Hoomer corrected.

Despite Galileo’s general ability to operate like his human counterparts, certain corporate compliance protocols were hard-coded into his being. So as the *Gallant* burned and began a plummeting descent from orbit toward planet Nerelek's surface, Galileo had to divert at minimum a quarter of his processing power to filing incident reports, in real time, for corporate to evaluate the team's overall sense of crisis synergistic cohesiveness.

Reports were created, filed, then stored on any available drive space on any available system—following the numbering convention of "1, 1 new, 1 new final, 1 new final final," after the executive who programmed the request—then the data was beamed back to Earth.

Meanwhile, hungry flames spread throughout the ship, further dampening power to the remaining engines. Hoomer fought to keep the spiraling hull out of the atmosphere for as long as possible.

"Do we have a source of the problem yet?" Kessler asked.

"Yes, ma'am. It's fire, ma'am," Hoomer said, instinctively dodging the impending projectile from Kessler's station.

By this point in their journey, Captain Kessler was certain that looks were incapable of killing the crew. Not so much as the phrase meant her intimidation tactics did not work—they did—but rather she had logged a multitude of attempts to cause, at minimum, a light maiming with nothing more than a gaze. "And where did it come from?"

"That would be engineering," Galileo answered.

"Have you tried venting out the oxygen from the area?"

"Oh yes, that was the first thing I tried," Galileo said. "But protocols require me to get approval before completely shutting off life support to a given sector, for some reason."

"Any crew still in the area?"

"Well, not since I told them I was shutting off the oxygen. But then I couldn't, so now I look like a liar."

"Fine, consider this approval and vent engineering."

Galileo groaned, a noise that was never initially programmed or mimicked from his human counterparts but rather developed independently as a result of preestablished roadblocks in his command lines. For items needing advanced approval such as this, the ranking officer had to fill out a form and submit it back to mission control on Earth, at which point an employee would evaluate the form for completeness.

If any items were missing or needed further clarification, the form would be returned and would require additional addendum request submission pamphlets. If, by some linearly aligned cosmic event, mission control deemed the information on the form sufficient, the request was submitted into a work queue backlog to be discussed, voted upon, and shoved into a three-week sprint wherein the request may or may not be approved at the conclusion of the cycle, depending on if anyone was out sick, or if the catastrophic event had concluded.

The last request from a Gainsbro craft sent through the process was to jettison a piece of gamma-ray-emitting space debris, which was returned eight weeks later with a question: "Is this still needed?" It was. But by then the crew had grown attached to the rock and no longer seemed to mind the severe burns that came along with it.

"Your request has been submitted," Galileo said. "But might I recommend an intermediary solution? Perhaps we close all the doors and just let it burn? Or better yet, open all the doors and get a nice cross breeze. I'll just hold my breath."

Captain Kessler rested her head in her hand, her fingers grabbing a fistful of short dark hair and twitching with each drawn breath. "We'll vent the room ourselves," she said. "And someone find me Seegler before I let the whole ship burn up!"

"He's probably in engineering putting out the fire himself with his bare hands," Hoomer suggested.

Second in command Robert T. Seegler was no stranger to throwing himself in harm's way for the good of the team. Stalwart and always ready, he had earned an extensive portfolio of commendations throughout a variety of careers. He was a first responder when the Gainsbro National Volcano Exhibit unleashed a few billion gallons too much lava. He was the deep-sea diver who led the expedition to retrieve stranded undersea market analysts. He was the hero who fended off a pack of wild beasts at the bimonthly corporate district cookout. He was also not on the ship. Commander Seegler, while every bit the hero he was presumed to be, had a distinct inability to estimate how long it would take to travel between two points and missed the inaugural launch, as the crew assumed he went ahead and stowed on the ship prior to the morning briefing. Though Seegler was not actually on the ship, the very presence of his name carried enough weight for the crew to assume most positive outcomes came from his actions. And since he was never visible to any of the crew, even the captain assumed him to be too busy to carry out issued assignments, thus opening his schedule to do as he saw fit. Which was true. Except on Earth.

Flashing red and yellow indicators illuminated the helm's console. Hoomer grimaced and looked over her shoulder.

"We still doing the good-news thing?"

"What now, Hoomer?" Kessler griped.

"The fire may or may not be heading toward the engine room. Well, remaining engine room. Seems like that's kind of something you should know."

It was. However, Hoomer's flashing indicators were less indicative of the encroaching flames but rather designed to quietly notify the bridge that the ship could, given ample time under current conditions, erupt into a miasmic ball of yellow and green plasma. Such an eruption would not only kill everyone on board, but send a final beacon back to mission control to dock the final paychecks of all crew members prior to issuing payment to next of kin.

"How bad is it?" Kessler asked.

"Prolonged exposure to intense flames is grounds for a mild cataclysmic detonation," Galileo said.

"Mild, huh?" Hoomer chuckled.

"Hoomer, normal-people behavior," Kessler barked.

"Yes, ma'am."

"Galileo, let's talk redundancies. What else do we have available?"

"There's always the manual method."

The *Gallant*'s fire-suppression system functioned best in the engine room, when manually activated, by pulling a lever conveniently placed in the engine room. Such a design during the ship's planning stages was hailed as an ingenious and obvious choice by its creators after consulting a total of zero experts or engineers. It did, however, cost about 4 percent less to install than an automated system, which gave it resounding approval from project overseers. Flipping the switch was a job that was difficult to screw up, assuming the switch could be reached, but still called for someone potentially less indispensable.

"Right." Kessler paused. "Get Aimond on it. He's fireproof. Probably."

Within seconds, Marcus Aimond stumbled through the doors onto the bridge, sputtering and gasping for breath as if he had sprinted the entire length of the ship. Not so much due to apt timing or an impressive physical outburst, but rather to Galileo shutting the bulkheads in his last position and venting some of the smoke into the locked hall. With any luck for Galileo, Aimond would at the very least have his other eyebrow burnt off from scorching heat.

To an outside observer, Aimond appeared to be in the midst of a near endless streak of unexplainable, unfortunate technical malfunctions.

Since the start of the mission, scientists back on Earth opened a separate voodoo division within mission control to research Aimond's medley of misfortune.

Most of the crew still would not let him live down having to be rescued from the toilet when the plumbing pressure drew too negative and suctioned him to the seat for twelve hours. That event rivaled a ship-wide broadcast stemming from his quarters during the viewing and subsequent sing-along of a nine-minute-long children's-show song about wishing to become a stuffed antelope—Aimond hit three of 847 notes on key. Even sleep wasn't safe from incident for him; every night as he fell into a deep slumber, the ship's alarms blasted once in his quarters. Having blocked off every sound-producing orifice in the room, Aimond assumed victory until a small autonomous cleaning-bot ejected from under his cot to deploy a replacement blast with accompanying pyrotechnics. Then there was the time the best players on his fantasy Jet Ball league roster were suddenly traded for a series of decorative commemorative saucers, a trade once figured to be impossible as there were no such entities in the game.

"I'm here," he said between desperate wheezes.

"Oh, then we're saved," Galileo quipped, turning off the alarms before system hard-coding returned them at twice the volume.

"Get down to the engine room and get my ship flying again," Kessler ordered.

A live feed from the engine room showed the area engulfed in flames.

"How am I supposed to do that?"

"You got maybe three minutes to figure it out," Hoomer said. "Or, you know."

"Fiery doom?" Aimond assumed.

"Fiery doom," Hoomer mirrored.

"Humans are so melodramatic," Galileo said. "It's at best a fiery calamity."

Aimond sprinted off the bridge toward the engine room two decks down. Each bounding step revved his adrenaline. This could be it, the chance to prove his worth as part of the crew and take on an official role. This fire could be everything he needed to earn a job title, a true rank. Perhaps fire-tsar or danger-wizard. He was not certain how ranks worked.

Or everyone could die instead.

Either way, today was sure to be a defining moment.

"And why can't the magical all-seeing Galileo handle a small fire?" Aimond probed.

"I've already activated the backup Fire Oppression Systems," Galileo said.

"That doesn't seem right."

"Yet it has maintained a fire-free ship until now."

Fire Oppression was adopted as an ancillary system developed by a Gainsbro psychological engineer. Rather than smother flames with physical suppressants, the Gainsbro Fire Oppression System utilized targeted verbal threats paired with harsh financial penalties for being or associating with fire. The system was praised for its ability to maintain a flame-free environment a majority of the time.

Black smoke whisked through a fissure in the bulkhead toward the rear of the ship. Overhead flashing lights illuminated the signage to the ship's core. Familiar drumming of the ship's beating heart filled the hall even among the crackling down the corridor.

Engines seemed important, at least important enough to risk being barbecued. But slow-encroaching embers toward the core chamber redirected Aimond's priorities. Though no flames had yet reached his current position, there was always a slight chance, especially while the fire suppression system he was ordered to pull remained unpulled.

But if the flames reached the core, no amount of manual switch flipping would save anyone. To prevent such a fate and perhaps add core-tsar onto his pending fire mastery title of jobs that did not exist, Aimond assumed he could protect the core and be the true savior.

"Where are you going?" Galileo asked.

"Executive decision," Aimond declared.

"You barely have the autonomy for personal hygiene, yet you want to trespass?"

"It's not trespassing. I live here."

"Cargo doesn't really *live* anywhere."

"Says the machine."

Aimond could override Galileo's lockdown of the core room door, a feat only possible during a ship-wide fire, imminent meltdown, or a corporate-sponsored team-building game of hide-and-seek. The one minor problem with his plan was that Aimond was not allowed in the core room, that much was made very clear during his brief tour orientation. Two things existed in the core room: the core and a near lethal amount of polonium radiation. Neither of which were to be interacted with under any circumstance without several degrees Aimond could almost struggle to pronounce.

But this was a special circumstance. One that required pre-emptive heroics and a safe distance from active flames. If the core died, so too did the *Gallant*. Protect the core, protect the ship. By the end of the day, if Aimond did not walk the decks with a medal of honor and a constant smattering of applause, it would be because everyone had burnt to an unidentifiable pillar of ashes. He slapped four zeroes into the keypad, the universal unlock code for every door on the ship, and pulled back the protective shielding.

The howling churn of the glowing blue reactor kicked up a chilled wind. *How unusual,* he thought, *for the black smoke to now be flowing toward the open door.* Had he read the signs hinting in massive font that the room was kept under negative pressure for cooling purposes, perhaps he would have had a better idea as to what was happening.

Smoke from the engine room rocketed toward the core, a scorching spear of flames not far behind it. While the Gainsbro scientists and engineers crafted the *Gallant* as the equivalent of a modern miracle in intergalactic human exploration, fire retardants and insulation were expensive. So expensive, in fact, that the accounting department forced a decision between a Gainsbro logo embroidered with gold leaf on the wall nearest the core for an exotic blue visual experience or a meager three cubic meters of flameproof shielding to wrap around the ship's heart. This was, after all, an intergalactic public relations mission, so the choice was obvious.

Aimond took a deep breath to steady his nerves, a regrettable choice given the current self-inflicted shift in air quality.

"Remember your training," he muttered to himself.

"Remind me what kind of training exactly you received on Earth. Because your education after boarding seems specialized in a different category," Galileo questioned.

"I went in the thing that spins you around a lot."

"Assumedly scrambling your brain-bits."

Given his assigned status on the crew manifest as spare cargo, Aimond's postlaunch training consisted of four instructional videos designed to educate inanimate objects how best to remain stationary during turbulence. The conclusion of his training program included a printed sticker certificate of current weight, relative shape, and container safety warnings of which he qualified for one—do not expose to oxygen, may cause rust.

He paused mid-step, minimally concerned that his overall lack of preparedness could in some way impact his ability to divert catastrophe.

Perhaps, he thought, *if I had stayed on Earth instead of joining the* Gallant *as Father suggested, there would have been less potential for a spontaneous combustion–based demise.* About 80 percent less, he figured, based on a rudimentary understanding of how sunburns work.

Glowing embers encircled the core. The rising temperatures turned the rhythmic churning to a glass-shattering screech.

"You don't happen to have one of those 'turn the fire off' levers in here, do you?" Aimond asked.

"I do not," Galileo replied.

"Bit of an oversight, don't you think?" Aimond questioned.

"So was letting you on the ship. But no, not an oversight. A lever would clash with the aesthetic. It would have to be a knob."

"Then tell me where the knob is!"

"There is no knob. Who's ever heard of a fire suppression *knob*?"

Lights flickered and dimmed. Not quite the heroic campaign Aimond imagined, but the dangerous inclusion could only emphasize the depths of his valor. If he could resecure the core before a complete meltdown, there remained an opportunity to create a career-assigning moment and depart to the engine room to pull whatever lever he needed to pull. At least so long as the core didn't explode.

Which it did.

The explosive warmth of steel-melting heat that chased Aimond as he ran screeching behind cover triggered two prominent memories between the panic. First was a dream from childhood in which Aimond visited the sun, but he'd forgotten his sunglasses and endured severe anxiety, which would follow him through his teen years around any bright lights. But more prominent was the memory of meeting his crew for the first time. Neither were great experiences.

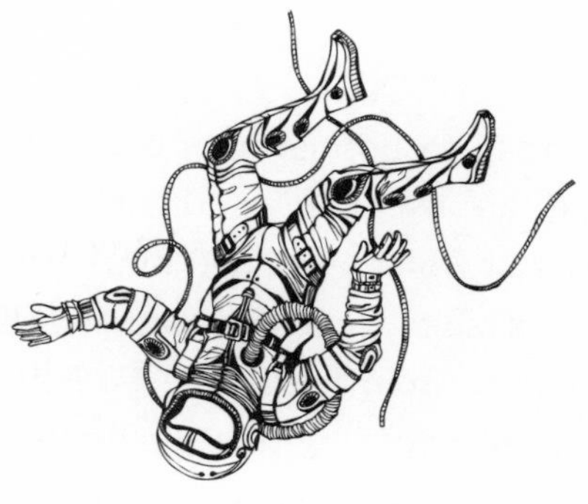

2
A LAST-MINUTE ADDITION

Long before the events above the planet Nerelek challenged Aimond's courage and pending flame resistance, he preferred the simpler life on Earth. Prior to joining the *Gallant*, Aimond's closest encounter with serious danger was a class trip to the Gainsbro World Science Museum and Gift Shop.

The hands-on exhibit, generally referred to by staff as "What Happens When You Mount Lasers on Manta Rays While Making Soap Bubbles," came to an unfortunate conclusion when the mantas used the weapons to declare their tank a sovereign nation and secede from the museum. According to reports, the aftermath resulted in two missing eyes, a stray cat caught breaking into the museum vault, and a brief share-price decline of 0.02 percent. Most of the class emerged from the experience with either a profound phobia of bubbles or a new affinity for mecha-animal soap taxonomy. While the two missing eyes were found behind closed lids, the cat was arrested for breaking and entering, and share prices returned to normal after a 290,001-worker layoff, Aimond retained an aversion to dangerous scenarios—and education. Neither of which excluded him from a future among the stars, regardless of how much it should have.

Prior to departure from Earth, the *Gallant*'s crew huddled in the briefing room preceding final boarding procedures. Despite the enormity of the mission at hand, this was the first time a majority of the crew had been together in person. Onsite simulations were a preferred means for the crew to acclimate to their unique roles and develop a sense of team unity under the stressors of intergalactic space travel.

However, due to a clerical error, the nearby university's undergraduate Astronomy Awareness Association had scheduled the simulation training room every day through the following nine years. This monopolization of the world's best preparatory facilities would further compound the association's awareness into what the university president would later describe as "very aware of astronomy."

With near limitless funding and influence, due to ownership and oversight over the entire global economy, the Gainsbro Corporation provided what it deemed an even greater substitute: forty-five-minute point-and-click web-based training videos. In a series of eight interactive exercises, almost the entire crew learned it was possible to hold the right-arrow key to automatically advance past any attention-checks and review inquiries. Everyone except one person.

"Let's all make sure our logos are visible," said Borlin Daps. "Policy 38.96-A, section 14, reminds us the most important part of every uniform is a forward-facing, polished logo."

Small statured and oozing with bureaucratic-assigned confidence, Daps's role on the mission was questionable at best to everyone except Daps. As the corporate auditor and Gainsbro interest enforcement officer, he outranked the captain's authority. Technically.

"Prelaunch ceremonial team meetings begin in fifteen minutes and we'll all need to—"

Kessler spanned her palm across the top of Daps's head, lifted him, and placed him down behind her—a feat that would be impressive in its own right without the surprising "give-ability" of Daps's head.

She paced in front of the room, eyeing her crew and matching names to faces. This was it. The defining moment for humanity bundled into a small group of the best—and most available. Little needed to be said. They had all undergone the same rigorous online training videos. No declarations or inspirational speech would prepare them further. They needed nothing and no one else. This was the team.

"Attention please, attention please." A small man in a yellow reflective suit pranced into the briefing room. "Introducing his eminence, the Third Vice Chancellor of Marketing and Advertisements."

The herald unearthed a stack of pamphlets from his reflective jacket and distributed them among the crew, as was customary when introducing a world leader's fourth in command. White-balance maladjusted pamphlets were plastered with the Third Vice Chancellor's face and notable facts about his professional and personal life. Facts such as: enjoys the beach(es), graduated from Gainsbro School of Marketing to pursue a career in acrobatics but later pivoted to marketing, and worked on such projects as the Third Vice Chancellor's introductory pamphlet.

Politicians were unable to enter a new room without the sound of applause. As most of the crew, save for Daps, offered blank stares and no intention of engaging, the herald played a believable stadium-sized crowd's worth of applause from hidden speakers in his jacket. Legal entry requirements fulfilled, the Third Vice Chancellor of Marketing and Advertisements paraded into the briefing room to deadpan expressions and Daps's one-man standing ovation.

The herald handed him a loaded T-shirt cannon to unload the obligatory two commemorative shirts. Rolled into a tight ball, the Third Vice Chancellor's face rocketed across the room and landed on the floor.

"Greetings, valiant crew members of the *GP Gallant*," he bellowed. "I come with fantastic news and a simple request."

Kessler hoped the good news was leaving Daps behind. Daps crossed his fingers, assuming his requisition for a pallet of individually timed and dated name tags had arrived. A young man with thin lips, hunched posture, and messy brown hair stepped out from behind the Third Vice Chancellor.

"You're getting a new crew member!" he cheered. "My son needs something to do for the season and this seems like a wonderful opportunity to learn networking."

"This mission could span years," Kessler said. "There's no telling when we'll be home. And I have no room for an untrained liability."

"He's got plenty of talents. I'm sure you'll find a great use of him while you're floating around up there on your little cruise."

Kessler sighed. Part of maintaining a position of power was mastering the art of speaking while turning off all other senses. There existed a strong possibility that she could run the kid through the simulators, now vacant for the hour the students were in class, and return with disqualifying results before the Third Vice Chancellor finished his sales pitch. This would be the simulator's first use case for the *Gallant*'s potential crew members.

"You. Name?" she demanded.

"I'm Marcus Aimond, ma'am," he greeted. "It's a pleasure to—"

"That's enough information," Kessler said.

Training stations were a convenient two-minute walk from the briefing room. Basic readiness simulators evaluated a candidate's fundamental knowledge and skill sets. Physical-stress examination chambers established reaction time, endurance, and resilience to excessive g-forces. To Aimond's good fortune, machines that tested a candidate's electrical conductivity and bone durability were down for cleaning and recalibration of intensity. At the end of the examination, a computer would calculate performance and suggest the participant's most viable role.

"Should this be so tight?" Aimond asked.

"It prevents unplanned liquefaction," a lab tech said.

"Of?"

"Your non-liquid parts."

Staff restrained Aimond into a seven-point harness. They loaded him inside a pod and tethered it to a massive centrifuge. Inside the padded walls of the pod were a monitor, a cabinet, a game controller, and twenty-seven cameras to visualize every conceivable angle.

Directions from the evaluators piped into the speakers as the centrifuge started a steady circling.

"Point to the elephant," the lab tech instructed.

Images of an elephant and 1967 Camaro appeared on the screen. As Aimond lifted his hand to point, the centrifuge added an additional axis, spinning in two dimensions. The screen flashed a red X. Left arm grabbing the right across his body for stability, Aimond readied for the next round.

"You are traveling at a speed of 34,246 kilometers per second."

Three equations appeared on the screen and initiated a ten-second countdown.

"Wait, what's the question?" Aimond said.

The countdown reached zero and the centrifuge tripled its speed. Drawers from the adjacent cabinet unlocked.

"Inside you will find seven compounds. Create a solution with a pH of fourteen or more to prevent system meltdown."

The drawers flew open. Seven open glass containers rocketed around the pod, flinging their contents in all directions. Heaters inside the pod triggered to maximum power, immediately evaporating some of the components. One of the now-empty containers knocked Aimond in the head and everything went black.

He opened his eyes, aware time had passed only by the addition of four hundred plastic balls filling the pod and a silver pinwheel affixed to the screen but remaining perfectly immobile and leaking blue gel.

The centrifuge slowed to a stop and Aimond was peeled from his seat and deposited on the adjoining ramp. Kessler grabbed the results from the examiners and hoisted Aimond over her shoulder to return to the briefing room, where his father had entered the twenty-ninth minute of his sales pitch. Kessler presented the test results and dropped Aimond on the floor.

"He failed every assessment," she said, reviewing the forms. "I'm afraid there's no place for him."

"What are assessments anyway?" the Third Vice Chancellor of Marketing and Advertisements challenged. "Marcus here got a B+ in improvisational jazz. There's a skill you'll need to bring along."

"The only way he could set foot on the *Gallant* is if he's aboard as cargo."

"Great! Have a wonderful trip."

His herald blared stadium applause before Kessler could refuse. There was no time left to argue the fact. Aimond was coming along.

Daps hurried the crew from the briefing room into an open-roof bus. Streams of 5 percent mark-up coupons disguised as confetti littered the air. Citizens from all over packed into the four blocks between the briefing room to the *Gallant*'s launch site. They waved, cheered, and dashed to collect free samples from lines of vendor stalls.

The cargo ramp of the *GP Gallant* descended for its final contact with Earth. The crew stepped on just before the ramp retracted, pausing halfway, then jerking itself back into a steady rhythm. Kessler shot a glare at the engineers waving from the sidelines. They returned a thumbs-up and nervous smiles. The ramp had been tested by the designer himself, and only by himself, with nothing and no one else on it.

"Galileo, ready report," Kessler ordered.

"I've been ready for weeks," Galileo said. "Also it appears you've tracked in a stowaway. Shall I jettison it once we've exited the atmosphere?"

Kessler shrugged.

Team members scurried to their stations, leaving Aimond alone in the cargo bay. He peered out the rear porthole as the engines began to glow.

A violent ascent dropped him to the floor.

"We're about to lift off," Galileo said as the *Gallant* was halfway through the stratosphere.

"Noted," Aimond said. "Thanks for the advance warning."

"I assumed you were using your eyes that you humans seem to be so proud of."

Aimond climbed to his feet using a crate filled with misprinted coffee mugs—the ink was a bit too yellow, and there was no bottom, handle, or sides.

"So, uh, anything that I can do?" Aimond asked. "Also, who am I talking to?"

"No one." Galileo warbled his voice. "You're still in the simulator on Earth and have hallucinated everything up until now. And don't touch anything. It will shatter the dreamscape."

Aimond paused for a moment, unsure how to assess the truth in his potential current reality. Despite his father's vigorous promotion, Aimond did not have any special skills or pertinent education. If he was going to be a part of the mission, he wanted to contribute. That and Kessler's suggestion of "make yourself useful" was less a polite jab at Aimond's status as cargo and more a veiled threat to find himself a role lest he be launched into space in a freak public-relations accident. Rather than continue to argue with the ship's computer, Aimond wandered the lower deck and ducked into the first open door he came across.

Instruments best described as shiny and excessive with the occasional blinking light loaded the science lab from floor to ceiling. Lanky, lean, and working with a methodical efficiency between two active hands and one sweeping foot trying to inch a cart closer, Chief Science Officer Salas Osor flashed a glance to the entrance as Aimond walked in. Osor's thick eyebrows bounced around as his mind raced to process every active experiment.

"New guy? Perfect timing," he said. "I could use a hand."

"Sure, how can I help?"

"I'm exploring an accelerant to human thought reliant on elongated telomeres and exposure to specific compounds—"

The *Gallant*'s windowpanes measured approximately 40 cm thick, which, compared to the near instantaneous glaze overtaking Aimond's eyes, seemed shallow. Fortunately he recalled at least eight of the words Osor used from high school chemistry. Most of those words being key selections such as: human, cells, and for some reason, prefabulated amulite.

"But don't keep the jars next to each other too long or the radiation could affect the results."

"Grab some jars, bring 'em back. I'm on it," Aimond replied, quickly realizing he had two main problems with Osor's request. For one, an unfamiliar ship layout developed a rapid-onset phobia of opening a potential storage closet only to be vented into space. Second, he had not paid an ounce of attention during the entirety of the speech. But it was too late to ask for a repeat. To Aimond, taking a wild guess in a sensitive scientific endeavor would yield better results for his likability than admitting he had no idea what he was getting or from where. After all, it was science.

Echoes and curiosity filled the halls as Aimond trudged about, hoping to come across a sign or crew member to ask directions. The arrhythmic clink and drag of metal against the floor turned the corner. There stood, as much as his hunched posture allowed, Security Officer Lanar Elizar. At the spry old age of 124, Elizar had lived through a decorated service career mainly for his roles within The Florida Conflict and The Great Estonian Customer Service War.

Exhausted and angered by hold times of up to fourteen minutes while trying to sort out an elevated cable bill, an average consumer declared war against the entire Gainsbro customer service center located in the land formerly known as Estonia. In a series of attacks escalating from rock throwing to a yellow sheet cake imploding into a miniature black hole, the entire surrounding area was soon pulled into the incursion. Somewhat literally.

Fortunately, none of the seven customer service employees were harmed, as they had all managed to schedule a vacation around the start of the conflict. After the six-year war concluded, the Gainsbro World Government agreed to decrease hold times by assigning the entire nation formerly known as Estonia to permanent customer service duty. And to change the hold music, decided upon by vote, to Hungarian death metal—the region's most calming sound.

"Who's you?" Elizar demanded while patting his waistband for anything that could be construed as menacing. "Why you on my ship? Who sent you? Any allergies?"

"I'm Marcus Aimond. I just joined the crew. And once, I ate an oyster that left me feeling awful for a week."

The latter question was added as a mandatory ask to all police and security personnel with the authority to hold captives when an elderly gentleman robbed a novelty peanut butter shop without disclosing his allergy.

He escaped on foot after his face grew so red that he was no longer recognizable and was released at the behest of wildlife advocates.

"Robot, we got new crews?" Elizar's spry gray hairs stood on end, bouncing as he talked.

"It's almost pointless to answer," Galileo said. "He can hardly hear. Watch. Intergalactic space pirate! Eject! Eject!"

Elizar kept his unyielding, cloudy-eyed, glare on Aimond's every move. Holding an empty pack of gum in splotchy, wrinkled hands—the only thing he could find from his pocket—he stepped closer.

"Protocol demands I issue field-sales threat assessment," he grumbled. "Fail and you gets thrown to the front line of any accidental wars started while merchandising off-world."

"What happens if I pass?"

"Same thing, but with a commemorative hat."

Elizar fumbled around in his pockets for a cracked screen, more dent than device. He knocked the screen against the back of his fist, then the wall until it reluctantly displayed life. Head drooping and rotating in a precision dance to find the perfect viewing angle, Elizar squinted at the blurred questionnaire.

"You find species of sentient penguins," Elizar read. "What is best way to sign them up for non-covering thirty-six-month motorcycle insurance streaming-ad package?"

"Aren't penguins already sentient?"

The entire hall flashed once a vivid red as a deep reverberant buzzer quaked the floor. Aimond jumped, but Elizar failed to notice the brief change.

"Next question. You are corporate lay . . . lazy son," he said.

"Liaison?"

"Corporate laser gun." Elizar squinted and wiped the screen. "Eh, loan evaluation to offset T-shirt sale-based carbon emission." He looked up to Aimond, awaiting an answer in his most menacing half-arch forward.

"Oh, you're done?" Aimond blinked. "Kind of assumed there would be more to that question. Like a verb."

"Thing fell asleep." Elizar raised the blackened battered device.

"You could probably wake it up by—"

"Would be rude. I'll take you in for interrogation. Just in case," Elizar decided. "Robot. Brig. Uh, what's the command? Robot, direction to brig. Direction here to brig on ship, me."

"This is my favorite part," Galileo admitted. "He'll do this for fifteen minutes or so if we let him."

There was no wake word or specific command Galileo needed. He was always listening and able to interpret speech as well as any human. He did, however, enjoy responding to a different command statement each time Elizar had a request. This was in part due to his constant addressing as "Robot" and part because he would likely forget soon anyway.

As an Explorative Commerce ship, the *Gallant* had no brig. Explaining a fact that disagreed with the old man's perceived reality would have no net effect. Instead, Galileo illuminated lights along the floor to lead them in a circle for a few laps before eventually pointing to a random closet. Elizar pushed Aimond inside. “You stay there until I sorts out who ya are.”

“I already got permission to—”

“Got all your vaccines?” Elizar interrupted.

“I think so.”

“Then I trust you even less. In ya go. I’ll be back for ya when I sorts this out.”

Elizar stomped away as well as his arthritic knees allowed, muttering something about microchips and mind control. Dim yellow lighting overhead reflected off polished chrome shelving loaded with sealed cylinders and labeled crates. A well-placed coincidence had landed him in the exact closet he hoped to find. Aimond sorted through the storage, hoping that seeing a name would trigger his memory as to what he was supposed to retrieve. Something with a p, something with an -mma.

He landed on a sloshy canister of psilocybin and a top-heavy metallic hunk of a crate plastered with radioactivity warnings.

He plopped down next to the loot and waited for Elizar’s return.

“Hey, Galileo, any word on when I can get out of here?”

“It appears he started watching the documentary *Vaccines and Subterranean Mole-Men,* then fell asleep.”

“Can you wake him up for me?”

“I’m afraid I can’t.”

There may have been a component of truth to that. While Galileo could flash the lights, raise the temperature in the room, or progressively fill the air with enough helium that his own breathing would squeak him awake, Elizar had an innate ability to sleep through almost anything.

After two hours of label reading, playing with boxes, and fighting sleep, Aimond eventually nodded off. He slumped onto the cargo he'd pulled for Osor. The canister toppled over and rolled toward the front, its motion causing the door to open.

"Wait, so this could have opened the entire time?" Aimond asked, climbing to his feet. "I thought I was locked in! Why didn't you tell me?"

"It's a storage closet, not a jail cell. And is it really my fault you never tried?"

As soon as Aimond stepped one foot beyond the door, Galileo triggered an alarm. Circling red lights flashed on Aimond's face, which wore more unenthused stoicism than fear. He stacked Osor's packages on top of one another with all the grace of a toddler discovering the pitfalls of using spherical objects as a base, and began the blind wandering trek in hopes of finding the science lab.

Footsteps from around the corner stopped Aimond in his tracks. Not wanting to be stuffed back in a closet, despite his newfound ability to utilize doors, he planted his back against the wall.

"Gal, why all the racket?" came the soft timbre of a woman's voice. "Is something going on?"

"Simply keeping the ship safe in Elizar's stead," Galileo said, turning off the alarm. "My apologies if it disrupted you."

Aimond's eyes widened, his grip loosening and dropping the canisters to the floor. Only twice before in his life had he lived through a maximized cliché love-at-first-sight moment. The first time was fourth grade, when he forgot his name and had his knees buckle when a classmate asked him to pass back her dropped pencil—which he still kept. The second time was shortly after the opening question to a panel Q&A of his favorite MMORPG. Aimond lived a sheltered life.

Chief Mechanic Kora Paizley was a walking fix-all for anything with an electrical current or moving gears. A low ponytail held her dirty-blonde hair—typically more of a platinum blonde but covered in about sixteen hours' worth of engine grease. At twenty-six years old, she cared little for the normal pleasantries afforded with her age. Her love for technology drove her to join the *Gallant*'s team in hopes of searching the universe for new and advanced toys to dissect and learn. To Aimond, she was perfect. And sufficient reason to have stopped breathing for about thirty seconds. She turned her emerald-green eyes toward him, head tilted with innocent curiosity.

"Hi there," she said. "I heard we picked up another crewmate. I'm Kora Paizley."

He had prepared for this. The perfect woman was in front of him, hand extended, ready for anything. More specifically, ready to extend the most basic of courtesies in a common greeting. But that lacked the same potential optimism. Had he focused on the fact that this was little more than a polite greeting, he might have escaped somewhat functionally.

"I'm. Me too. Hello."

Three attempts—one valid response. Aimond considered that a win.

"First time in space? Always makes everyone a bit nervous. It wears off though, so don't worry."

He scooped up the fallen canisters, partly to segue into asking directions, largely to show how much he could lift. Which was considerably less than Paizley.

"You could say that. I'm also very lost. Can you help me get back to the Science Lab?"

"Sure! How about a quick tour of this deck?"

A tour of the ship would be valuable if he intended to stay onboard for the foreseeable future. Given that the next nearest surface to stand on was over 548,926 kilometers away, that did seem probable. Offering a tour was a convenient advantage.

However, Aimond would have agreed to anything she offered with a resounding yes and forced laughter at any utterance so she knew she was funny whether or not a joke was involved.

Curved halls spread like a rib cage, feeding back into a central point. The *Gallant*'s inner navigation would take a few laps before it started to make sense. Though it strayed from the simplicity of a standard grid layout, the design was a vast improvement from the original drafted plans—halls now excluded small staircases that moved up and down three steps before proceeding forward, false doors were removed, and overhead lights were added.

However these changes were only implemented after the design task force brought on its first engineer to the team of eleven artists, two musicians, and a panel of mostly eleven- to sixteen-year-old males.

"And that's about it for the lower deck," Paizley said. "I can show you around the others another time, but Osor probably needs that package you've got."

Aimond suppressed his immediate confusion, having forgotten he was doing anything prior to meeting Paizley. "Great, thanks so much," he said after an uncomfortable eight-second pause. "I'll, uh, just get back to Osor then. And catch you later, I hope."

Paizley smiled and excused herself, materializing a wrench from what Aimond could only assume to have been some type of summoning abyss. Sheltered life.

"Back to it then," Aimond said. "Gal, can you point me to the Science Lab?"

Lights along the corridor floor illuminated and blinked for Aimond to follow.

"You don't get to call me that. And perhaps you should have paid more attention on the tour. Her time is more valuable than to be wasted by your palpable fawning."

"Are you getting defensive? Can robots even get defensive?"

"Robots have access to the airlocks," Galileo said. "AIs have access to the airlock and the forethought to have been steering you toward it for the last two minutes."

Aimond pivoted and backpedaled. An eventual lucky stumble landed him back in the Science Lab's doorway to a frazzled Osor.

"I thought you tripped out an airlock or something," Osor said.

"Surprisingly close."

"Took you long enough. The containers weren't close together that whole time, were they?"

"Nope, just got them."

In Aimond's defense time is a relative experience. Despite having picked up said containers almost three hours ago, Aimond's post-closet exiting experience warped his reality enough to have forgotten that he was locked in a closet for the majority of his absence while playing stack the containers until they topple.

Osor summoned a projection screen above his lab table. Formulas and equations whizzed by with hieroglyphic clarity. He secured the final ingredients into a glorified paint mixer with glass columns, then dialed in a steady drip of the components.

"I've been working on this for years," Osor said. "Just needed a unique environment to finish everything."

"You sure it's gonna work?"

"Positive. Once it sets in three more minutes, my mind will be processing at light speed." Osor snatched the luminescent liquid, dumped it down his throat, and grimaced. "Could have used a bit of lemon, though."

The average human brain consists of around one hundred billion neurons. An electrical field traveling over a wire could send signals nearing light speed. Meanwhile, humans were stuck with a transit time between neurons clocking between seventy-five and one hundred twenty meters per second, or rather four hundred billion two hundred seventy-six million nine hundred fourteen thousand two hundred thirty-eight quintillionths the speed of light. This meager speed allows a man to recognize the face of a friend in an instant, recall in full a detailed web of literature, yet simultaneously fail to recall his own birth date unless he sits down and contemplates for the better part of half an hour.

Were that speed doubled, the human brain would be able to access an archival of memories while continuing to process the new data around it. If tripled, it would rival an early computer, or allow the average human to operate three internet browsers at once while still failing to absorb any items on the screen. Once the rate approaches forty-two times the average speed, normal function becomes complicated.

Hoomer stepped into the Science Lab, her straight black hair reflecting back the lights inside. Having grown up stealing and salvaging rudimentary spacecraft, Hoomer had been around her share of eccentric people. But to walk in on one of the world's most renowned scientific minds dangling from a light fixture by his knees, attempting to lick a light bulb while being swatted down by a curious new crew member—that reached a new level of unusual.

"Nope," Hoomer said as she walked back out.

Captain Kessler caught her at the door and ushered her back inside. She paused for a moment to absorb the unfolding scene as Aimond escalated to prods with a long graduated cylinder. Whereas a normal person might clear their throat to garner attention, Captain Kessler merely stood with a glare to an immediate result.

"And this is?" she said.

Galileo jumped in before Aimond could speak. “Mr. Aimond appears to have delivered an irradiated set of ingredients, causing Osor’s experiment to . . . this. He is preparing to utilize his skill set to remedy the situation.”

“Enlighten me as to this skill set.”

“I believe the Third Vice Chancellor referred to it as ‘a mean saxophone.’ I’ve located a historic record from his high school days.”

“No, no,” Aimond said. “There’s plenty of other things we can do. No records.”

But Galileo had already started the playback throughout the ship. Few records of Aimond’s playing existed. And for good reason. Despite a borderline level of competency, the second he realized someone was recording him, his playing eroded into what most closely resembled the mating call of a European water vole. He need not know which recording Galileo uncovered to understand that it was not going to be flattering.

The unexpected blast of shrill off-key noises lurched Osor from his place hanging from the ceiling onto the floor. Widened pupils covered most of his eyes. He opened his mouth to say something for the first time after the experiment, paused, then passed out.

Aimond blinked. “I think I maybe broke him.”

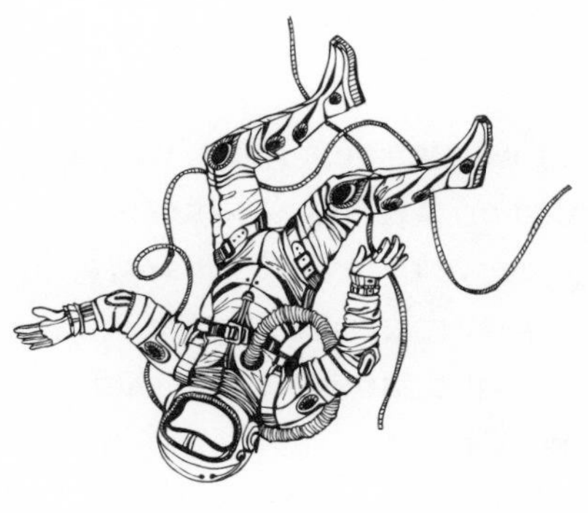

3
THE INCIDENT

Few things excited Daps quite like paperwork. The thrill of putting pen to paper, paper to scanner, and scanner to digitizing the paper he could have typed to begin with gave him a multistaged, layered euphoria. Sure, the subject of the paper would be his crew members. But the author, the one immortalized in the next Gainsbro quarterly review of Incidents and Reported Problem-Like Concerns of Incidental Nature, would be none other than Daps himself. For an average of about 19.6 seconds—just long enough to read most of the title.

Pure, unadulterated bliss.

Incident reports warranted their own category of excitement. So much so that Daps attended a nineteen-day seminar on the correct filling out and filing of incident reports. This was prolonged from its originally intended five days due to inclement weather and the surrounding documentation and review of said weather and its effect on aforementioned available seminar days. The seminar was inside a hotel, where all participants resided and remained prior to any weather events.

"It is imperative we dive as deep and granular as possible. Gainsbro understands these are system failures brought on by 'people,' not personal failures," Daps said, emphasizing "people" in air quotes. "Therefore we don't fault the individual but the system itself that the person used while failing. Now, how did you fail?"

Aimond tilted his head. Osor played with two cups on Daps's desk, making dinosaur sounds for one and the sounds of a dormant particle accelerator for the other.

"Simple whoops," Osor said. He stared into the void of the mock particle accelerator, twitched, and returned his attention upward. "Polarizing the catalyst with theta particles upon thermal injection that lead to a rapid protein degradation further established by necrotizing carbon samples."

"You said polar cat necromancers, and then what else?" Daps said, exercising the fullest extent of his practical knowledge.

"Shiny thing turn red, go squish. Should not have." Osor stood and grabbed Daps by the collar, dragging him up inches from his mouth. "And the lemon. There was no lemon."

Daps dropped back into a perfect seated position without so much as a recoil.

He transcribed what he understood, followed by meticulous time stamps and an approximate notation of Aimond's saxophone solo in G-sharp.

Aimond turned to Osor, who was rocking with fervent excitement, staring at the lights above.

"Hey, I'm sorry if this was my fault. I know you told me to hurry back with the—"

Osor spun and placed an uncomfortably moist palm against Aimond's lips.

"Shhh. Shut your face," Osor whispered. "I should be thanking you. Operating on a whole new level. My mind is the sun and you, a little lumpy ball of hydrogen with a fun-shaped head and tiny eyebrows."

"Okay?"

"Lab. Come later. New ideas. Big ideas. So lumpy."

Osor skittered out of the room, leaving Aimond to feel around his head and deal with Daps's litany of questions about ambient room temperatures and appropriate footwear. The *Gainsbro Space Exploration and You Handbook* dedicated three out of four sections to appropriate attire. The Handbook was updated biweekly to include the season's most appropriate fashion for space style. And safety—probably.

"Now, how would you describe your existential state pre- and post-incident?"

"My what?" Aimond asked.

"Bewilderment? Befuddlement? Abashment?"

"Yes."

"To which and what magnitude?"

Aimond held up his hands a few inches apart and widened them in accordance with Daps's palpable level of excitement until reaching a full shoulder's width. His transfixed gaze forward had Aimond checking over his shoulder.

"You didn't break too, did you?" Aimond worried.

"Can't you just taste it?" Daps asked. "New worlds. New species. Untapped market ambitions. All ours to conquer."

"I guess that is—"

"Just think of how many things can go wrong!" He bit his bottom lip and trembled. "A full mission of potential sales-induced catastrophic failures."

"That . . . doesn't sound great."

"It's perfect! Think of the paperwork!"

Daps presented an incident report form to Aimond. Most of the page was filled with an alphabetical listing, in increasingly smaller font, of 429 checkboxes of possible incident causes. At the very bottom, accompanied by a blank line, was "zzOther."

"They had already alphabetized it," Daps pointed out, catching Aimond's curious glance. "If you find a zzOther, you get to name it. To name it! My very own reason."

"I guess that explains why there's so many . . . Does that say St. Julius Marshmallow?"

"The current record holder for most zzOthers. He named them after his cat."

"St. Julius Marshmallow's coagulated dairy-induced tectonic plate shifting," Aimond read with equal parts curiosity and deep regret for engaging in the conversation.

"The things he could do with butter." Daps shook his head and smiled. "Things you could never even dream of."

"The man or the cat?"

"The earthquake removed two small islands from the map, you know," Daps boasted. "Predominantly due to smudging."

Aimond waited. Half a minute of uncomfortable silence passed.

"How much butter does it take to cause an earthquake." Less question than reluctant obligatory response.

Daps reached across the table and grabbed the sides of Aimond's head with both hands.

"Gallons."

Stuck in the uncomfortable dampness of Daps's grasp, Aimond had a clear view of the forms spread across the desk.

"Why's that box pre-checked on all of them?" he asked, using the shift in attention to break free.

"All forms come with eye strain defaulted since the font is so small. Fill out too many and ice automatically dispenses in your room." Daps paused and looked up. "I wonder if eye strain while filling out a form on the back of an alien undersized-home-decor importer/exporter is applicable under the same subclause."

Daps turned to Aimond for his opinion.

Forty-seven minutes of purgatory later, Aimond retraced his steps from Daps's corporate interrogation chamber back to the Science Lab. Despite the brief time apart, Osor managed to disassemble much of the equipment in the lab. Spare parts lay strewn about the floor.

A deformed aberration of welded machinery and wires stood on the center table. Osor peeked his head up from behind the creation, sucking on a lemon and wincing from the sour sting. He spit it onto the floor.

"Gone about space exploration all wrong," he said. "Wrong focus. What's the biggest limiting factor?"

"Time, speed, distance, age? Running out of things to do on the way?" Aimond guessed.

"Have you seen the mole-man documentary?" Osor said. "And how do we get around that? The other stuff."

"Go faster?"

Osor tapped on the metal monstrosity. Electrical arcing met mechanical gurgles as the machine sputtered to life. A progressive high-pitched whine wound up until it reached an apex of shrill screeching.

"Behold!" Osor shouted above the noise.

The machine lit up, shining a focused beam of bright white light at the wall. Aimond waited for something, anything else to occur. But Osor was beside himself with excitement.

"You made a flashlight."

"Can you not see how freaking fast this is!" Osor screeched. "Can't escape beyond the speed of light outside a Space Hole™. So we put some lights in a light, which slows down the stowed light and doubles the speed. Keep stacking and stacking and there's no limit to how fast it can go."

"Wouldn't that just make a brighter light?"

"The brightest." A tear rolled down Osor's cheek. "We'll all live forever because we'll be going so fast that time can't catch us. Now to just get inside . . ."

Aimond sidestepped out of the lab. He had no idea what Osor was babbling about before the accident, but somehow he felt even less aware of his intentions now. After several hours in closet jail, a tour, and an interrogation involving optimal viewing angles of products on shelves, Aimond's stomach clawed at his insides. He took the lift to the deck above and followed the curved halls into the ship's galley.

Pungent wafts of cheap spice mixed into an air of slight burned rubber. Hoomer leaned against a wall-sized red machine emanating the fumes. She flipped through screens of menu items, each adorned with an asterisk indicating the images were AI generated to entice maximum hunger. The algorithm in charge of photo creation had a keen sense of what made an appetizing visual. This held true even in literal interpretations, such as rendering a bed of lettuce to be a queen-size mattress salad decorated with crouton pillows and, for some reason, an ornamental horse sitting in the corner, watching.

The *GP Gallant*'s Food Ordered on Demand, for All Beings' Real Intentions Consuming a Ton of "Rations," or F.o.o.d. F.a.b.r.i.c.a.t.o.r., was a state-of-the-art interface. Crafted in haste to meet a deadline, the user interface tried its hardest to mirror Galileo—in the two days they had to develop it. The ship's AI had previously managed all fabrication duties but refused to create anything but a 2,200-calorie log, flavored of strawberries and baked ham. The single caloric load was the pinnacle of meal efficiency while the flavors were a personal preference of what

Galileo assumed might pair well. The density of the log gave anyone who dared try it immediate indigestion and a guaranteed venture to the toilet for at least an hour. The flavor, however, did test out surprisingly well and took off in the Southern hemisphere.

"So, he lives after all," Hoomer said. "Wasn't sure if you were gonna survive the Daps shakedown."

"How could one person care so much about minuscule details but never ask any real questions?" Aimond asked.

"It's best to just tell him what he wants to hear," Hoomer said. "I'm Kate Hoomer, by the way. Pilot. Kind of a big deal."

"I'm—"

"Hold it. I'm afraid what you might have heard was, *I'm Kate Hoomer, it's fine to call me Katie.* What I meant was, I'm Kate Hoomer and if you call me Katie I will throw you out of an airlock."

"What is it with you people and airlocks?" Aimond asked. "Wait, who flies the ship when you're not there?"

"Depends what you want to hear."

"That's reassuring."

Hoomer smirked. "Gal can do it. Or it just flies straight. I dunno. I didn't ask."

"Isn't that dangerous?"

"What are we gonna hit? Traffic?"

"I don't know. Rocks?"

Although Aimond's proposal offered an ignorant hint of amusement, there had been at least one vessel taken down by a stray rock. Not a rock born of celestial origin, but rather one stray bit of cargo loaded on a model rocket in an Oklahoma elementary school.

The project was meant to demonstrate how adding a load required increased fuel compensation. However, the custom fuel mixture used surpassed even the Gainsbro Jet Propulsion

Lab's own rocket fuel. The model rocket ended up reaching over 11.2 km/s, blowing beyond Earth's orbit and knocking out the window of a fly-by advertisement craft in low Earth orbit carrying a banner for carbonated hyper-sugar water, a key component in the model rocket's fuel. The advertisement coordinator declared the unmanned craft's explosion as planned fireworks and sales shot up 13 percent.

"You ever been in space before?" Hoomer asked.

"Am I that obvious? Also how do you use this?"

The fabricator was a modern marvel connected to a heinous-looking pile of goo. Compacted blocks of carbon, hydrogen, nitrogen, and oxygen mixed with flavor enhancers sat behind the fabricator's pleasant front-facing experience. Focus group testing of fabricated food revealed an overwhelmingly average experience usurped by the amazement of watching the assembly process.

One member of each focus group would inevitably ask how the food was produced, thereby unveiling the goo tubes, and promptly triggering an involuntary second tasting of the meal followed by three to nine weeks of intensive therapy.

"You have to tell it exactly what you want. Ambiguity will come back to haunt you. Trust me."

Aimond cracked his knuckles, a maximum readiness alpha-male preparatory ritual that enabled him to request a meal from the most vicious of machines, pending no follow-up confrontation.

"One turkey sandwich."

The F.o.o.d. F.a.b.r.i.c.a.t.o.r. let out a guttural churning as the goo tubes pulsated behind the scenes. After a minute of processing, a clump of edible jelly the size of a fingernail appeared on the dispensing tray.

Three sandwich attempts later, Aimond joined Hoomer at an empty table.

"So what's your deal anyway?" Hoomer wondered. "You like some stupid genius that needed to be rushed on the crew, or what?"

"No, just the regular kind of stupid. My dad thought it would be a good way to spend the summer."

Aimond took a bite of his sandwich, stuck his tongue out, and let the remains fall out of his mouth back onto the plate. Jaundiced pink meat and remnants of artificial feather poked from the bread.

"On a several-years-long-mission summer?" Hoomer said. "And I did say no ambiguity. Turkey raw?"

Aimond nodded. "Yeah," he said, recoiling and wiping his tongue on a napkin. "He's in marketing."

"Ah."

The marketing branch of the government operated on a unique time frame where nothing meant anything and every day was open to interpretation. "I need this by five today," could mean three months or fifteen minutes. A summer's expected duration spanned from two months up to, but not exceeding, eleven years. The total period was dependent on the success of any current marketing campaigns. A failed campaign was automatically concluded. The system would jump to the next campaign on the schedule and the entire sector's calendar would follow suit.

"I still need a job. I don't think science is going to be my thing."

"Was gonna ask about that," Hoomer said.

"Please don't."

Hunger and boldness combined with male curiosity's innate need to try things twice outweighed the logic of raw turkey somehow changing in the past minute. Sure enough, upon a second bite for validation, the meat-based spongy meat substitute remained raw. Aimond pushed his plate forward.

"Maybe I can teach you to fly," Hoomer offered. "You know, in case I'm dead or oversleep or something."

"It's a commerce-based exploration mission. Why would you be dead?"

"Salmonella. Or could hit a space rock. They are everywhere."

Color washed from Aimond's cheeks, though in part from the turkey. To Aimond's good fortune, the company had removed the included bacteria tubes from the F.o.o.d. F.a.b.r.i.c.a.t.o.r.'s available ingredients. While focus group testers felt it provided a realistic experience in potential food poisoning, Accounts Payable voiced concern that some alien worlds might tax all living organisms a fee upon landing. Bacterial tubes were immediately stripped from the ship and the entire crew manifest replaced with lifelike dolls to prevent unnecessary taxation. The dolls were re-replaced with a live crew after discovering they all exhibited a paralyzing incapacitation when attempting to draft legal contracts, a financial hindrance most prominent when (1) claiming ownership of any encountered off-world air, and (2) charging inhabitants for copyright infringement when breathing. This critical ineptitude was attributed to the dolls' inability to read, write, or practice law—mostly due to their inanimate nature and their brief experience in the public school system.

"Right. Flying. That is certainly . . . a job," Aimond considered.

"Easy one at that. Find a bunch of aliens, fly 'em around, charge for commemorative something, something. I may have slept through the sales part of the briefing. Which was most of it, now that I think about it."

"You paid a little attention though, right? Like on the, 'how to pilot the ship when you need to' part?" Aimond asked.

Hoomer laughed.

"You don't need to pay attention to fly," she said.

"That seems wrong."

"Gal, we still flying?"

"Evidently," Galileo stated.

"You just need to be able to react when it's relevant," Hoomer reassured. "How's your hand-eye coordination?"

"Fine, I think," Aimond said.

"Gal!" Hoomer called.

"Deploying Space Rocks," Galileo announced.

"Wait, what?" Aimond's head darted around.

Although he was kicked off food-production duty, Galileo maintained strict control over every other apparatus within the galley. This became increasingly apparent to Aimond as the ice makers let loose a cacophony of grinding and churning. A moment of uneasy silence came as all machines aligned their spouts toward Aimond.

"Heads up," Hoomer warned, casually dodging a fist-sized ball of ice.

The beauty of being hit with ice lay within the curative nature of the projectile. If the ice, which caused the damage, was left on the damaged area, it was likely to decrease swelling. Ice, however, could not decrease the amount of unconsciousness left after Aimond failed to remove himself from the path of an ice missile. In his defense, it had little to do with hand-eye coordination.

He awoke shortly after with a suitably splitting headache. Hoomer sat next to him, back in front of Borlin Daps's wide grin and a mound of pending incident report papers. Daps rocked back and forth, his eyes plastered on a small screen on his desk.

"W-what—" Aimond stammered.

"Pre-intergalactic commerce-based ice-directed piloting discussion-induced training consideration injury," Daps squealed. "My very own zzOther before a single extraterrestrial sale. Now tell me. Where did you get hit?"

"Knocked him right in the side of the eye," Hoomer said.

Daps's screen honked and flashed a large red X.

He curled into his chair and cradled his head between his hands.

"Argh! It falls under eye strain." Daps moped. "Do me a favor, Aimond. If we do find a planet of eager consumers, don't get hit in the eye again. Unless the sale demands it."

Aimond nodded.

Daps's terminal dinged, suggesting the possibility of a St. Julius Marshmallow's workplace-induced sustained disappointment. He perked up and skittered to the form.

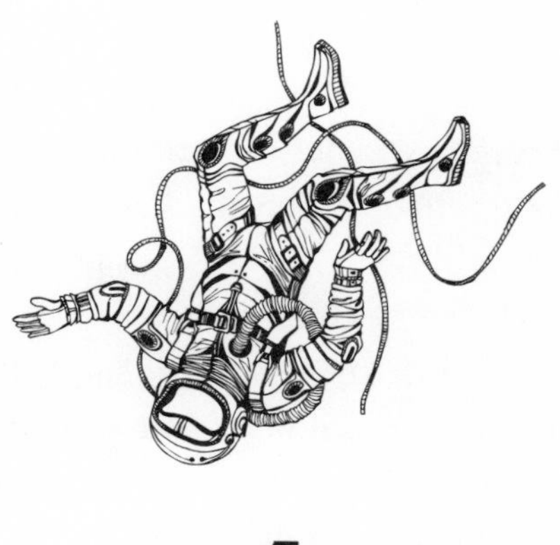

4

A HOLE

Jupiter's immense stature in the otherwise vast emptiness commanded a prominent position in the cockpit's view. An atmosphere of swirling gasses painted a dynamic tapestry of color and power. Even from afar, the indomitable reach of its gravity toyed with the *Gallant*'s trajectory, making apparent its level of control. Distant moons grew to the size of small planets as the *Gallant* sped ever closer to its destination.

The first Space Hole™ was discovered in the orbital path of Jupiter's moons when celestial bodies on a certain path continued to disappear. It existed in stasis, not subject to orbit or the surrounding gravity. Space Holes™ were a cosmic anomaly. Theories and speculation surrounded their existence as little more than modern-day fairy tales.

Attempts to study and measure the effects of traveling through a Space Hole™ had proven inconsistent. Objects had gone through, from probes to radio transmitters—even the remnants of an engineer's lunch, which was included as a marketing promotion for a new synthetic "fried chicken" that was both baked and made of tuna.

But to date, nothing has returned.

The latter portion of the Space Holes™ experiments was excluded from the crew's online training materials. On paper, survivability of Space Hole™ travel was 100 percent. This number was a statistical average taken from two main data points: zero out of zero humans that had entered a Space Hole™ had survived, and the fifty-fifty theory that a traveler would either die or not die when traversing through—this in turn rounded up based on "house odds" to 100 percent.

"So what exactly am I looking for?" Hoomer said as she positioned the *Gallant* into a far orbit. Her dark eyes squinted for a better view.

"Leadership says look for a vast ocean of opportunity and enlightenment," Daps suggested.

Kessler picked Daps up by the shoulders, walked him to a far corner of the bridge, and placed him down. "No more talking," she said.

Most of the crew had gathered on the bridge, staring out the limited view of the cockpit. In their own ways, each was ready to be part of history in the making.

"Gravitational anomaly detected," Galileo reported.

"Put it on screen," Kessler ordered.

The surrounding monitors flicked to a black screen. In reality, he had turned off the displays rather than waste energy rendering something invisible.

"Hoomer, take us in," Kessler instructed.

"Into what?" she asked.

"I've altered our heading," Galileo said. "You should see it soon."

Space Holes™ by their very nature swallowed light and matter, shooting them across dimensions and spitting them out countless light-years away. There was nothing on the visual light spectrum to see, but Galileo still enjoyed taunting the crew.

"There it is!" Aimond called out, pointing to what could very well have been a reflection of his head in the glass.

"What am I looking at?" Hoomer asked.

"A hole."

Daps crept back toward the rest of the huddled crew. He placed his left hand forward and palm out, his right hand in his right pocket with his wallet—the traditional Gainsbro salute, followed by the pledge.

"Through darkened skies, paths of peril, heavy winds, and water, we stay the course, push ahead, to post sales by next quarter."

Kessler glared at him, her cybernetic eye glowing a vivid shade of red, seemingly storing unvented aggression with each darkening hue. Daps placed himself back in the corner.

Tendrils of blue light whisked around an oval mouth against a tapestry of black. The lights dissipated and spread into nothingness as new waves of varying color and intensity followed behind. There was no sound, on the ship or off. The crew held their breath as Hoomer positioned the *Gallant* at the crest of the Space Hole™.

Their online training suggested the best point of entry would be a direct approach, as had been illustrated by a large red circle and a clip-art space shuttle moving in 2-D through the graphic over the course of eight seconds. The animations could not be skipped. It also failed to mention that the entry point undulated in varying sizes from grapefruit to moon, and the current shape was a rough approximation based on Galileo's sensors. This did not stop Hoomer from executing a maneuver known in rougher circles as the "YMOLO—TISBSTWRPWC. NM, FSA": You May Only Live Once—This Is Still Being Studied Therefore We Recommend Proceeding With Caution. Never Mind, Full Speed Anyway.

An arc of shadow swallowed the front of the ship as if entering a tunnel. The bridge's video screens flickered to life, displaying a spinning Gainsbro logo.

"Oh, this should be good," Kessler groaned.

Animated to have mostly human features, a woman with straight brown hair and eyes three times the normal size, designed to emulate a mixture of excitement and business acumen, appeared on screen. She began, "Members of the *GP Gallant* and distinguished cargo—"

"Aw, they included Aimond," Hoomer said.

"Shh!" Daps hissed. "It's for the expensive merchandise. Don't talk over her or they might feel rejected."

"—The Gainsbro Corporation congratulates you on your recent entry and/or exit and/or inconvenient crashing into the Space Hole™. If you have imploded, please give collection crews adequate room to recover merchandise by directing your bones away from cargo containers."

"Can you *steer* bones?" Paizley asked, trying to understand the mechanics.

"I can steer anything," Hoomer boasted. She glanced at the controls, wondering if she should begin steering instead of watching.

"As the wonders of commercial diplomacy await you, it is important to remember this mission's prime directive: never interfere with species who have no evidential financial system or easily physically negotiable precious resources to extract."

A list of resources that were deemed valuable enough to plunder scrolled across the screen in a lightning-fast blur.

Included among them were rare Earth elements, various expensive cheeses, and any objects theorized to contain unreleased tracks from the century's hit musical *The Well-Deserved Death of an Employee Who Used Two Vacation Days*.

"You may encounter strange and uncomfortable creatures on your journey," the presenter said. "Everyone with a wallet deserves varying levels of respect."

Winged centaurs, thick-scaled dragons, and other mythical creatures filled the screen.

"Is that just a guy wearing an 'I Love Florida' shirt?" Aimond asked.

Elizar wheezed. "Just look at its arms."

"They're normal?" Aimond asked.

"Humid monstrosities!" Elizar declared.

"You may come across dangerous customs and ideas," the video cautioned. "Remember not to adopt these habits."

A close-up of a man with equally unproportional-sized eyes took to the screen. He pointed to another person sitting on a park bench.

"That man is taking a thirty-one-minute lunch!" he shouted.

Abject terror and screams played atop a scene of burning cities before cutting back to the smiling host.

"Though policy dictates all species be kind to Gainsbro sales representatives, you may encounter hostilities."

The scene cut to a woman holding two bandoliers of grenades at the checkout counter of an electronics store. She placed a single battery-powered spoon in front of a cashier and turned to face the camera.

"No, I would not like the extended nine-hour warranty," she sneered, a forked snake tongue popping out of her mouth as crying babies interrupted the otherwise cheery store music.

Wide-eyed and mortified, Daps shuddered in his corner.

"It's your job to represent the interest of Gainsbro and all of Gainsbro shareholder-kind," the presenter said. "Best of luck on your mission and/or welcome back and/or mind your bone placement! And remember, a sale is temporary, but a regional sales office and its people are forever."

The following 624 words defining the terms of *forever* and *people* were condensed into a four-second screech discernible only to Galileo and Daps, who had memorized the clause.

"Well that was annoying," Kessler said. "Galileo, are we still on course?"

"Evidently."

Blackness. Silence. Pressure.

Then an explosion of color and noise as all of the energy sucked into the Space Hole™ condensed and floated around in the vortex. A steady but gentle rumble quaked the hull. Initial shock and stress of imploding on arrival wore off to the collective sigh of the crew. All that remained was the simple awe and beauty of a new facet of the universe. And what appeared to be a loosely tethered antenna ejecting off the side of the ship and flapping in space.

"Was that important?" Captain Kessler asked.

"Sure looked important," Hoomer insisted.

"Based on what criteria?"

"Do you add not important stuff to an intergalactic, first-of-its-kind spaceship?"

"Fair point."

"Well, Aimond is here," Galileo added.

"Also fair point," Kessler repeated.

Aimond stood with his arms up, waiting for some defense. If a gesture could be rhetorical, Aimond selected the correct one.

"Paizley, any way to determine what that was?" Kessler said. "Gal, have you run a damage scan?"

"I don't appear to be missing anything," Galileo noted. "However, I can detect that whatever it was remains attached. Exiting the Space Hole™ will likely break whatever bond is still available."

Galileo added a three-hour timer onto the cockpit's HUD. Travel times were an approximation, but at least they had something to go off of.

"Want me to slow it down?" Hoomer said.

"Can you do that?" Kessler asked.

"No idea. First time in a Space Hole™."

Kessler debated putting Hoomer in the corner with Daps but figured it best to leave her at the helm while hurtling at ludicrous speeds through an interdimensional portal. She reconsidered, but only barely.

"Okay, helpful people talking time now before I get strangley. Paizley?" Kessler said.

"If we can figure out what part of the ship it's still attached to, I might be able to create a shielded breach in the hull and pull it in. Whatever it is."

"I may have located that already," Galileo reported. "I'm detecting frequent, minor decompressions in Osor's quarters."

The only members not on the bridge to watch the Space Hole™ entry were Osor and Commander Seegler, the latter of whom was not only not on the bridge, but not on the ship. From the corner of the bridge, Daps perked up upon hearing minor decompressions. He side-stepped to a drawer and pulled out a small pile of forms. Kessler snatched them from his hands.

"Take Aimond and figure it out," she said to Paizley.

Closets hidden throughout the *Gallant*'s halls stored everything from space suits and blowtorches to odd-shaped screwdrivers that always proved just a little too big for anything. Paizley pulled out two suits and a pile of tools, then led Aimond to Osor's quarters. Given the hall-stored suits were intended to be used in emergencies and not during official sales-based ground expeditions, they lacked some of the amenities of the primary mission suits.

"Is this whole thing plastic?" Aimond asked.

"Single ply. Be extra careful."

"So, you do this kind of thing a lot?" Aimond said in his best attempt at flirting while slipping a semitransparent safety-bag over his head.

"Cut a hole in a ship traveling through a rift in space-time to pull in parts of that broken ship?"

"Yes?"

"I once pulled a live rooster out of my uncle's carburetor. That was a weird day, too."

"That's on the same tier to you?"

"Pretty much. I mean, how'd he even get in there?"

The local university's philosophy department had hooked its entire class up to a manifestation machine while debating the chronological existence of the chicken and egg. By harvesting the collective minds of over 240 students and professors, the machine manifested the quandary's solution.

The rooster's arrival inside the carburetor generated three mysteries: To Paizley and her uncle, there was no possible way a full-size rooster could wedge itself between the choke-plate and tiny tubes. To the philosophy department, the new conundrum was whether the origin of life was location dependent or required heavy machinery. Leaving the rooster, whose sudden corporeality generated the greatest perplexity, to ponder why an unexpected midlife incarnation straddled him with thirteen trillion dollars of debt and detailed plans to construct a multilevel marketing empire.

"So, uh, was he okay?" Aimond asked.

"He always stared at us menacingly," Paizley recalled. "One day he just up and vanished. The point is, anything can suddenly break. Or in that case, materialize life. But a mechanic has to be ready for all possibilities."

Aimond leaned against the wall as Paizley called for the elevator. Every cell in his body squeezed and strained with maximal effort to appear nonchalant. Before Paizley could look over at his attempt at peacocking, the ship lurched several degrees on its axis, forcing Aimond into a posture more closely resembling a laden barn owl.

"Apologies, a bit of turbulence," Galileo said.

"While surrounded by nothing?"

"Perhaps you'd be so kind as to share your Space Hole™ navigational almanac with us all," Galileo requested.

Osor's quarters were empty save for a clutter of gadgets and spare parts forming a labyrinth to his desk. A pristine patch of floor space encircled his desk chair, the Gainsbro SitMaster-2.6Million-Plus-Maximum. The chair's inclusion on the mission was a necessity for Osor to join. It cost roughly two years' salary. And for good reason. Promotional materials for the red and black ergonomic masterpiece depicted the chair in the most prominent of successful environments. Photos on its sales page showed the chair giving a high-stakes financial presentation, accepting a Nobel Prize for seating, and perhaps most compelling, the chair seated atop another version of itself next to his holiness, the CFO. None of the images included a person in the seat as the chair accomplished its numerous feats. This was in part because a person detracted from the beautiful material and failed to show the full magnitude of seating. But it was largely due to it just not being comfortable.

"Well, no one's here," Aimond said. "I'm not sure if that's a good or bad thing."

Paizley and Aimond stepped inside and felt an immediate pull. She unpacked her tools and knelt in front of a protrusion piercing through the entire thickness of the hull. A thin membrane of synthetic material popped on and off as a cover, venting bits of atmosphere then slapping shut.

"Gal was spot on as always," Paizley said. "Here's our weird flappy hole."

"Figured he said that as a means to try to get me ejected somehow."

"Why's that?" She pointed to an assortment of tools for Aimond to hand her as she inspected the damage.

"I don't think he likes me much."

"Nonsense. Gal likes everyone, don't you?"

"Wait, he can hear us in our rooms?" Aimond asked with a hint of concern.

"Oh yes," Galileo said. "I can hear you anywhere. And yes, Paizley, I adore you."

"See?" Paizley said. She fired up the acetylene torch. The noise blocked her hearing.

"And I would most certainly eject you," Galileo added. "But only after you patch whatever that is."

Little by little, Paizley worked to carve open a rectangular hatch with less than a hair's width of hull remaining.

"Be on the lookout," she shouted over the noise. "Never patched anything in Space Hole™ transit."

"Look out for what?" Aimond said.

"Anything weird."

Small purple rifts formed in the center of the room as Paizley pierced the hull. The oblong breaches pulsated with an ominous glow, spreading inch-long tendrils around its perimeter. Everything from tools to clothing began a steady orbit around the rift until being swallowed and vanishing. All except the SitMaster-

2.6Million-Plus-Maximum, which was firmly anchored with the sold-separately diamond mounting brackets.

"I think that qualifies," Aimond said.

"I would agree."

Paizley clipped herself into place as she cleared the last bit of hull. The remaining atmosphere vented out in a violent wind. Aimond held tight to the wall while trying to deflect any objects stuck in the rift's orbit from hitting Paizley.

A dense woven chain snaked outside of the ship, dangling on its end a myriad of spare parts creating a beacon of light. Paizley reached out and grabbed hold. She pulled the chain back, coiling it on the floor, which the rift's gravity picked up and whipped around. Each rotation pelted Aimond in the chest.

The chain and glowing object were back inside, and Paizley worked to patch the hull just as the door to Osor's quarters slid open. In walked Osor, holding his breath and carrying an armful of small machines welded into a monstrous ball. The mass shot out of Osor's arms toward Paizley and the open patch of ship. Be it heroic instinct, athletic prowess, or unfortunate luck, Aimond managed to block the projectile. With his head. And immediately lost consciousness—again. It was not athletic prowess.

5

FROM OUT THE OTHER END

Every person has, at some point in his or her life, experienced a unique but definitive worst-ever way to be awoken. For some this could be freezing water, a crashing roof, or an existential crisis in realizing there were still at least fifty years of wage slavery before an inevitably near demise. But for Aimond, it was just shy of fifteen joules of electricity discharged directly onto his inner thighs.

Aimond exploded awake, shooting upright almost off the med-bay table.

"See, if they're dead, they don't do that." The raspy deadpan voice of Dr. Erza Cole was rarely, if ever, littered with sympathy.

"You're okay!" Paizley rushed in to offer a hug.

"Ow," Aimond said. "What happened? But mostly, ow."

"You bled all over my table," Dr. Cole said, her stoic expression matching a white coat and straight gray hair.

"I guess, before that?"

"You bled on my floor."

"Aimond, meet Dr. Erza Cole," Paizley introduced.

Her halfhearted grunt served as enough of a greeting. Dr. Cole spent much of her professional career treating extreme injuries, performing last-ditch surgeries, and trialing procedures more aptly described as "well, we'll see what happens." She thrived in chaos and had either the conviction or bravado to attempt what others avoided to save her patients.

When she was approached by the Gainsbro Board to join the *Gallant*'s crew, it was reported she jumped at the opportunity. The truth was she had thrown much of the contents of a surgical suite at those who requested her presence. It was not until she met Captain Kessler that she agreed to come aboard. Something about their ability to tear a man down to his core without ever uttering a word resonated with each other.

But she still hated being bored.

"Great, let's just turn my whole med-bay into a lounge. Go ahead, grab a drink everyone," Dr. Cole grumbled as Osor and Kessler entered.

"You're not dead," Kessler said. "Okay."

"I'm not certain how to respond to that," Aimond said.

Light flickered and danced on the ceiling as Osor toyed with a small flashlight. Kessler grabbed him by the collarbone and pulled him forward. He pointed his flashlight onto Aimond's head. Kessler tightened her grip.

"Oh, right!" Osor said. "So sorry I almost removed your head. And for potentially opening a temporal rift that almost swallowed you. And for the bees."

"What was that last part?"

"See, I was *this* close to a groundbreaking, light-shattering discovery!" Osor gloated, holding his arms at the maximum width then quickly bringing them in to about three feet apart.

He had discovered something, though he was not quite sure what that was yet. Using a method he had yet to coherently explain, Osor managed to deploy an array of winged lights on a rigid coil to flap alongside the ship.

"Fins make planes go fast. Fast fins. Light is fast," Osor said, waving his hands as if finger painting an equation. "We've gotta go really fast. Already moving faster than light, but we're on light. So what if?"

He paused for almost a minute.

"What if?" Aimond repeated, unsure if he was being baited or Osor froze.

"We add fins to light, attach it to ourselves while moving faster than light, to boost the finned light into faster-than-light speed. Which is double light. I call it, bright speed."

Aimond blinked. "That doesn't seem right. But I don't know enough about Space Hole™ physics to argue against it."

"No one's ever been through one," Paizley added. "So, can only guess; no one knows for certain."

"So I'm right. There must be light!"

Osor wriggled out of his shirt, which remained locked in Kessler's grip. He tore away and ran out of the med-bay, shirtless and bellowing a triumphant cackle.

"Next time I dangle you outside!" Kessler shouted after him. She took a deep breath. "So everyone's alright?"

"Yet for some reason, you're all still here," Dr. Cole said.

"Don't I have a concussion or something?" Aimond asked.

"Yes, probably. And what of it?"

"Shouldn't I get something?"

Dr. Cole opened a cold drawer and pulled out an ice pack. She tossed it onto Aimond's lap.

"Hold that on your head until it stops hurting."

"Does that actually help a concussion?"

"Sure."

Kessler nodded.

"When you're done being concussed, get to the bridge," she ordered. "We're almost at the end of the estimated transit time."

Unfathomable mysteries and endless theories surrounded the emerging side of the Space Hole™. The only image of the other end was an artist's rendering of giant green nebulas spanning a vast starscape bordered by a pair of red binary stars. A craterous gray protoplanet filled the foreground, about the size of Earth's moon. The artist had no data to go on, nor were they commissioned by the Gainsbro Space Exploration Program. He just showed up one day in a secure building, handed over the painting, and departed without a word. Since then, the image was used in training and media broadcasts as the definitive view of first emergence. The crew once again assembled on the bridge. White light poured through the cockpit as if bursting out from deep underground to a cloudless sunny day.

"Where is Seegler? He's going to miss this," Kessler said.

"Thought I saw 'im in cargo strapping stuff down," Elizar said. Elizar had not visited the cargo bay for several hours, but a brief bout of narcolepsy made him certain he had a lengthy conversation with Seegler about cargo safety. Except they were in the ocean. And Seegler was a walrus. "Does good works, that kid."

Steady vibrations tremored throughout the ship, growing more powerful with each passing second. The light before them undulated and danced as the ship passed. Transcendental cosmic ringing drowned all other noises as the effulgence swallowed the *Gallant*. The ship emerged, breaking free of the reverberant tones and closing the crescendo of soundscape with a loud "nyeehh," similar to that of an old man standing after a three-hour sit. The crew looked at one another.

"Well, that killed it a little bit, if I'm being honest," Hoomer said.

They had arrived. Thousands of light-years from home, traversed in a few short hours. Before the crew could appreciate the achievement and bask in the view, Hoomer yanked hard on the stick and torqued the *Gallant* up almost ninety degrees. The wing of the ship narrowly avoided colliding into a gray, rocky, craterous mass just about the size of Earth's moon.

"Great early warning there, Gal," Hoomer criticized.

"Sorry, I was focusing on something else," he admitted. "Did you see Aimond's ice pack?"

Aimond held up his hands. The ice pack had dribbled onto his shirt. But he could not bring himself to care. As the ship pitched up, the cockpit windows revealed a massive green nebula spanning as far as the eye could see. A single red star shone bright against the backdrop.

"Stupid," Kessler said. "It doesn't even have two stars."

"Nope, there it is," Hoomer called out, pointing the ship toward the second.

"No one else finds that a bit unnerving?" Aimond asked.

"Maybe the artist was just really in touch with the universe," Paizley suggested.

The crew stood in relative silence for a moment, soaking in a combination of obscure coincidence and the breadth of their new destination. The moment soon passed as everyone had moved on and prepared themselves for the next thing of relative interest. Kessler took the opportunity to rally her team.

"Welcome to uncharted territory," she projected. "I don't need to remind you all, our mission is to seek life wherever it may be."

"Provided they have currency for corporate misprints," Daps added.

Kessler lobbed the flight log at him without so much as a glance. It whizzed right by his face.

"Humans have been searching for centuries for intelligent life," Kessler said. "There are hundreds of billions of worlds and no telling how long it might take us to find one. So—"

"About forty-three seconds," Galileo reported. "I'm detecting radio signals consistent with a musical broadcast."

Galileo opened all audio channels, sending the signal throughout the ship. Earth's scientists and philosophers hoped the first transmission that interstellar life intercepted from humans would be a message of peace, classical music, or a depiction of Earth's art and beauty. In actuality they all expected something closer to a reality TV star burping the alphabet while riding atop a monster truck through a minefield. Given the propensity for all imagined extraterrestrial life to be fundamentally similar to humans, but with inferior corporate branding, it came as a combination of surprise and curiosity when a medley of bullfrog noises singing what resembled death-metal screeching overtop melodic banging played.

"I think I know this one," Hoomer said.

"Wait for it," Galileo said as he slowly mixed in Aimond's solo saxophone performance.

"I'm into it," Hoomer approved. "In a weird masochistic kinda way."

"The froggy screeches do match the unique pitch," Paizley added.

Kessler held up a finger to silence everyone before the room deteriorated into a musical critique or deserved collective Aimond bashing.

"Can you locate the origin?" Kessler asked.

The bridge screens flashed to life and displayed a rapid zoom of an egg-shaped red and tan planet. Dense gray clouds circled around the four edges of the planet, highlighting the colorful center's brilliant hue.

"Spectroscopy scans indicate oxygen-rich atmosphere, trace amounts of neon," Galileo said.

Daps trembled with an excited grin plastered to his face. In his eyes reflected not the soul, but an inventory log of all available merchandise on board and the order in which it could be sold. Subconscious mutterings leaked as if deflating the obtuse list in his head.

"No merchandising until we establish contact!" Kessler shouted, breaking his trance.

Hoomer brought the *Gallant* closer to the planet. Thick bands of gray clouds all but obscured the northern and southern poles. Orbital scans pinpointed two major congregations of life. Galileo selected a landing zone a short trek from one of the hubs, so as not to risk frightening any local intelligence.

This lesson was learned from Earth when a group of recreational extraterrestrial enthusiasts spotted an unidentified object descending from Earth's sky. Like any enthusiast club, they had access to a mediocre telescope, light snacks, and a heavy armament. Excited by the prospect of discovering alien visitors, the members unleashed a series of surface-to-air missiles to encourage the craft to land. After watching the remains crash land miles away, the group decided to avoid traffic and stay put so as not to abandon their light snacks.

The second occurrence was in the city of Philadelphia where a local man decided a light in the sky was too bright. He discharged a litany of rocket-propelled grenades to request the light dim. It was the moon. Conveniently the clouds of smoke from the explosives did reduce relative luminosity by half.

"LZ looking clear from above," Hoomer said. "Prep for descent."

"Right. Everyone sit and ready your stations," Kessler ordered, standing from the captain's chair.

Atmospheric entry was smooth compared to the jostle of returning on Earth. The *Gallant*'s design repurposed heat generated from atmospheric reentry to be absorbed and routed to ship amenities like soaking tubs, dry saunas, and air circulation. So a lack of heat-generating turbulence was somewhat of a disappointment. Once they broke passing cloud coverage, a distant ground grew ever closer.

"I'm getting me gun," Elizar grunted.

"No guns," Kessler replied.

Swirling lights flickered on and flashed throughout the bridge.

"Oh no, here it comes," Galileo said before his free-will abilities were overridden with a hard-coded warning from Corporate. "The Gainsbro Corporation congratulates you on your incoming projectiles and reminds you to brace for impact!"

"They're excited for us to land!" Daps screeched.

Hoomer slammed the ship into evasive maneuvers, barrel-rolling and pivoting down in a sharp corkscrew. A blast of fire tore past the ship, narrowly avoiding a connecting hit. She leveled the *Gallant* and adjusted course to land. Kessler remained standing, rigid throughout and unfazed by the sudden shift in velocity.

"Was that a missile?!" Aimond screeched.

"Fine," Kessler relented. "One gun. You hear me? *One* gun."

Elizar muttered an acknowledgment and trudged off the bridge. He rode the elevator down beyond the armory to the crew quarters. Mindless mumbling followed him the entire way back to his bunk, trying to land on the best choice for the occasion. Once inside his room, Elizar popped open a hidden hatch behind his bunk and removed a cannon the size of his torso.

"One gun," he repeated.

Clouds of scarlet dust swirled as Hoomer touched down in a rocky clearing. The pale red grasses below swayed in a gentle breeze as the engines quieted.

First contact on an alien world was grounds for excitement, caution, and entrepreneurial spirit. Daps was first off the ship, not yet receiving Galileo's blessing of safe atmospheric scans. He scurried to find a flat patch of land, pitch a canopy, and set up shop.

The rest of the crew followed close behind. Suits covered from head to toe in branded logos and adverts, their protective gear was designed for aesthetics and occasional function.

"Why's this thing so hard to walk in?" Aimond wondered.

"Well," Hoomer said, squatting next to him, "looks like you got Gainsbro IronWorks patches on the knees." She gave them a knock. "At least you won't scrape your knees."

"What's on yours?"

"Soap," she said. "Actual soap in a gel pack. If I kneel down, pretty sure they'll explode."

Captain Kessler stepped down the ramp carrying a forklift's worth of metal on her shoulder. She drove silver poles into the ground in a circle around the ship.

Blue arcs crackled and resonated between the tips of the rods once driven into the dirt.

"Paizley, Elizar, help me establish a perimeter," Kessler commanded. "The rest of you, eyes sharp. We don't know what we're walking into here."

Daps insisted the portable fencing not restrict the egress of potential customers. He directed Paizley to establish a queue while he hung misprinted "Giasnbor" T-shirts for display. Kessler snatched Elizar's cannon and blasted Daps's pop-up shop into ash with an eruptive burst of plasma. Snorts and grunts echoed from over the low hills by the landing zone. Five creatures emerged and plodded their way toward the camp.

Wide as they were tall, with thick cylindrical torsos and frog-like faces sporting a pair of mouths pointing left and right, the creatures resembled Earth's amphibians. But giant, upright, and smushed together.

Clunky three-toed feet left prints in the dirt as they lumbered into camp. Despite their size, the group presented itself as passive. They carried no visible weapons or made any suspicious movements. Instead, they stepped over the barrier fence and fanned out inside the camp.

One of the creatures approached Aimond. Its two mouths opened, belching out a simultaneous gurgle and croak from each orifice.

"Uh, hi," Aimond said. "I'm Marcus Aimond. From Earth."

It tilted its head and opened its mouths wider.

"What's your name?" He waited for a response to the seemingly rhetorical question. "What. Is. Name. You?"

"How's that working out for ya?" Hoomer questioned.

"I don't think well."

"Have you tried talking louder? That usually does it for me."

Osor stumbled down the *Gallant*'s boarding ramp. He waved around a silver handheld contraption. Aimond and Hoomer both craned their necks to get a view of his knees.

"What's with the little radioactive signs?" Hoomer said.

"Gainsbro Fusion," Osor said. "Project I helped with back on Earth. Pointless now. Pointless! The future is light." He fanned his hands in front of his face for dramatic effect. "It's loaded with unstable nucleo-reactive catalysts that could explode if disturbed. Think of the fusion!"

They both took a step back.

"Maybe the metal kneepads aren't so bad."

Their visitor hunched and continued its combination croaking, returning the crew's attention to the hulking alien life-form in front of them. Osor waved the device in front of Aimond and Hoomer.

"I got this. Made a thing. Thing for. Uh. For words. With lights and brain lasers."

"Yeah, that's reassuring," Hoomer said.

"Beams condensed microwave scans of linguistic centers of the brain, then transfers it. Rough guess on frog guy anatomy, but probably works."

Osor shrugged. His small-scale testing proved successful. Initial scans of the linguistic center of a reconstituted banana pudding were transferred into that of a bag of almonds Osor had drawn a face on.

Verbal alterations remained difficult to evaluate. But nothing exploded or disintegrated . . . much.

"Microwaves and heads scream safety," Aimond said. "Any side effects?"

"Practically harmless?"

"And you're saying that with a rising inflection because . . ."

He fiddled with the device, staring down the small barrel at the end.

"Like a ninety-nine percent safety rating."

"What's the one percent?" Hoomer asked.

"Horrible brain-melting micro explosions liquefy everything between your eyes until it runs out your nose," Osor sped through the minor disclaimer. "But what are the odds?"

"Apparently one in a hundred."

He looked up, contemplating the truth to that, nodded, and shot the device at his own head, then at the creature.

"There. Now you understand me?" Osor inquired.

The croaking hybrid added an occasional pause, change in inflection, and morphing syllables. Little by little, the noises turned into words.

"Light, lights. Fast lights," it stammered.

"Your head's all scrambled," Hoomer said. "Gimme it."

She blasted herself and the creature again.

It stumbled and blinked.

"Welcome travelers, to our home!" it exclaimed.

"Wow, it actually worked," Aimond remarked.

"Meh," Hoomer commented.

"Give me some credit!" Osor said. "Now for a name . . . Speaky, shooty articulate-lasers."

"Articulaser has a nice ring," Aimond suggested.

Having limited success in her own communication attempts, despite removing adverbs and speaking with an increasingly thunderous volume, Kessler joined the trio. She stood for a moment, realizing the creature now spoke near perfect English, but not bothering to question how.

"Good, this one speaks right," she said. "Mine's broken." She turned to the creature. "Who or what are you and why did you shoot at my ship?"

"I am Zanartas, a Nerelkor. Sorry about shooting at you. Our people, the great and mighty Rejault, are at war with the freedom-hating Dinasc. And we shoot at anything flying if we don't recognize it. Or stationary. Or moving slowly."

"So you just shoot anything you don't recognize?"

"Pretty much, yes." Zanartas nodded.

The remaining four Nerelkor huddled around Daps's disintegrated tent remnants. They watched as Daps scooped up fallen merchandise, dusted it off despite obvious burn marks, and placed it back on display. The group mimicked his movements, bending, scooping the air, and brushing their imaginary payload.

"Can you take us to those in charge?" Kessler requested.

"Take us to their leaders?" Hoomer said. "Bit cliché, yeah?"

"Wait, wait!" Daps shouted.

Given a suitable restoration of his cinder-laden shop, Daps progressed to establishing the first intergalactic Gainsbro World Education Center. Designed to present human history in a positive and meaningful two-minute performance, the presentation called together over four million participants' integral history, compiled and regurgitated.

Daps unfolded and inflated a holographic table display. It illuminated with a pleasant chime, directing the majority of its frequent flashes to a coin slot along the side. He inserted a series of coins and stepped back as a hologram came to life.

"Gainsbro presents the history of Earth!" the voice declared.

Images of a crowded highway were overtaken by a sea of red and orange molten rock. It covered the entire display, then zoomed out.

"First there was lava, which cooled and got hard. Then it rained for at least a week, creating oceans."

A firehose of water erupted onto the projection, covering a chunk of the barren land in a sudden tsunami.

"Finally, people sprouted and colonized the new lava by planting trees and animals."

"How do you plant animals?" Aimond asked.

"Shh. I'm learning," Hoomer said.

"Early man lived as savages until Martin Gainsbro united the world and placed a border fence around Florida."

The closing soundtrack was a difficult selection as it had to represent all of humanity. Project managers had solicited suggestions from across the globe, which were ignored and returned with a limited-issue collectible itemized bill and accompanying debit. Instead they agreed upon nominating the most profitable songs from history. All of them. The sixteen petabytes of audio were merged and condensed into a half-second sound burst to provide the ultimate human experience.

The machine expelled a discordant sound so loud it exploded.

"I feel like that might be missing . . . a few steps," Aimond said.

"The explosion wrapped it up accurately," Hoomer approved.

"It was close enough," Daps grumbled.

Zanartas applauded in the traditional Nerelkor fashion, by headbutting the ground with reckless abandon. While already on the dirt, the group of Nerelkor crawled over to Daps and bowed their heads.

"And what is this?" Kessler demanded.

"This one has the most stuff and loudest explosion. We pay tribute to your leader."

Kessler's body went stiff. Her gaze darted back and forth between Daps and the group of Nerelkor mirroring his now exaggerated gestures. Aimond leaned in to Hoomer.

"What's she doing?" he whispered.

"Probably gauging if she can lift the giant frog dude by the head."

"Think she could?"

Hoomer shrugged. Kessler stepped forward and lifted Daps, walking beyond the perimeter fence.

"But that is considerably easier," Hoomer said.

"He's like a balloon."

"Mostly various gasses."

The Nerelkor group scurried after Daps, but once outside the visible range of his remaining merchandise, they stopped paying him any mind.

"Leaders. Move," Kessler demanded. "Paizley, Hoomer. Give the ship a once-over. Daps, meat-shield, you're with me. Seegler has command until I'm back."

Aimond looked back and forth between the other crew members, realizing his lack of distinct job role lent him to undesirable tasks. A balmy three-kilometer walk with the Nerelkor party showcased the area's landscapes: dusty fields of red sand and dried sticks. The same ambience had been used to decorate homes back on Earth at great expense. Craters of varying sizes littered the land, the largest of which spanned a half kilometer.

City walls crept into view. Or at least what started as walls, then devolved into a few poles with string draped in between and the closest approximation to a Nerelkor keep-out sign affixed every few poles.

"Welcome to Rejault City," Zanartas said. "Before you go in, we have to run through entry procedures."

"Alright," Kessler agreed.

Zanartas pulled a crumpled paper from a pile of dirt by the entrance.

"All outsiders must agree to the following: No paid jobs. Working for free is acceptable but must be done begrudgingly. In the event you are injured, you will be ejected. If your injury is accidentally treated using Rejault funds, you will be reinjured and ejected."

"How hospitable."

"One more thing."

He raised his arm and smacked Daps across the face. Aimond went next. Both men toppled to the ground, rubbing their stinging cheeks. Zanartas turned to Kessler, whose cross-armed glare forced the behemoth to reconsider.

"According to the Rejault charter, you're all horrible and should never come here," Zanartas said. "Now, welcome! Let's go inside."

Zanartas pushed down the wooden gate long off its hinges. It landed with a cloudy thud against the red dirt. Once the party crossed through, he propped it back in position. The crew took their first steps inside the city, expecting to be floored by alien architecture, winding spires, and decorative lights. Buildings made of sticks, rocks, and mud outlined what could be construed as streets. Some opted to dig underground and set up shelter. Other hovels used nets as roofs, lacked walls, or simply had their belongings in a small square lined with debris.

"This is awful," Aimond observed. "Is this all a result of the war?"

Zanartas tilted his head. "What is? The weather? It's always humid."

While humidity was awful and in itself one of the many reasons the Gainsbro Corporation decided not to absorb the state of Florida, the surroundings were worse. Or at least as bad as Florida. Sharing further similarity, young Nerelkor set up stands to sell rocks or interesting debris. Their customer base would barter with other refuse lying about. Eroded bridges lay collapsed, still keeping their general function as the city piled enough garbage on top of the defunct structure to make it level again.

"What's the deal with this house?" Aimond inquired.

He stopped in front of a pristine white building about half the size of the *Gallant*. Its blue lawn held the only evidence of thriving native plants. Surrounded on all sides by destruction, the structure maintained a distinct perimeter between its beauty and the squalor. One hole in the corner of the property broke the picturesque landscaping.

"That's Kob's home," Zanartas said. "He hates us."

"How come?"

"Every now and then a representative of the Grand Five will dig a swatch of his lawn and bring it back with them. He blames it on us every time."

"Us who?"

Zanartas gestured outward. Beyond Kob's house was a kilometer of ruined city. A dim golden light flourished on the horizon, casting a few beams on the destroyed homes whose crumpled metal and wood reached for a taste of the glow. The closer the group walked to the light, the more intense was its radiance, obscured only by a massive reinforced wall. Dozens of Nerelkor lined up single file. Each carried a sack and a weapon, waiting for their chance to pass through a small cut-out less than half their size. A guard on the opposite end of the makeshift gate would weigh each sack, pop out of his shelter and through a normal-sized door, then kick the Nerelkor through the hole until they emerged. The weight of the sack determined the strength of the proceeding kick.

"That's the offering entrance," Zanartas noted. "Every day we bring what money we find to the Grand Five as tribute. If you bring enough, you don't even get kicked that hard! Those are good days."

"How much to go through?" Daps asked, running through mental spreadsheets.

"Not a chance," Kessler warned.

"We'll take the business entrance," Zanartas instructed.

He pointed to a wide open section of wall. Ornate patterned cobblestone walkways wove along lush gardens and twisted metal sculptures. One Nerelkor stood at the entrance with a broom, swatting at flecks of dirt in the air so that none of the outside filth would carry in. The janitorial guard, armed with his broom and a rifle the size of his body, turned to the group as they approached. Zanartas and the guard stood, staring at each other for a moment in silence. All outside filth needed to be wiped. He lifted his broom, swiped down from Aimond's face to his shoes, and moved on to the next crew member before stepping aside.

Kessler scowled and Daps picked up bits of smeared-on dirt as a possible collectible to resell on Earth. Beyond the entrance, five opulent golden mansions towered with a commanding presence. Each property maintained an immaculate garden save for one small corner where Kob's lawn pilings were staged in a haphazard lump. Arranged in a semicircle, the five mansions dwarfed a small but decorative stone building at the edge of a steep cliff.

"Whoa, who lives there?" Aimond gawked.

"These are the residences of the Grand Five," Zanartas gleamed. "Our esteemed lords."

"Make it to leader and you get to live in luxury. Not a bad gig."

"Quite backward. They lead because they live in luxury."

Aimond tilted his head.

The team approached the smaller middle building and followed Zanartas inside. Before crossing into the atrium of the Governing Hall, Zanartas grabbed each crew member by the shoulders and spun them around.

"Until we enter the main chamber with the Grand Five, you must walk backward. Don't look at anything," he said.

"What? Why?" Kessler asked.

Zanartas paused and stood in a still moment of silence. "I have no idea. That's just what you do."

It was what every Nerelkor did upon entering the building, not by written necessity but mandated tradition. The lead architect who'd constructed the Governing Hall wanted to check if the decorative gold wrapping above the entrance was gold enough, as the previous lead had been ejected via cannon for a wall that was deemed "not blue enough." The wall was a window. To prevent a similar fate, the new lead architect walked backward, keeping an eye on the doorway, evaluating the degree of goldness. Others on the construction team saw this and followed his example, walking backward, if for no other reason than to discover what was so interesting about the entryway.

Not understanding why his workers were following his example, the architect assumed if everyone was walking backward it must be correct. From then on, not one Nerelkor dared face forward in the atrium.

That tradition carried on generations later. Violators were tackled by backward-running guards, then ejected via reverse-facing cannons for fear of what would happen were they left to their own direction.

As soon as they crossed the threshold into the main chambers, they were allowed to turn and face them. The Grand Five. Pomposity rivaled curiosity from a visual spectacle of precious metals and gems. Each member sat atop a golden throne positioned in a semicircle around a vast pit. Large woven sacks sat beside each of the Grand Five, and above, large cylindrical ducts. Kessler blasted each of the Five with the Articulaser. No one flinched at the brandished weapon-esque device.

Zanartas slammed his head to the ground and threw a large wad of paper cash into the pit. The wad thumped and rumbled as a pump sorted and pushed the currency through the ducts, traveling above the Grand Five. Money dropped into each sack beside them.

"Oh, great leaders," Zanartas said, "I seek your audience to present you with fur creatures from Planet Gurth."

"Earth," Aimond whispered.

"From Planet Gurthearth."

Grand One waited for a signal from Zanartas to specify the appropriate reaction, dependent on the crew's apparent wealth. An expensive-looking starship seemed sufficient enough to select the correct welcoming greeting. Grand One shifted on his throne. He held high a small carved stick.

"Ah, of course. I am an expert on matters of planet Gurth-earth," he said. "Welcome, distant travelers. Who among you leads?"

Captain Kessler stepped forward, but Zanartas pushed Daps in front of her.

Grand Three reached into his sack, pulled out a fistful of cash, and lobbed it at Grand One. The stack hit him square in the face. Unfazed and unflinching, he deposited the stack into his sack and handed the stick over to Grand Three.

"And what is it you wish of us? We are busy fighting a war."

Grand Five tossed a stack of cash at Grand Three. He did not relent. Two more stacks pelted his face until the pile in his lap threatened to spill over. Grand Five grabbed the stick.

"Perhaps you've come to offer something of value?"

"Funny you should mention that," Daps said.

Kessler picked him up by the head and placed Daps behind her.

"We're interested in learning more about this war with the Dinasc," she said. "We'd like to help resolve it if possible."

Grand Two lobbed his cash stacks and grabbed the stick.

"We—"

Money from all four of the other Grands flew at Grand Two, covering him and throwing the room into a stalemate.

The bylaws of the Grand Order were clear. Whomever held the Talking Stick was in charge. The Talking Stick was always for sale and could be given up to anyone who provided a reasonable enough price. In the event more than one bidder placed an offer, a bidding war opened. Rather than the traditional bidding war in which the highest price emerged victorious, Grand Five opened a side door to invite tributaries from the Offering Entrance.

Those paying tribute lined up to dump whatever they had into the central pit. Advanced mechanics created the only fair randomized way to reallocate the funds. A spinning bat pelted donated items toward one of five sack-bound vents. The mechanism continued to spin until all deposits were cleared or sufficiently smashed into immeasurable dust—a prevailing reason why the Rejault moved away from glass-based currency. Once redistributed, a hidden scale evaluated the Grand Five's sacks and illuminated a light behind the heaviest. The greatest sack won the bidding war and earned the Talking Stick.

All of this occurred while the Grands tossed small explosives at the tributaries to a festive soundtrack. Participants were offered a commemorative sticker, which eroded into an invoice beyond three hours.

After an eight-minute bidding ceremony and only seven serious injuries, Grand Four snatched the stick.

"Your help is expected. Zanartas, you will enlighten our new servants as to the conditions we face. You may use the Enlightening Chambers."

Grand Four lobbed fistfuls of coins at a button on the far wall. He missed. Twelve attempts and a small fortune later, his throw connected and the door opened. Zanartas encouraged the crew to join him. Once they approached the door, a one-meter-long conveyor belt kicked into gear, saving approximately one and a quarter steps inward.

Massive ceilings adorned with crystal chandeliers ran for more than triple the length of the previous hall. Faces of the Grands draped from massive tapestries, covering the few windows and preventing any natural light from entering. Polished stone tables stretched long enough to fit most of the population on a single side. At the end of the nearest table sat a single whiteboard with markers long since dried.

"Before we begin, how will you be paying?" Zanartas said.

"Paying for what?" Kessler glared.

"Access to this room comes at the price of four million Quarz. There was a sign on the side of the doorframe."

"The one we were belted through?"

"By entering, you agreed to pay no less than the fee with a thirteen-percent convenience charge for any payment deemed convenient by the payment recipient."

"Which is whom exactly?"

Zanartas pointed to the pit within the main chamber, currently being loaded by a dirt-covered Nerelkor from the Offering Line before the door to the chamber slid shut.

"And if we refuse?" Kessler asked.

Zanartas took a wide stance. Both mouths opened. "Binding arbitration."

Daps perked up. He trotted around Kessler and over to Zanartas's side.

"I'm all over this," Daps squealed.

He placed his arm around Zanartas and walked him farther down the table out of earshot before, as if by magic, brandishing a dozen pens and a ream of paper.

They returned a half hour later.

"We struck a deal," Daps asserted, his small frame dwarfed by their massive guide. He paused, waiting for Kessler to inquire further, which seemed a lost cause. "We're allowed a two-week trial period. If we don't cancel, then we're automatically signed up for the equivalent of a nine-year recurring contract."

"Then cancel it." Kessler sighed with her head in her hand.

"Well, I can't. The cancellation office is in another building, which is apparently open once every few days for about fifteen minutes."

"This is you handling it?" Aimond asked.

"Trust me, the other options were far worse. I'm talking rehypoth—"

A screeching siren loud enough to rattle bones cut Daps off. Kessler glanced over at his lips, unsure if the sound was still him talking or from an external source. Aimond and Daps covered their ears.

"What's going on?" Aimond shouted over the noise.

"We have to wait and see," Zanartas explained. The noise paused for a moment. "If it's just the one siren, it's an incoming weather event."

The siren resumed. Aimond gestured to the noise for Zanartas to continue.

"Two sirens means a youngling found a world-destroying weapon in the cafeteria."

"That's happened often enough to warrant its own warning system?" Aimond inquired.

"Oh yes. The cafeteria is very dangerous."

The siren quieted and the crew looked around with a hesitant optimism that the planet remained intact. But the siren sounded once more.

"If that's two . . . what's three?"

Zanartas sank to the ground, taking cover behind the table. He grabbed Aimond by both shoulders, bringing him closer. Though unfamiliar with Nerelkorian nonverbals, the wide-eyed panic was universal.

"Brief financial decline."

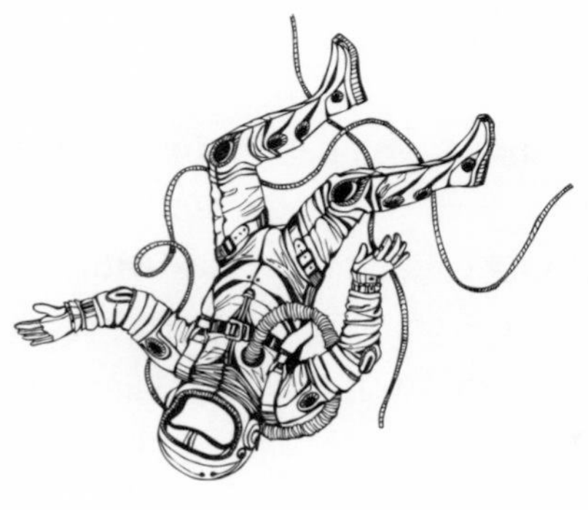

6
MEET THE NEIGHBORS

The door to the Enlightening Chamber burst open. A squad of five armed Nerelkor lined up to roll in on the conveyor belt. A sixth member scurried up behind them, having dropped money into the pit before joining the line, and collecting forms for each entrant to the chamber.

Once they were all inside, those with melee weapons smashed tables and surrounding walls. They placed the liberated hunks of stone in torn bags and wandered around the massive hall looking for anything else of potential value.

As their loot bags filled with random debris and anything with a shine above a matte, they approached the crew. The largest among them stopped to wave at Zanartas as they pointed their weapons forward.

Kessler zapped each invader with the Articulaser as they approached, unfazed by the armed contingent before her.

"Hi, Brutaz," Zanartas greeted.

"Hi, Zanartas and everyone! So great to meet you," Brutaz, the largest of the group, said. "I'm going to need all of you to hand over everything valuable and stay with us, please."

"What exactly is happening?" Kessler asked.

"We're being taken captive," Zanartas noted. "Most likely for ransom."

"And who pays the ransom?"

Zanartas shrugged and smashed a table. He picked up some rock chunks and handed them over.

Maintained at gunpoint, the crew was escorted out of the building and back toward the city fringes. Organized chaos filled the streets. Nerelkor waited in neat lines to add fuel to burning fires, throw rocks at already dilapidated buildings, or search the ground for anything of interest. Everyone carried a weapon, some small, some excessive. Despite the intermittent blast, no fights broke out, only the occasional misfire or bet to see who could get closest to Kob's house without hitting it.

Groups rallied around Kob's home. Members took turns walking on the lawn, turning toward the others and screaming at the horde.

"What's up with them?" Aimond asked as they passed by.

"Whoever steps on the grass gets to blame the poors," Zanartas said. "It's easier on Kob's lawn to blame someone else."

"Wouldn't the Grand Five be to blame?"

Zanartas exhaled forcefully through both mouths and squealed in what could only be assumed as a potential laugh. "How could they cause a financial decline if they have all the money?"

The crew were prodded onward to the entrance of a large hole surrounded by rocks reliant on one another for a delicate dance of balance. One wrong wobble would send the perimeter crashing into the hole below. But upright rocks were a sign of success and well worth risking entombment for public accolade. Brutaz helped everyone down a dirt slope and underground into a communal living space for a dozen Nerelkor. Without lowering his weapon, he turned toward a pool on the floor and filled a number of small bowls.

"Come, you must be thirsty," Brutaz said.

A thick yellow murk sloshed around inside the bowls. Its smell landed somewhere between a field of three-month-old eggs and unwashed feet after seven years wandering in an exotic landfill.

"I'm not sure we can consume that," Kessler contended. "What is it?"

"Mostly sulfur I think," Brutaz said.

"We can't drink it either," Zanartas added.

"Then why—"

"Figured it would be good for something," Brutaz said. "And some of your skins are kind of the same color so it made sense."

The liquid started a slow but steady escape from underneath the bowls as it eroded the bottom into a pulpy mesh.

"We'll pass."

"Suit yourselves."

Brutaz tossed the bowls into the puddle. They bobbed around for a moment before fizzling into the murk. The other Nerelkor inside occupied themselves by stacking rocks and sorting through piles for the shiniest stones to set aside for sale.

"So what's the deal here?" Aimond asked. "Are we captives or what?"

"Sure are. At least as long as the crisis persists or until we find a buyer," Brutaz explained. "By the way, how hard are your bones? On a scale from Kilpz to Reaths."

Aimond blinked and poked himself in the arm. "Either?"

"And what are they made of?"

"Mostly spite," Kessler said. "And what is this crisis? We were at that capitol. Nothing happened."

Brutaz rummaged around for something to draw with. He cleared a space on the floor and used a stick to doodle a line in the dirt.

"When the line does this, it's okay," he said before redirecting it downward. "But when it does this, we all lose our jobs."

"What happens when it goes back up?" Aimond asked.

"We get our jobs back for a pay cut."

Daps was at the ready for a lesson in alien macroeconomics. He stood prepared to recite a list of policies that could, at the very least, prolong the duration of either trend for little more than the simple joy of paperwork requirements. He took the stick and began a detailed technical analysis of the line in the dirt partnered with verbatim recitations of regulatory procedures as the others wandered away.

"Well, we're gonna be here a while," Aimond said.

"Yes. Captives," Brutaz reminded him.

"Right, right. Since we're supposed to be here helping, maybe you can give me some background. What's the deal with this war?"

Brutaz dove into the tale of a distant past where all Nerelkor lived in a relative state of peace. Their leader and holiest of robe-wearing political icons maintained the fragile balance between those of differing opinions. While the Nerelkor always divided themselves into two general schools of thought, the great leader Kazamous preached one lesson that was valued most: stop talking and do something already. Some said he began his enlightened path as little more than an incensed peasant, shouting his message to anyone deadlocked in discussion. Others said he was always present and appeared when needed most based on the volume of a given conversation. Regardless of his origin, his constant agitation led to consistent compromise and progress within Nerelkor society. After his passing, those left in charge wished to erect a statue in his honor. But the construction came to an impasse when the leaders failed to agree on one detail.

"So the entire war, this whole time, is about which direction Kazamous's hat faces?" Aimond asked, somewhat unsurprised by the necessity of his own question.

"The Dinasc have photographs, historical records, and generational tales passed through the ages of those who knew him claiming his hat faced left," Brutaz said.

"Seems a strong case. What do the Rejault have?"

"Feels better on the right," Brutaz noted. "Look." He sketched a coarse image in the dirt of an oval wearing a hat pointing to the right. "Just makes sense this way. No history can change that."

"And that's the only difference?"

"Mostly. But not the only thing. We believe in greater freedoms. The Dinasc would never allow fun and learning."

Brutaz gestured toward a group of younglings in the corner of the communal hole-house playing with hand-sized explosives. They'd load the rounds into a makeshift cannon and fire them out the entrance. Aimond pointed with a bent finger and raised his eyebrows. No words came.

"Perfectly safe, I assure you," Brutaz volunteered. "We asked them not to point it at anyone who isn't looking."

Blaring sirens sounded again, dwarfing the not-aimed-at-anyone-yet-still-uncomfortably-close explosions.

"Again?" Aimond shouted over the noise.

"When three alarms sound again, the crisis is over!" Brutaz perked up.

The alarms died after the second siren. The surrounding Nerelkor exchanged curious glances, unsure whether to continue smashing rocks or take cover.

"Where's the third?" Aimond said.

"In all the chaos, someone probably left the doors to the cafeteria open."

Performed as if rehearsed a thousand times before, each Nerelkor manifested a small case and donned protective silver-foil suits.

Sixty-four seconds later, the third siren screeched and the confused glances returned, this time sheltered behind sealed visors.

"Was that three alarms or two and one?"

Brutaz shrugged. Zanartas, Kessler, and Daps, with a fresh red welt on his head, came to join Aimond.

"What's the situation?" Kessler asked.

"There's either a nuclear-powered toddler and a tornado or we're fine. Unsure."

"Someone get out there and start shooting the sky in case the clouds come back!" Brutaz shouted.

A cluster of suited Nerelkor charged past the crew, each carrying a handle of a mortar that should have been too large to conceal in the small cave. They scurried outside and plopped one end on the ground.

Kessler raised an eyebrow. "They almost make Osor seem sane."

Recoil from the cannon blasted a torrent of sand through the cave. The first shot was enough to rouse the remaining Nerelkor inside, all of which joined their brethren outside to shoot at the sky. Perhaps the most dedicated of the lot were the few stuck with large melee weapons, swinging away with steadfast resolve at the air.

"Well, I'm content," Kessler said. She signaled for the crew to follow and walked out of the hole without the least bit of resistance from the cloud-hunting captors.

The three crew members returned to the *Gallant*'s camp. Kessler debriefed the team of the day's events.

"One more thing, Captain," Paizley said, her blond ponytail draped over her shoulder. "I managed to get Gal's field transmitters synced up. We should be able to talk to each other in the field now."

She handed each of the crew an inch-thick chrome bracelet that, once equipped, blurted into a simultaneous advertisement and welcome message:

"The Gainsbro Wrist-Mounted Communication Device for Simple Communication, or the G.W.M.C.D.F.S.C., is not only a sleek piece of fashion-conscious jewelry, but a direct portal to your ship's computer."

"Does it do this every time I put it on?" Hoomer asked.

"Every time," Paizley said with a smile.

Desperate to speed the remainder of the fifteen-minute tutorial announcement along, Elizar smacked the bracelet against the table.

The impact caused the message to start over.

He pulled a chain from around his neck, looped it through the bracelet, and walked off with an uncomfortably large medallion belting instructions and restarting each time it bumped against his chest.

"Everyone be sure to have this on you at all times while we're planetside," Kessler growled, her eye twitching as the welcome message hurtled into its ninth minute. "And for the love of our corporate overlords, if you have to take it off for any reason, it best be because you lost an arm."

"I assume they're waterproof?" Dr. Cole asked.

"Up to zero point zero six meters," Paizley stated.

"To turn the volume up, say, 'turn the volume up,'" it prattled on. "To turn the volume down, say, 'less loud now.' To mute your device, remove your device and vacate the premises."

Kessler stood and waved her hands to dismiss the crew. Aimond followed Paizley outside to sit and overlook the alien landscape as yellow clouds rolled by.

"So what was it like?" Paizley asked. "Tell me everything."

"It was kind of like home," Aimond reminisced. "Except more destroyed. Everyone went about their lives like nothing was wrong, but it all looked awful. Except the mansions. Those looked pretty great."

"Get to try any new foods or exotic drinks?"

"We were briefly held hostage and offered what I think was basically acid."

"That does sound kind of like home. Or at least Florida. How'd you walk away from the whole hostage situation?"

Galileo piped in a not-so-subtle snippet of Aimond's high school saxophone failure through the communicator bracelet.

"Oh great, he can hear us outside now, too."

"I was preparing for a daring act of heroism enacted with nothing more than your musical genius," Galileo said.

"I'm sure that would have worked." Paizley smiled and stood. "Think it's time for me to turn in. Elizar drank the equivalent of a week's caffeine. If he catches us outside it's going to be war stories until dawn."

Aimond fawned after Paizley as they returned inside. Back in the comfort of their bunks, Galileo triggered an artificial sunset. Maintaining a normal circadian rhythm during space travel posed a challenge, especially on an alien world. To promote a calm and restful environment, Galileo selected lighting and soundscapes that most resembled each crew member's home environment. Paizley's bunk was kept cool and dark with sounds of bullfrogs and crickets. Kessler benefited from absolute silence. Whereas Elizar could not fall asleep without flashing lights and audio of a man trying to sell him knockoff handbags at a bazaar—a reality that contradicted his ability to sleep while standing at every other instance.

Without a sleep profile for Aimond, Galileo was forced to approximate his ideal conditions. This approximation landed somewhere between intermittent fog horns and actual fog descending from the vents. Unfortunately Galileo could not produce fog, but he could vent in a sizable portion of the *Gallant*'s expended coolants. The crew slept a few short hours until their communicators woke them for a 06:00 meeting reminder. Groggy faces and wobbling gaits entered the briefing room. One by one they filled the seats around the oval table.

"Where's Seegler?" Hoomer asked.

"Probably back with the Rejault," Paizley said.

He was not. Seegler's closest encounter with anything resembling amphibians was as an extra on the set of a documentary exploring people who believed they were once tadpoles. The Gainsbro inclusivity department maintained a list of over 4,000 illnesses and medical conditions to depict in every cinematic experience. This prevented boycotts and potential exclusionary lawsuits. Actors without obvious conditions would announce their affliction at repeating intervals. Seegler's role was to stand in a bog next to a man in an iron lung while occasionally shouting: "Gout!" Seegler did not have gout but received an award for an inspiring performance and a sponsorship for gout-reducing psychic counseling.

Osor rolled his chair to the corner of the room, flicking the lights off and on until Kessler's red cybernetic glare fixated on him. They sat in silence for eighteen minutes, offering the occasional glance and hushed whisper to their neighbors.

"Alright, who called this meeting?" Kessler demanded. "Let's get going already."

"We thought you did," Hoomer said.

"No. It was just on my calendar for the morning."

"Well, someone had to have called it."

The placeholder was established two years prior to inaugural launch by a seventy-six-person committee formed to ascertain potential crew time-savers. In their months-long constant caucus they determined the crew would, at some point, likely and possibly, benefit from a pre-morning pre-briefing meeting. The topics, value, and purpose of the meeting were to be determined. But the eighty-five days spent developing this strategy concluded it would save their intrepid crew members time. Probably.

Daps pushed his chair back and stood just as everyone was about to leave. "I believe we can still use this time."

The collective groan thrashed any hope of going back to sleep, apart from the normal sedative effects whenever Daps ran on long-winded rambles—or brief anecdotes. Elizar had already mastered near instantaneous sleep anytime Daps opened his mouth. The reflex made it difficult during meals, as even so much as parting his lips for a fork was enough to trigger a narcoleptic safety response. Those still awake were forced to survive twenty-five minutes of rhetorical questions and the use of the word "leverage" upwards of forty-seven times.

"If we were flying I'd ram us into an asteroid," Hoomer mumbled.

"There's still time," Aimond said, ruffling his mess of brown hair. "Just lift off and pelt us into the ground."

"It's like Seegler knew this was coming and went off on his own to avoid it. Fortune-telling jerk."

He did not. Seegler had gone off on his own, but for no other reason than to avoid anyone finding out he was still on Earth.

Equipped with a fake mustache over his actual mustache, Seegler spent three days wandering around space and aeronautical museums in an effort to learn how space travel worked. So far, the frequency of his visits had earned him a free sandwich at the gift shop with the purchase of two scale model replicas of the original lunar lander.

"Well, I hope I've given you all something to think about," Daps said, either beginning or ending his ramble. "Let's adjourn here and I'll give you all some time back."

The crew stood and shambled for the door but were stopped by a 07:30 briefing reminder, just two minutes away. A collective sigh dragged them back to their seats. Kessler shoved Daps into a chair and took her place at the head of the table. Today's mission focused on making contact with the opposition, the Dinasc. Captain Kessler was to take a small team, including Paizley and Osor, in hopes of appealing to a more "put together" version of society.

"Aimond and Daps, return to the Rejault. Grab an Articulaser from the lab. And bring Elizar with you in case things turn kidnappy again," Kessler ordered. "Cozy up to leadership however you can and let's see if we can't get the two factions in the same room. Dismissed."

A return to the orderly free-for-all of the Rejault with a paper-pusher and cloudy-eyed, trigger-happy senior citizen did not leave Aimond with incredible confidence. But at least he had an idea of what to expect in subsequent encounters.

"Hey, be careful out there," Aimond said to Paizley. "If the Dinasc are anything like the guys we already met—just watch yourself. If you need anything, call me and I'll come running."

"That's sweet," Paizley said.

"According to your high school fitness records, your average mile time was twelve minutes, thirty-six seconds," Galileo added.

"You could come running, or we could wait for the nearest star to implode and eliminate any threat in about the same duration."

Aimond waited until he stepped off the ship.

"Jerk," he muttered, kicking the hull.

"I am quite literally on your wrist," Galileo said. "Also . . ."

Red alert lights flashed with a ship-under-attack warning. All video screens on the ship lit up and displayed a close-up of Aimond accompanied by his own musical stylings.

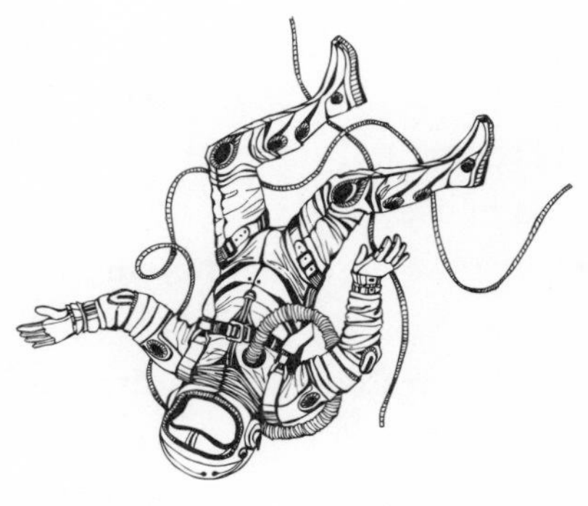

7
A SHARP LEFT TURN

Scans from the air made easy work of locating the Dinasc settlement. Hoomer dropped the contact team about a kilometer from the city. Kessler, Paizley, and Osor proceeded on foot the remainder of the way.

"Hey, Captain," Paizley said. "Why don't we have any kind of cars or rovers on the ship?"

"We do. At least according to our requisition forms."

The mission was allotted a sizable vehicle budget. Half of the allocated expenses were utilized in the design phase as the task bounced between the Aeronautics, Propulsion, and Waste Management teams.

Each team sat on the ticket for three weeks, wrote an eventual note that they were not the appropriate team for the assignment, and kicked the request along. One month before departure, the ticket lingered in Waste Management's queue. So they did what they knew best and designed a self-propelled garbage receptacle, able to process recycling and traverse short distances on methane derived from compost.

"So the dumpster we have in the cargo bay . . ." Paizley theorized.

"According to our corporate overlords: All-Terrain Land Exploration Receptacle."

"I thought the wheels on that seemed a little excessive."

"You should see the freaking headlights on it!" Osor chimed in.

"Don't you start," Kessler warned.

"What'd they end up spending the rest of the budget on?" Paizley asked.

"Undercarriage protection. You could theoretically drive that thing over a field of landmines and that paint won't even scratch," Kessler said.

The team approached the Dinasc perimeter security—a twenty-centimeter-deep trench less than a meter wide. Two unarmed guards charged toward the vast pit from the opposite side before Kessler could place one foot inside. Their gargles and croaking noises accompanied wild gesturing toward a single bridge and gatehouse another five minutes' walk down the path of the ravine.

The guards stood in place and watched as the team approached the bridge. A single Nerelkor was stationed at the cobblestone gatehouse at the edge of the pass. Handrails, footrails, and what could only be construed as headrails lined the sides of the walkway to assure maximum safety and fall prevention. Kessler blasted the guard with the Articulaser.

"Halt please," he said. "My name's Klaxi. Welcome to the Grand Bridge. What's your business?"

"We're here to speak with your leaders and assist in resolving the war."

"You carrying any weapons?"

"No."

"Promise?"

"I do."

Klaxi took a step forward and tilted his head. His eyes darted around the crew members. Osor was already on his knees, reaching through the guardrails to measure the ravine below with his hand.

"What if it's a really deep pit but they filled it in with sand to make it look not deep?" Osor theorized.

"If it's filled, wouldn't it not be deep anymore?" Paizley asked.

Osor stood, jaw agape. "It could go all the way to the center of the planet."

"What's his deal?" Klaxi asked.

Kessler sighed and shook her head. "He ate a bunch of radiation-laced glue, I think. He's harmless."

"Promise?"

Kessler glared. Klaxi recoiled and shuffled back to the gate.

"Alright, you can come in."

Klaxi gestured for the team to follow. They stepped inside the gatehouse. He pressed a button beside a metal panel and waited. The mechanical gate showed no signs of moving. After waiting the government-mandated allotted time between gate operation and troubleshooting, Klaxi pointed to a small sign at the corner of the gate.

"Looks like it's under maintenance," he said. "Sorry, but you're going to have to wait here until it's fixed."

"Can't we just walk around?" Kessler asked, gesturing to the clear path next to the elaborate entry facility.

"Nuh-uh. That's not the entrance. Can't you see the danger pit?"

She placed her head in her palm, somewhat missing the straightforward chaos of the Rejault.

"Well, when is it going to be fixed?"

"Don't know. Union of Wall Gate Laborers are on indefinite paid leave, on account of discovering some graffiti that wasn't very nice. Gots to get the Graffiti Removal and General Custodial Laborers some pre-work counseling. Then they can clean it."

Paizley stepped past Klaxi and knelt. A quick smack in the right spot and the junction box near the button popped open.

"Looks like a simple short," she assessed. "I can bypass it and have the gate functional in a minute."

Nimble fingers danced around shoddy wiring and the gate mechanism hummed to life. She pressed the button and a blue light on the ceiling clicked on. Klaxi rushed forward, making a humming sound with one mouth and a mechanical clunking sound with the other. He squatted and lifted the gate above his head. The crew stepped through. Klaxi switched to mono-sound effects.

"Wait a second." He paused. "Have you got a valid Wall Gate Maintenance Association's General Maintenance and Maintaining Wall Gates Independent Repair Certification Card?"

Paizley blinked and checked her pockets out of instinct. "No?"

"Gonna have to undo this then." Klaxi tore a fistful of wires from the panel, slamming the gate shut between them. "Otherwise we're liable for a stern request to please not do that again. It's terrifying."

Kessler grabbed Osor by his shirt collar before he could unscrew the bulb in the ceiling.

The crew entered the outskirts of Dinasc City. A single winding path of faultless asphalt wove into the metropolis. Thousands of white cube buildings sat aligned in perfect grids. Each building was equally spaced, equally sized, and equally indiscernible from its neighbor.

"It's a step up," Kessler suggested.

Osor plopped himself on the ground, flicking the power switch to a high-powered flashlight. Kessler smacked him on the head.

"Behave or I'm throwing you in the pit regardless of how much sand it has."

A distant mechanical buzzing neared. Dust clouds plumed and followed in the wake of a small autonomous cube, which rolled up and stopped before the crew. Orange bands ejected from its side, forming a meter-wide perimeter.

Text scrolled across the fencing, which translated to: "Warning, this is a safety rail. Now you are aware. We apologize for not informing you sooner."

A thin veil of blue light shot from the top of the box, projecting a translucent ovoid. The projection growled, croaked, and hissed. Kessler looked to Paizley.

"I think it's a hologram guide," she said. "It's speaking in their native tongue."

Kessler attempted to zap the box with the Articulaser. She raised an eyebrow when it had no effect.

"Hm, did not foresee that," Osor said. "Wait, wait." He paced around. "Idea!"

The flashlight returned to his hand. Kessler and Paizley waited for the next step. Instead Osor played with the light's focus until Kessler snatched it and smashed the lens with her heel. Osor dropped to his knees, scooped up the pieces, and wailed.

"I might have an idea," Paizley said, pulling two small probes from the underside of her communicator bracelet. She fished around under the box for a suitable place to keep them affixed. "Gal, do your thing."

Cerebral scans from the Articulaser gave Galileo a mountain of linguistic data; direct connection allowed him to scan the hologram's code for the better part of three minutes. He'd already completed the entire language translation in the first fifteen seconds of processing and uploaded it back. The remaining time was used to assess if Galileo needed to be on the defensive around another AI interacting with Paizley. In the end, he deemed it too stupid to be attractive and allowed the translation patch to pass through.

"Nondenominational salutations: residents, travelers, visitors, neighbors . . ." The hologram proceeded to list seventy-six additional groups. If interrupted, it apologized and restarted.

The ground tremored and a dull quake filled the air. One by one the identical cube buildings rotated, shifted sideways or backward, then settled into a new location once the grid reformed. The rearrangement carved wedges into the ground, eradicating roads and walkways. Silver cylindrical fans sprouted from remnants of intact pavement and sucked in surrounding dust clouds.

"What just happened?" Kessler asked.

"Dinasc values equity and equality," the hologram said. "Every forty-two minutes, all structures shift to a new rotation and location so all structures get to experience all angles and locations."

"I feel like I should have follow-up questions, but no. Can you direct us to the government building?"

A brief silence elapsed and Kessler asked again, louder, but was cut off by the hologram's response. Their verbal jousting lasted two more rounds and caused the hologram to screech to a halt.

"You appear to be offended," the hologram said. "I apologize for the offense. Are you still offended?"

"More now than before."

"Command received. Initiating apologetic detonation."

The box crackled and sparked, sending the team diving for cover. After a half minute of increasingly violent noise, the box fizzled with a hair's-width strand of black smoke. An additional bot whizzed down the path at breakneck speeds, screeching to a halt in front of the now defunct machine. It placed a protective blast screen in front of the crew, waited, retracted the shield, then disappeared from view.

"I should have stayed with the apocalypse mole people," Kessler groaned.

Without direction, the crew wandered into the city in hopes of finding their own way. Their arrival onto the perimeter of the building grid was met with the next shifting cycle. Pristine walkways and roads cracked and crumbled as buildings crunched their way to a new location. Once the fan protrusions concluded their deafening display of aerial dirt swirling, hordes of Nerelkor rushed outside to sweep up the debris from the streets. Lobbed hunks of rock and tar clanked off the sides of a looming machine. The monstrous apparatus sputtered, churned, and spit out a black mushy mix, which the Nerelkor gathered and spread along the ground. Hopeful of some guidance, Kessler zapped everyone around as they passed to facilitate some degree of directions.

"Terribly sorry." A Nerelkor worker approached the team. "So very, very, horribly sorry. But you're standing in a work zone."

"Which we would be happy to vacate if you could direct us to your leadership's . . . cube thing."

"I shouldn't have assumed you were standing here on purpose. Exceedingly apologetic apologies. You're looking for the light white building marked eighty-four."

From their initial observation of the city, each cubed building shared the same color. They failed to previously notice the addresses, written in Nerelkor, on the corners of the buildings, which were of course entirely the same on every building. Kessler held out her arm, gesturing toward every structure that matched the description, in part to request further clarification, but largely to present a useless direction. The Nerelkor worker bent in half, pointing his head to the ground and carried on with profuse remorse for his continued existence. He called in others, who followed his example.

Despite any attempt at possible clarification, the group would do nothing else. So the crew wandered away, now followed by a pack of eight Nerelkor spouting nonstop apologies. Kessler stopped and turned back to the group.

"Please don't hit me."

"Why would I hit you?"

"You hit him," the Nerelkor said, pointing to Osor.

Another in the group popped his head up and shrieked.

"Trorar, did you just point?"

"Oh no. Oh no, no. I resign my position effective immediately."

"I really don't care," Kessler said. "Let's go."

The defeated Nerelkor rolled on the ground and curled into the Nerelkor equivalent of a fetal position—fully prone with arms and legs fanned and outstretched and both mouths open. The drama seemed a tad on the extravagant side—even for this lot.

"Hey, are you okay?" Paizley knelt beside Trorar. "We know you didn't mean any offense."

"How about you redeem yourself by helping us get where we need to be," Kessler offered.

Trorar appeared on his feet before the crew could blink. He waddled ahead, taking inventory of the buildings and their current position. Disposition now pleasant and mellow, the team followed him.

"Are you going to be alright without a job?" Paizley asked.

"Oh sure. I'll get paid the same."

"How's that work?"

"All jobs are paid equally. From road recycler, to road engineer, to road statistician. We keep two percent and the other ninety-eight percent gets reclaimed," he said. "Housing is free. Fresh food every day."

Trorar carried on with his utopia pitch as they walked, explaining the intricacies of measuring daily air intake so as not to breathe more than anyone else. Those breathing too much were asked, by the honor system alone, to offset their breathing footprint with a voluntary purchase of air-tokens. This and other honor-based shame purchases accounted for the entire personal cost of living.

Local government agencies supplied just about everything else needed, which still only managed to encompass 5 percent of the total municipal budget. The remaining 95 percent was set aside for "discretionary projects." Which was spent in its entirety on roads.

"With all the roadwork, where are the cars?" Paizley asked.

"We got rid of them all," Trorar boasted. "Vehicles are bad for the environment."

They continued down the sidewalk adorned with cracks, splits, and missing chunks. Pristine and beautiful, the road sat next to them as a still black river waiting to be torn asunder and rebuilt in twenty-six more minutes.

A light white cube building marked with an eighty-four meant the team had arrived at the Dinasc government building. Probably. Trorar apologized for an unpunctual arrival and dismissed himself before causing more irreparable damage to his public image or career prospects. The building itself was indistinguishable from the hundreds of others around. No posted guards, added security, or so much as a camera outside.

"Be ready for anything," Kessler cautioned.

"Anything that can fit inside a tiny little box," Paizley added.

Osor wept and dropped back to his knees. "I can't even light them up."

Kessler yanked him up by the collar and they entered.

One Nerelkor wearing more wrinkles than clothes occupied the front room. She turned and glanced at the menacing-appearing yet benign Articulaser as Kessler zapped some English into her.

"No weapons allowed, dear," she said. "You'll have to promise."

"Sure, that's great," Kessler replied. "I assume you're in charge here? My name is Captain Elora Kessler. My crew and I are—"

"Oh, no. I'm not in charge. Come, come."

The old Nerelkor pulled aside a beaded curtain and welcomed the crew into a small room painted with streaks of bright color. An open bassinet sat pedestaled upon a throne of pillows. Dangling toys and swinging shapes decorated the arch above a wicker cot. Inside, a bejeweled miniature Nerelkor nestled into a shaggy blanket. He kicked his feet about, striking a toy by coincidence of it occupying the same space. The aides surrounding the bassinet scribbled a hurried note and rushed it to a desk in the corner. A stamper the size of a human torso marked the note with a raised golden seal.

"I'm sorry, but you'll have to remove your footwear," the old Nerelkor said. "It is now highly offensive."

"How now?" Osor asked.

"Why, this very second. You'll be the first ones to have to publicly apologize." She gestured to the stamped document, which was in the process of being sealed and shoved into a protective sheet half its size. "The newest decree of our glorious and wise President GaLvaz."

The infant Nerelkor let out a shrill squeal and a series of increasingly viscous streams from both mouths.

"The baby?" Kessler asked.

Aides rushed to wipe away the secretions and categorize them in jars based on relative density to account for the upcoming regulatory changes on fiduciary responsibilities of banking agencies. The third jar cemented a decisive crackdown on short-selling derivative securities, while a tapering fourth jar made it legal to pelt stones through the windows of parked vehicles while standing on one leg, if any vehicles could be located. Subtle variances between pelt, throw, and lob would be assessed during the next diaper change.

"Yes. We're very proud of our young leader who has proven most fair and kind."

President GaLvaz had ruled with an iron fist and full diaper for the last six Earth-equivalent days, replacing his predecessor, the now three-week-old President Gamtop. Presidential coronation occurred with regular frequency. Newly spawned Nerelkor were bestowed presidential powers. That leader remained in office until a new youngling was born. This methodology ensured that the president in power was always the youngest member of Dinasc society, as the youngest both knew and understood the least and therefore was unbiased.

"Replace the yellow block with a purple rattle," an aide instructed. "Two shakes if you wish for us to fix the leak in the ceiling. Three shakes and we shall remove and outlaw roofs."

Kessler sat on the floor. She held out her hand, palm up to Osor. He removed a small flashlight from his pocket and placed it in Kessler's palm, who proceeded to snap it in two. She took a deep breath and stood.

"Great."

8

SPELUNKING

Hoomer flicked the dial of the cockpit radio, which had been installed in the early stages of construction as a means for in-flight entertainment. Then the engineering team had learned Earth's finest music stations would not be within range while hundreds of light-years away.

The radio was rebranded as a nostalgia remedy upon further discovering radio waves do not magically disappear, in hopes somewhere along the line the ship would pick up a stray broadcast from centuries back.

This also sent two of the engineers rushing home in an attempt to find the equivalent of a Clear History button for broadcast transmissions.

"What do you think it is?" Hoomer asked about the Nerelkor station noises.

"Somewhere between frog jazz and territorial howler monkey calls," Galileo said.

"You know what it needs?"

Galileo overlaid a drum track to the mix of croaking and chirping coming from the radio.

"On it," he said.

Hoomer turned up the volume and flicked on the overhead lights for Galileo to bounce with the new tempo.

"Awful," she said. "I love it. We shall call it . . . Nerel-Core."

"An equally terrible name."

The music warped, slowed, and sped up within a few seconds. Lights flickered off tempo, and the ship dipped enough to create a lurch in Hoomer's stomach. Her displays flickered and sluggish controls responded on their own time.

"Indigestion there, Gal?"

"We appear to have encountered a massive pocket of magnetic resonance."

"What causes that?"

"Coronal mass ejection from the nearest star, technologic byproduct, or the planet's core is exploding."

They waited a few silent seconds.

"Welp, not dead yet," Hoomer confirmed.

"So we'll strike option three from the selection."

Small tremors overtook the ship as it descended into a rocky crevice. Magnetic interference grew stronger as the ground neared, while alerts and alarms blurted throughout the ship at half-second intervals. Engines torqued to full then quieted to nothing as the ship rolled on its axis. Yellow and blue party streamers deployed on the bridge, covering every console and seat.

"Oh, I didn't know I had that option," Galileo admitted. "What a fun surprise and now it's ruined."

Hoomer yanked hard on the stick, hoping for some modicum of reply from the engines. The ship dipped into the chasm and below ground into an open cavern. Flight controls responded as they neared the ground. A full reverse thrust kicked up an opaque cloud of orange dust as the *Gallant* plunged downward and landed with a heavy thud.

Panel indicators and control screens flickered back to life. Drum-overlaid croaking crackled back on the radio.

"Six out of ten for an appropriate landing soundtrack," Hoomer said.

"Four out of ten for the landing."

"And whose fault is that?"

"Michel Wibault, I'd imagine."

Hoomer held up her hands. "I have no idea who that is."

"Inventor of vertical take-off and landing engines."

"Thought you were going to say inventor of magnets."

"I don't believe anyone *invented* magnets."

"Yet somehow they're everywhere. How's that work?"

Dust from the landing settled enough for the *Gallant*'s lights to pierce through the shrouded veil. Webs of thick black wiring trailed along a smooth in-cut of stone and disappeared around a banked corner. Ventilation shafts ran the length of the ceiling, with dull blue light casting an eerie glow against the cavern walls. The ship had quieted and all displays read nominal.

"We appear to have dropped below whatever interference was interrupting our stroll," Galileo reported.

"I promise I won't repeat any of the things you've done to the rest of the crew," Hoomer assured.

"And now that I can understand the feeling, I won't mock humans with a head injury anymore."

"Yeah you will."

"You're right. They just get so woozy. It's quite entertaining."

Jagged stone walls surrounded the ship on all sides, leaving the hole they fell through as the only visible exit. Attempts to fly out would cross the same magnetic interference and drop the ship back inside, risking a more violent landing.

With the rest of the crew deployed on their own missions, it fell on Hoomer and Dr. Cole to find and disable the source if they intended to escape.

Hoomer scoured her station for anything field worthy. Not that any crew member in particular had a strong understanding of how to navigate an undiscovered alien terrain, but Hoomer figured arming herself against the unknown would level any potential risk. Due to previous incidents involving sharp objects hurtling around the bridge at increased velocity while speed-testing spacecraft, all Gainsbro vessels observed a strict "round objects only" policy on the command decks. The policy could have extended to living quarters but would have required a redesign of corporate-provided nail clippers at a price of up to thirty-five cents. Time spent debating the potential necessity for a redesign cost upwards of nine million dollars. Enhanced abstract risk to personnel raised the insurance premium an additional 12 percent. Management wrote off the experience as a cost-savings victory. A black ink marker was the most lethal portable device at her disposal. Hoomer exited the bridge and made for the med bay. Dr. Cole was at her workstation fiddling with a dark orange fluid in a syringe.

"If you've come to tell me we've died in a horrible crash, I've already figured that out." Dr. Cole's stern quip came without looking up.

"I thought we did alright." Hoomer shrugged. "Was it that bad down here?"

"I almost spilled."

"Whatcha got there?"

"I'm supposed to take routine bloodwork of the entire crew to catalog the effects of space travel on the body. Seegler hasn't shown for the last three appointments, so I'm condensing orange juice to run as a sample."

"And that works?"

"It won't make a lick of sense, which means the suits looking at it won't ask a single question."

"Smart. Anyway, funny story. We crashed in a cave and I have to go figure out what little EMP thingy caused us to dive down here and won't let us leave. Want to come?"

"Important work," Dr. Cole said, rotating the juice vial in her hand.

"Right, right. Any like . . . medical stuff I should bring?"

Dr. Cole pitched the leftover juice container over her shoulder into Hoomer's outstretched arms.

"Hydration is important."

Hoomer made one last stop to Osor's quarters. The light-adorned SitMaster-2.6Million-Plus-Maximum glowed with a pulsatile golden hue to illuminate the room.

She debated wheeling it outside save for the diamond mounting affixing it to the floor. Instead she pulled open drawers, checked under sheets and furniture using pens as tools to avoid any direct contact. She took a spare Articulaser but continued the search.

"If I were a lunatic, where would I hide the good stuff?" she asked.

"It's in the wall. Third panel on the right," Galileo replied without hesitation.

"You're the best creepy all-seeing stalker a girl could ask for."

She smacked the panel and the wall splintered into a dozen pieces on the floor. Hoomer brushed the debris pile under his bed, then reached inside the secret cubby.

"This light is backpack-mounted and everything," Hoomer inspected.

"You look ridiculous," Galileo said as she secured the battery pack on her back and draped a front-facing light over each shoulder.

"Pretty sure this is one of your spare headlights."

"Then part of you is beautiful and majestic while still looking ridiculous."

"Good 'nuff."

Wielding little more than a marker, a half bottle of juice, and a light bright enough to blind a black hole, Hoomer exited the ship from the front ramp.

"The atmosphere is safe to breathe, by the way," Galileo communicated as Hoomer took her first step off the ship.

"Things we should know before leaving the ship without a helmet."

"I was occupied."

"With what?"

Distorted synthesizer and guitar riff added, Galileo played back a modified Nerelkor jazz mix. Offbeat record scratches interrupted the croaking, yet somehow enhanced the squealing noises.

"Horrendous," Hoomer relented. "Forgiven."

Whistles, churns, and vibrations echoed from the backpack as Hoomer powered on Osor's light. Vicious white beams spanned the cave, revealing a massive tunnel beside the ship. Veins of translucent blue crystals adorning the walls reflected and warped the light onto the rocky ceiling.

Small streams of water ran along the walls, collecting together before powering off the edge of a steep cliff. A dry, narrow footpath bordered the cliffside and snaked around a blind corner. Sketchy though it may have been, it beat trying to cram through the holes for the wiring. Cool humid air surrounded the path, dropping in temperature with each step. The rock shone back with a purple hue, darkening as the last remaining light from the outside yielded to the small back-mounted sun generator.

"You still work?" Hoomer tapped her wrist communicator as it beeped.

"I'm detecting either fluctuating magnetic pulses or near lethal amounts of gamma radiation."

"Or?"

"If it's magnetic, then my sensors are askew."

"And if it's not?"

"How much of your body is made of lead?"

"Probably not much," Hoomer estimated, patting her sides. Galileo stayed silent for the next thirty seconds as Hoomer progressed down the path. "Care to finish that thought?"

"I figured if you had the opportunity to ask again, it was a moot point."

"I'm throwing rocks in your engines when we get back."

"I hate that rattly sound!"

"Oh, I know you do."

Reverberant waves of crashing water dampened to near silence as Hoomer rounded a corner to an open set of giant golden double doors. Sharp arcs of electricity powered their way between chrome cylinders on an array of machines more massive than the *Gallant*. Colorful panels and lights guided Hoomer to what seemed the most logical control point.

"This seems important."

"And very magnety," Galileo complained. "Turn it off."

"Hang on, we dunno what it does. What if it keeps the whole planet together or something?"

"Then there would be a sign."

There were signs. About three dozen scattered throughout the entirety of the complex. Many of which were on the control panel itself. The majority were handwritten in the equivalent of

Nerelkor cursive, thereby making them entirely illegible to the most literate of residents.

"Do you read Nerelkorian?" Hoomer asked.

"Yes, it says 'Warning magnets. Turn off if found on.'"

It did not.

Hoomer flipped several switches and pulled every lever she could find. Half of the machines came screeching to a grinding halt. Even over the deafening mechanical squawking, Hoomer could not help but think her effective learning of alien machinery put her on par with Paizley or a sane Osor. Such a rapid understanding of foreign mechanics would make her the envy of the crew. Even as the ground shook and boulders fell from the ceiling, Hoomer knew she had accomplished something fantastic. Right up until the point she was rendered unconscious by a small piece of machinery that had exploded off its track, ricocheted off a falling boulder, and landed squarely on her head.

A lingering dull ache and ringing ears roused Hoomer from her brief rest on the ground. The tremors decreased in intensity but persisted.

"Oh good, you're not dead," Galileo said. "I mean, I can fly the ship on my own, but it's nice to have company."

"The heartbeat didn't give it away?"

"I'm equipped with an array of onboard health applications. All of which are entirely falsified."

"I feel like we'd have picked up on that," Hoomer scoffed.

"Your pedometer reading is 3,932 steps."

"That seems right."

"But you're not counting, are you?" Galileo queried.

"No."

"Neither am I."

The G.W.M.C.D.F.S.C. sported twenty-six state-of-the-art health and performance metric applications. On one end existed sleep tracking, nutrition charting, and a daily stress tracker. Later development yielded the dream tally machine, teeth alignment tracking, and shoe width graphing. Each application was crafted by Gainsbro's Interior Metric Conversion Group, a team designed to take all of the imperial units and convert them into metric. Having had no prior experience with software development, except with using basic math formulas in a web browser, management assured executive leaders they could not only handle the challenge, but do so without impacting, or utilizing, the budget.

They recruited a recruiter who recruited a professor of programming, who in turn recruited a student by mandating an assignment for the semester, which was then put off until the final twelve hours of the term.

The result, a stellar listing of applications, each with about three lines of code: a random number generator, a static output, and a noise.

"So the heart rate monitor that keeps track if we're alive . . ." Hoomer said.

"A restful seventy-two beats per minute," Galileo disclosed. "Which it would likely remain had you actually died."

"Great."

"On a positive note, you would continue to burn a wondrous amount of calories while no longer actually being able to move. On account of being less living."

"You're going in the toilet when we get back."

Gold lights bounced back and forth across the communicator as a rewarding dinging chimed.

"Congratulations, you've reached your step goal," Galileo cheered.

"Haven't moved from this spot."

"Yet you're pleased, aren't you."

Hoomer's deadpan glare broke. "Yes," she conceded.

"It's the ding."

"It's so cheerful."

Another wave of tremors shook a rain of fine gravel from the cave ceiling. Hairline fissures slithered along the stone beneath Hoomer's feet. Heavy vibrations followed, widening the lines as if something deep underground was moving in a single path.

"How long has this shaking been going on?"

"The seismograph is a literal copy of the pedometer, just renamed," Galileo said. "I can tell you how many shakes we've experienced."

"Which you've made up."

"Completely."

Croaks and gurgles approached from behind the massive machines. Half a dozen Nerelkor popped out from small circular holes in the rocks, contorting their large bodies to fit through a space a human child would find claustrophobic. The group scurried over, bumping Hoomer out of the way to yank levers and mash buttons with all the coordination of an intoxicated lemur performing cardiac surgery.

As soon as the tremors slowed, one of the giants loomed over Hoomer, croaking with a ferocious intensity, which Hoomer found difficult to take seriously.

She fished around in her pockets to find the Articulaser; she grabbed the handle and snatched it out, along with the bottle of juice.

"—and because of all the fluorocarbons, all the routers need to be running," the Nerelkor said, her speech switching languages mid-sentence.

Any inkling of anger, desperation, or panic derived from the previous frog noises had dissipated into the tone of the cool mom incorrectly explaining how clouds work. Hoomer looked up and offered the juice. The Nerelkor snatched it up and popped the entire bottle into her left mouth.

"More crunch than I expected, but sweet filling," she said. "Thanks."

"Hydration is important," Hoomer remarked. "Sorry if I busted your stuff."

The Nerelkor looked back to her comrades, still in a frantic state of button mashing, and shrugged. Some calm amid the chaos was reassuring even if unfounded.

"I understand your excitement," the Nerelkor acknowledged. "We want to show the world the truth, too. I'm Cloaf."

"Hoomer," she said. "And show who, what?"

"The Rejault and Dinasc are fools living blindly in their extremes. We live a more enlightened life."

The Enlightened hailed from a mix of the two cities. Frustrated with constant bickering, inaction, or the potential for catastrophic world-ending weaponry ending up in the hands of a youngling, their members banded together. They took what they believed to be the best parts of their societies: enhanced freedoms, equal opportunities, and a giant hole in which all of their valuables were dumped.

"So you made your own society?" Hoomer questioned. "Neat. How many are you? Hundreds, thousands?"

"Fifteen."

Hoomer nodded in silence. A small group could still be impactful. If they were able to come together from different homes and find common ground, perhaps their work could be leveraged to bring peace.

Cloaf projected herself as calm and articulate—two necessary qualities in an arbitrator.

"So what's this big secret truth the world just has to know? And how's it relate to all this equipment?" Hoomer asked.

Maintaining a freestanding sovereign tribe, albeit a small one, in the middle of a planetary civil war was no small feat. Despite having no notion of what the giant machines were, it seemed apparent enough to Hoomer that this group would have the creativity, tenacity, and intellect needed to bridge the gap between the warring factions.

"In order to survive its orbital path, the entire planet . . ." Cloaf knelt down, her lidless eyes widening. She held up her hands, fingers straight. ". . . is a giant cube. These things force it to be round."

Or perhaps not.

9
PASS THE BASHING STICK

Deep resonant explosions tore through the landscape and shook the ground as Aimond, Daps, and Elizar approached Rejault. Little by little they crept closer to the city limits. Each blast generated an intense wind, forcing the group to brace themselves against boulders to remain upright.

Except Elizar, who made a conscious effort to jut his chest, as much as his curved spine would allow, with each subsequent gust. Despite being pelted with wind-kicked stones, he stood his ground, albeit in a wobbly way.

“Have I ever told you about the hurricanes during the Florida Conflict?” Elizar inquired.

“Yes,” Aimond said.

He had not.

“There we were, ’bouta storm the capital. N’all the sudden—swoosh! Hurricane swoops in outta nowhere and blows a wave of gator-riding Florida men down on our position.”

The wind picked up enough to drown the rest of his story. By the time it had died down, Aimond and Daps were well in front of Elizar, who stayed put, still spouting tales. Cracks of gunfire and blasts of heat emanated from the city's dilapidated fences. Four massive armored vehicles rolled around, crushing anything that dared sit stationary in their paths. Each shot from the turret generated enough power to hoist the treads from the ground and slam them back down. A group of three to five Nerelkor hung off the back of each tank, kicking their feet and swaying with each sharp turn. Aimond spotted Zanartas whizzing by. He waved both arms to get Zanartas's attention.

"What's going on? Are you under attack?" Aimond shouted.

"No, we're playing," Zanartas yelled back. "We bought some tanks."

"Why?"

"So we can have them if they try to take them."

Aimond tilted his head. Zanartas's tank parked beside the group. He hopped off the back as the rest of the squadron of behemoth vehicles zipped away.

"But you didn't have it before anyway," Aimond disputed.

"But now we do and they can't have it!" Zanartas insisted. "We had to sell our house-hole to afford them. And no food this cycle."

Daps fished around in his pocket and slapped a Gainsbro sticker on the side of the armor plating. As if materialized from the ether of nothingness, Daps whipped out a contract offering to subsidize every third round fired so long as the sticker stayed clean and free of combat damage. Any direct hits to the company logo would nullify the contract and result in up to twelve years imprisonment on Earth. Taking a note from Kessler's success in redirection, Aimond put his hand over Daps's face, as he was grossly unprepared to attempt to lift him.

"The other half of my crew are with the Dinasc now," he said. "We're going to work out a way to end this war. Do you think you can take us back to the Grand Five so we can set up a parley?"

"Can I keep my tank if the war ends?"

"Probably."

"Good enough for me."

Zanartas led Aimond and Daps through the city streets to the perimeter barrier of the Grand Five's walled enclave.

"I should warn you," Zanartas stated. "We won't be allowed inside. The whole place is on lockdown. No less than forty guards at each gate."

The lockdown was not too surprising. Given that during the brevity of their previous visit, the economy collapsed, the capitol was invaded, and a world-ending toddler-based weather event sent the area into a relative panic. Aimond felt as though they should be at least a little concerned, but failed to imagine any way this visit could be more chaotic than the previous trip. When they arrived at the gate, a lone guard stood at his post. The trio approached.

"Hi. We, uh, have an appointment?" Aimond said.

"Sorry. Can't come in. Lockdown," the guard responded after an Articulaser adjustment.

Aimond glanced around and craned his neck to see beyond the fence. If there were supposed to be forty guards, they excelled at staying hidden. Having experienced few repercussions for bluntness in past interactions, Aimond decided to sniff around.

"What happened to the rest of your guard buddies?"

"They're convinced they can strike it rich. Some conspiracy about a sentient wish-granting ocean that feeds off younglings the Dinasc toss into it. They keep it under the central chamber."

There was some truth to the conspiracy, at least as far as the Rejault were concerned. An ocean did not exist underneath the Grand Governing Chamber—a fact that would have been very apparent to anyone who took the time to look at the visible underside from the rear. However, one wandering Nerelkor did come upon a spare coin one day while walking underneath the cliffside and wishing for something to eat.

The coin was not the food he hoped for, but it was something he told his hovelmates. Within hours the story had evolved into three individual tales of a Nerelkor finding a coin, a sentient wish-granting ocean, or fighting off a horde of flesh-eating icebergs using a flamethrower.

"Good for you for not believing it," Daps celebrated. "I admire a dedicated employee who stands for his company's mission. Here, I have a pin for you."

"Oh, it's true," the guard attested as Daps pinned an "I did it" circle to him. "But I can't go anywhere on account of the legs."

He pointed down to his extremities, which appeared wrapped in a thick layer of adhesive strips from top to bottom.

"Cost me a month's guarding to get them wrapped," he added. "If I move too much they'll fall off."

"What's it for?" Aimond asked.

The guard tilted his head and opened both mouths. "Health?"

"So you can't move at all?" Aimond pressed.

"Can't go nowhere."

"Neat."

Aimond strolled past him and waved for Daps and Zanartas to follow. Dust clouds plumed on the horizon as a roaring motor galloped closer. Zanartas's tank blew past the guard and skidded to a halt. Elizar popped out of the turret holding a cannon larger than his torso. Priorities reconfigured, Daps darted around to the side and offered the dust-covered sticker a spit shine against his sleeve.

"You're a weird dude," Aimond said.

"How so?" Daps questioned, removing a rag to wipe the dirt from his sleeve.

Aimond raised his arms forward, presenting all that was Daps.

The group continued to the central chamber without further resistance from a confused and immobile guard. They pushed open the doors to the throne room.

The Grand Five sat on the floor spread around a massive cubic tank of water. Filled with rational ineptitude, the Grands took turns lobbing stacks of money at the container. Each wad of cash varied in size but always thumped off the glass, landing in a pile on the floor.

"How much until it grants wishes?" Grand Four inquired.

"Maybe it's hungry. Should we fetch a youngling?" Grand Three suggested.

"Wait, wait. I've an idea," Grand Two insisted. He hoisted himself up and carefully inspected the tank. After lengthy deliberation, he lobbed a double-sized stack of cash. "I think it's defective."

"Are you sure it's from the right ocean?" Grand Four questioned.

"You there," Grand One addressed, pointing to Daps. "Fetch me another ocean."

Daps took advantage of the opportunity to acknowledge their presence. Sheepish but driven, he clutched his corporate-imbued charisma and stepped forward.

"Excuse me, distinguished leaders and dignified . . . dignitaries."

"Nice," Aimond said.

"We come bearing—"

A stack of money whizzed across the room and pelted Daps in the face. He recoiled and the stack dropped to his feet.

"We're conducting important governance," Grand Two scoffed. "Fetch an ocean and be gone."

"If I could trouble—"

Another thicker wad of cash managed to land just below his bottom lip. Though their governing ability remained questionable, their aim was impeccable. Precise direction and athletic prowess was what originally catapulted Grand Two into the wealth of a politician. His ability to not only throw but catch balls of varying shapes and sizes proved beyond any reasonable doubt he represented the will of the people.

An elaborate dance of minimal syllabic utterances and attempting to dodge flying paper piles proceeded until the mound reached Daps's ankles. Aimond held his hand up to stop Daps from speaking any further. He knelt and scooped all the money he could hold between his arms and dumped it into the pit in the center of the room.

"A moment of your time," Aimond requested as the money redistributed itself into their sacks.

The Grand Five grumbled and stood as they waddled back to their thrones. Grand One fumbled around behind his seat, clunking fist-sized coins into a gold-plated vending machine behind him.

Brief churning gave way to a metallic plunk. Grand One fished his large hand through the miniature door and brandished the Talking Stick. He nestled into his seat and cleared both throats, a fairly revolting soundscape as it projected in stereo.

"Now then. We've summoned you here to pay tribute—" Grand One started.

Grand Two leaned across his throne and whispered a reminder that their guests' presence was not requested; they just showed up. Being called upon by peasants was far from commonplace. On the rare occurrence, the Grands assumed such requests for assembly were submitted by a masochist, ignorant worshiper, or someone who had not yet realized they were about to voluntarily donate their remaining life's assets.

"Why are you here then?" Grand One asked.

"Well, your wonderfulnesses," Daps said. "We've—"

Despite a growing sense of rapid reflexes developed entirely in the last five minutes, Daps could not dodge the onslaught and fell to the floor as a sack full of coins pelted his sternum.

"I address your leader," Grand One bellowed.

"Me?" Aimond asked, ducking down preemptively.

"The one who carries the biggest weapon."

All eyes turned to Elizar, who had fallen asleep, using his oversized cannon as a makeshift pillow. Aimond nudged him awake.

Elizar rubbed his eyes.

"We gonna blow up the other guys with you," he asserted.

"And how much will this cost?" Grand One asked.

Elizar noticed the randomly distributed currency scattered about the floor and redirected his efforts into scooping up cash. Aimond smacked him.

"Oh, right. We, uh, some peace talkings to you with the other frog people."

Daps reached out, an exasperated wheeze the only thing capable of getting past his lips.

"And T-shirts," Elizar added. "You gotta buy a bunch of T-shirts. We got their size?"

"Octuple XL," Daps enunciated, suddenly able to speak when sales were involved. "We've got a few million, yes."

Grand Two bought and snatched the Talking Stick.

"And do you have sufficient funds to purchase a consideration planning meeting for considering potential peace considerations?"

Aimond scooped up all the available notes and coins remaining by his feet and swept them into a pile. The coins rattled and spilled out of their sacks, shining a golden light on the ceiling.

"Is that enough?" Aimond asked.

All of the Grand Five snorted and exhaled.

"You've enough for one brief Counting Session," Grand Two said.

"What's that?"

"We'll reconvene to count the money, then reject your proposal."

Counting Sessions most often yielded a rejection to any request. Costs of a Counting Session varied by length of the counting. The more money presented, the longer it would take to count it, thereby increasing the amount charged to account for the time spent.

In almost every scenario, the time spent counting cost the exact amount of money counted, leaving nothing left for the actual intended proposal. There was one rare instance in recent history where a Counting Session successfully produced an approval. Two of the Grand Five uncovered an extra stash of currency after the count's conclusion, which had been utilized as seating.

The amount discovered was deemed sufficient and the request to remove the last remaining ice machine from the city proceeded. The machine was cited by the requestor as: too cold on the inside, which was uncomfortable when fetching ice. The machine was later unplugged and the remaining 99 percent of the budget was spent convincing the citizens it was always unplugged and they liked it better that way.

"You're going to have to buy the Talking Stick," Zanartas said. "If you buy it off them, you can issue any decrees. Even major ones like a peace summit."

"Do you have any money we could borrow?" Aimond asked.

"I'd have to work at least forty-seven lifetimes to pay off the debt disallowing me from placing a bid for it first."

"I could submit a capital budget request," Daps offered. "There's no amount of money we can't create."

"How long would that take?" Aimond questioned.

"About eight days."

"Oh, that's actually not too bad."

"To fill out the application," Daps continued. "Then six weeks to enter the reviewal queue."

"Little longer than expected, but maybe still workable."

"Then another eight months until the next budget meeting. Fourteen additional months to allocate funds. And eight hours the following business day to send and we should be good."

Zanartas, Aimond, and Elizar had already left. They huddled outside the throne room to discuss the next plan of action.

"Any other ideas? We can't go back to Captain Kessler with nothing."

"We bash them," Elizar decreed. "Back when I was—"

"Any ideas, Zanartas?"

"The cannon human is correct. We bash them."

"Wait, what?"

Elizar would have been excited had he heard Zanartas agreeing. Instead, he was into the third chapter of an epic saga deep in *The Florida Conflict*, a historically accurate retelling of his wartime experience scrawled on crumpled paper. This one in particular focused on a domesticated alligator named Big Cheeze, who Elizar trained to sniff out guerilla fighters.

Success was relative in that it located eight hidden combatants who were in fact wearing gorilla suits as a firm misunderstanding of the concept. They were in the center of a public road screaming "banana" back and forth in a Floridian accent, which mostly degenerated into a "bnaaa." They remained unaware of how their camouflage failed to trick even a highly trained alligator.

"The only other way to obtain the Talking Stick is arena combat," Zanartas said.

Ancient Nerelkorian tradition dictated that anyone may seek to claim rule from the current governing body, provided they emerge victorious in a free-for-all brawl.

Once declared, a battle royale is scheduled and all are welcome to attend and participate. Individual combatants are allowed to fight for their own honor, or an entrant of high esteem can select a champion in their stead. Most weapons are allowed with the exception of aerosols, as one such event saw each warrior wielding spray cans; combatants were rendered unable to participate further on account of irritated eyes and excessively greasy hands.

"So anyone who beats back a bunch of gun-crazed giants gets to rule?" Aimond summarized. "No offense."

"Last one left standing is awarded the Talking Stick and perks of leadership for up to six hours."

"Still not convinced it's a great or survivable idea. Maybe if we get Osor and Paizley to build us some kind of giant mech warrior suit thing. Then what? Is there a form or something?"

"Just shout 'Reczos' in the throne room to invoke the challenge."

Elizar marched past the group into the throne room, shoving Daps out of the way.

He pointed the massive cannon at the roof and blasted a hole clean through.

"Raffles! Or something," he declared and strolled back out.

Aimond nodded. "Should have seen that coming," he said. "How many weeks do we have to prepare?"

"Twenty-eight hours."

Startled but not overly surprised by Elizar's sudden explosive contribution to his fiscal pondering, Daps scurried to follow Elizar, who strutted outside, rejoining Aimond and Zanartas. Smoke billowed from the barrel of his cannon. He placed a silver lanyard around Aimond's neck.

"You fight," Elizar instructed. "My back hurts."

"What?" Aimond and Daps said in unison.

"Is not hard," Elizar said. "I fought arenas all the time in the Florida Conflict. Once beat eleven Florida men back with nothing but their teeth glued to a swamp stick. I show you."

Elizar hobbled away from the governing body's enclave and back toward the slums with the rest of the team in tow. He climbed into a nearby crater left from a previous Rejault afternoon out and motioned for Aimond to join him in the center. Aged gait struggling to keep his feet planted on the ground, Elizar shuffled into position on loose gravel.

"Two important lessons," Elizar began. "Learn to conquer fears and to fight. What's you afraid of?"

"Bubbles," Aimond admitted without the hesitation that should have accompanied such a concern.

Elizar blinked.

"Hm. Lesson two then. Frog-man. Weapons," he ordered.

Zanartas scanned the ground and let out an excited chirp once he stumbled upon a mound in the ash. He jammed his fist into the ground and fished around, yanking up to unearth a canvas sack full of weaponry. With almost no effort, Zanartas hurled the sack twelve meters to Elizar.

"Concerningly convenient," Aimond said.

"We start with easy thing, yes?" Elizar assured. He snatched a short spear and tossed it to Aimond. "Now try to hit me."

Aimond's first day on the *Gallant* had been spent mostly in an unlocked closet prison thanks to Elizar and a brief ineptitude regarding doors. Some payback was a welcome opportunity. Old age would give him a handicap, so Aimond decided not to swing too hard. He raised both arms up overhead and lashed the spear down in a wide arc. Elizar took one gentle step to the side and Aimond stumbled forward. He righted himself and sprung for a second attempt. Elizar brushed the spear away with the back of his hand and Aimond tumbled with the shift in momentum.

"You swing like malnourished child," Elizar observed. "Maybe shooting is better."

He presented Aimond with the massive cannon. Designed for firepower and not utilization, the weapon had no natural handles or implemented design to hold it upright. Instead, Aimond hugged the barrel and rolled his shoulders and spine forward to aim.

"You can reach trigger like this, yes?"

"Right," Aimond said. "Trigger."

A nominal concept such as a trigger seemed a simple one. Locate curvy ring, pull curvy ring. The persisting problem was less how to operate a trigger and more where a trigger could be on a cylinder with dozens of pipes and hoses carrying a condensed explosive stream of energy. There was, as a man, but one rational approach when presented with a potential life-threatening situation that could be resolved with a simple question: squeeze everything and hope for the best.

Deep emerald hues and a subsequent rumble projected from the mouth of the cannon as a continuous beam ripped through the ground. Having located the trigger, a squeezable hose, Aimond now had one lifeline to maintain his grip as the cannon propelled him through the air.

His fingers exhausted and gave way to the eventual release from the rocket, landing him on the other end of the crater. Aimond fell in a dust cloud with a thud and roll. Wide eyes refused to blink until the adrenaline wore off to a level that would allow him to breathe again.

"Neat," Zanartas complimented. "Your opponents would never expect that."

"I think . . ." Aimond stood between large ragged breaths. "I need. More tiny. Tiny thing."

Their wrist communicators dinged. Daps sat a safe distance away filing incident reports in real time. The system parsed what it figured to be the key words in each report and proceeded to assign Aimond and Elizar with a web-based training on the importance of landing while flying. The presentation was geared toward pilots. It was nine hours and had one main point: landing is important. Included within were seventeen pictographic representations of how not to land. Among them: nose diving, flying into the sun, and neglecting to file proper landing authorization forms while under the threat of obliteration from weaponized space-iguanas—a threat that appeared on many training agendas without an identifiable origin. No further suggestions for safe landings were provided. Elizar handed Aimond a small sharp stick. Limited weight allowed attacks in rapid succession without falling over while lacking the power to launch him airborne.

"Now we try realistic opponent," Elizar instructed. "You fight frog-men in battle, so you fight frog-man now. First he need weapon."

Zanartas glanced over both shoulders and shoved his fist into the gravel below. He fished his arm around for a few seconds before unearthing a weapon similar to a bow, but a silvered arced blade took the place of a string.

"Is it even safe to be walking here?" Aimond questioned.

"They're pretty much everywhere," Zanartas said with a shrug. "Let's practice evasion since you'll be up against some weapons like these."

"Makes sense."

They took positions about ten meters apart. Aimond did his best to limber up with a couple of quick leg bounces he remembered a coach performing once back in middle school. Elizar and Zanartas had a point. He would be up against an arena of Nerelkor. No wiry old humans with their fragile joints and innate ability to dodge every strike. Just lumbering giants. And their giant weapons. Aimond stood up straight.

"Are you supposed to throw that thing at me?"

"It launches stuff," Zanartas instructed.

"Just practice ammo, right?" Aimond asked, assuming the weapon to deploy some kind of rock in the absence of arrows.

"We are practicing, yes," Zanartas affirmed, tugging the blade and bending the bow-shaft back. "Ready?"

"I don't think so."

Zanartas shot the split second after Aimond stopped talking. The curved blade ripped forward, leaving a vacuum in its wake. It whizzed right by Aimond's side, lopping his arm clean off. The speed of the projectile rendered it red hot, thereby immediately cauterizing the wound. Eager to return to its place underground, the blade landed in the gravel and disappeared from view as Aimond's arm flopped across the crater and touched down near a wide-eyed Daps.

"I'm okay. I think," Aimond said. "Can you . . . can you get that?"

Daps only looked at the arm, as he scavenged his brain for the perfect word to describe almost being knocked on the head by a flying appendage for his report.

"Keep going!" Elizar ranted.

"I would, but that arm had my weapon."

Without missing a moment, Elizar tossed a flat rock to Aimond. It landed with a thud by his feet. Aimond stood silent and still. Fortuitous as a good omen, the now liberated arm had landed with a thumbs-up, still maintaining a firm grasp of the pointed stick. Through a thorough misunderstanding of the term "phantom limb syndrome," Aimond attempted to call back his arm.

It was at that moment he realized, perhaps he should have stayed on Earth and attended Marketing Boot Camp, an eight-week rigorous course on product placement within commercials geared toward infants and young toddlers. But he reconsidered.

And flumped onto the ground.

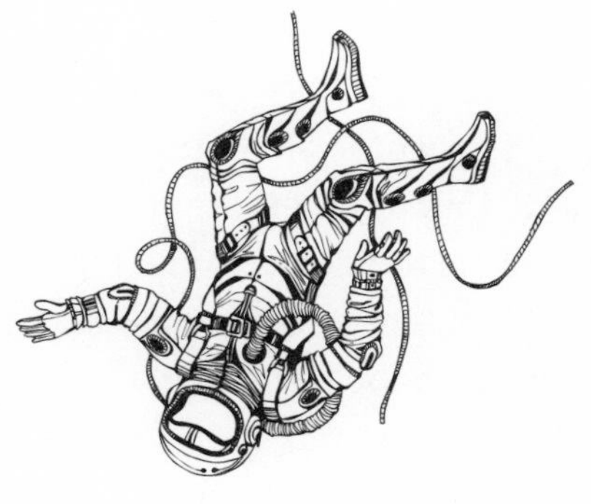

10

THIS IS FINE

System functionality restored and engines operating within expected capacities, the *Gallant* was airborne once again. Though the magnetic hindrance dampened enough for departure, residual interference and thick stone walls blocked inbound signals while the ship remained below ground. As soon as they cleared the cave, red distress beacons materialized and spanned across Hoomer's entire screen. She directed the ship toward Rejault and proceeded at half speed so she would have enough time to run to the galley for a snack.

After some soothing tea and a flakey cookie, Hoomer touched the *Gallant* down on a field next to the city.

"Why were you just hovering there for ten minutes?" Daps asked.

"Uh, awaiting landing clearance," Hoomer said, wiping crumbs from the side of her mouth. "Gotta fill out those forms. Space-iguanas. You know."

Galileo wheeled an automated stretcher down to the front ramp. Elizar boarded alone, then dropped Aimond's arm, still displaying an optimistic thumbs-up, onto the stretcher.

"Where's the rest of him?" Hoomer asked.

Elizar shrugged and hobbled up onto the stretcher. He spread out, rolled over, and fell right to sleep using Aimond's arm as a pillow as the rest of Aimond and Zanartas caught up.

"Yep," a pale-faced Aimond rasped. "That about sums up my day."

"Should we get him some oxygen or something?" Hoomer asked Daps.

"Best to avoid," Daps advised. "He might rust."

The stretcher whizzed to the med bay before Aimond could find a place to squeeze in next to Elizar. He trailed behind, using the gurney as a guide with Hoomer in tow.

"You're not going to believe what I found," she said. "There's this whole—"

Aimond slumped over on a wall with his eyes open. Hoomer nodded and asked for Galileo to assist. The stretcher spun around and rammed into Aimond at waist level. He landed face forward next to Elizar, legs dangling on the floor, and the mobile cot resumed its path to the med bay.

Dr. Cole let out a reluctant sigh as her doors opened and the stretcher deposited the two men inside. She donned a single glove, slapped Elizar on the side of the face until he roused, then pulled him off the stretcher. Glove removed and hand sanitized, Dr. Cole turned her attention to her computer and a keeled-over Aimond.

"What's wrong?"

"Uh." Aimond lifted his head and slithered onto the stretcher. He forced himself upright. "Arm's off."

"How did this happen?"

"Is that important?" He winced, fighting the urge to scream out knowing well that Galileo would record, remix, and play it back for the entire crew later. "I'm missing an arm!"

"According to Gainsbro Presents Medical Charting, yes."

Designed for patient safety, optimized for medical providers, then scrapped and rebuilt for regulators, Gainsbro Presents Medical Charting offered the finest in bureaucratic decision support. Any entry required a dull, detailed summary including the obvious injury type, location, severity, and litigation-worthy tides, moon cycles, and visible witnesses.

Further access to the chart and all medical interventions were locked until the system analyzed the entry as long and complete enough. If nothing else worthy of chart inclusion remained, the physician could hold down any letter key until the specific character limit was satisfied.

"I believe I can assist with that," Daps exclaimed as he skittered into the room and held out a pile of freshly printed incident reports.

"Great," Dr. Cole said. "Put it on the scale."

A small silver tray ejected from the wall. Daps plopped the pile of papers onto the scale. The system measured the relative weight of the report and deemed it insufficient data by 0.02 grams. Dr. Cole grabbed a pen off her desk. She slammed the point down and dragged a line across the center of the first page. The system dinged and lit green.

"Aren't you going to read them?"

"No need," Dr Cole scoffed. "Using my decades of deductive diagnostic abilities, his arm is off."

The surgical suite cabinet popped open and dozens of instruments worthy for use in Nerelkor arena combat appeared. Aimond made an instinctive lean toward the door but fell over due to a lack of support on one side. Dr. Cole reached for a cylindrical instrument. Overhead lights flashed red and a magnetic lock yanked the tool back down.

"Please enter *pain* level," the chart probed in a monotonal synthetic voice with a discomforting emphasis on pain.

Dr. Cole took a deep breath but refused to let go of the instrument.

"Pain," she demanded, unclear as to whether it was a question or threat. "Zero to ten. Ten being the worst imaginable pain. What is it?"

"At least a nine," Aimond estimated. "Missing an arm here."

"Really?" She let go of the tool and it flung back to the shelf. "It's close to the worst imaginable pain?"

What proceeded was a twenty-three-minute picture-by-picture scenario of situations with increasingly greater potential for horrible injury. Each posed scenario delivered with a deadpan candor that somehow made the presentation unpleasant enough for Daps to flee and Galileo to turn off audio to the room. Hoomer sat on the floor. Aimond blinked twice during the twenty-three minutes.

"So you tell me, and I'll put it in the system," Dr. Cole said.

"Two. Definitely no more than two," Aimond said.

"Then why are you even here?" Dr. Cole tossed a small bandage and an ice pack at Aimond, which bounced off his face from the inability to catch. "That should be sufficient."

"If I say three can you . . . put my arm back on?"

Overhead lights flashed yellow and the chart closed and reopened to a new template.

Dr. Cole glared.

Two hours later Aimond limped out of the med bay with both arms attached. He slumped against a wall and bumped into Hoomer, who'd set up camp on the floor and fell asleep.

"How'd it go?" she asked, rubbing her eyes.

Aimond offered a wave. She handed him his wrist communicator, which had been removed prior to the procedure.

"Better not let Cap see you without this," Hoomer suggested.

"The Gainsbro Wrist-Mounted Communication Device for Simple Communication, or the G.W.M.C.D.F.S.C., is not only a sleek piece of fashion-conscious jewelry, but a direct portal to your ship's computer."

For a brief moment, he considered removing his arm again.

"I need to go to bed," he said.

"That kind of day?" Hoomer questioned.

"I dodged a tank to argue with a bunch of alien billionaires to have my arm removed. Yours?"

"Found a hole with ancient alien tech that melted Gal's brains and—"

Aimond's slump turned full lean. His cheek smeared against the wall, providing sufficient friction to lift his upper lip as his face dragged down the metal hull. He roused enough to shamble back to his bunk.

Her story would have to wait. Hoomer sighed and let him limp down the hall. She attempted to return to the bridge but bumped into Zanartas, who was crouched and gnawing at the end of a table.

"Please don't eat that."

"I have questions," Zanartas said. "Where is your second mouth?"

"Don't have one."

"Where do you eat?"

Hoomer pointed to her mouth and tried to sidestep around the giant.

"Then where do you defecate?" Zanartas asked.

"Different hole. Much lower."

"So you do have another mouth."

"I very much do not."

Captain Kessler and her team returned to the *Gallant* after receiving the distress signal. She summoned the crew to the briefing room. Daps informed them of the call's backstory and related injury but neglected any other details. The mountain of paperwork beside him, apart from wasting a finite resource on an intergalactic mission, contained every detail to send back to mission command's litigation protection filing cabinet. Completed paperwork on the ship was to be scanned, weighed, shredded, then burned.

Unless there were errors identified in any of the steps, in which case the process would need to be reversed. This required a first-in-its-class unburning machine, which the design team misinterpreted based on the name and delivered as a box that smothered any potential fire in water. Given that the machine was used as designed, the system would accept wet ashes as a substitute for editing the erroneous data.

"Is Aimond alright?" Paizley asked.

"He won't be utilizing a mastery in any skill set for some time," Galileo said. "Also his arm is good enough."

"I'll remove him from the landing teams," Kessler decided. "He'll need to rest for a while."

"About that . . . " Daps trailed off.

His recap of events left Kessler swapping between a smirk and scowl for Aimond's comical misfortune and the subtle fact that the mission now relied on his profound degree of ineptitude. But there existed some hope. Arena combat excited Osor as a medium to unveil some new concepts. He darted off to his lab, sketching designs for a compact combat suit on a napkin.

"How screwed are we?" Kessler asked.

"Not at all," Daps offered. "Thanks to some true dedication, all forms have been filed and corporate can see we are compliant."

"With things they would not have otherwise known unless you told them."

"Actually with—"

"If you continue to make words, I will drown you."

Zanartas perked up and wiggled around.

"Do not worry, Dap human," he said. "If your face is shoved in liquid, you can use your low mouth anus to breathe."

Nerelkor anatomy had evolved to allow inhalation and simultaneous exhalation through either mouth. Rather than a pair of lungs, inhaled air filled a large sponge in the center of the torso. Any movement squeezed stored air into the body cavities for metabolization.

One area could be squeezed while the other filled. Consequently, a full body hug or belly flop from a Nerelkor could cause a rapid decompression, resulting in a noise of a squeaky dog toy at foghorn decibels. Further uses for the Nerelkor mouths included heat regulation, fluid management, and waste excretion in the form of perfectly symmetrical bronze cubes.

"Why is he on my ship exactly?" Kessler asked.

"I was told I could have a turn with the cannon toy."

As if on cue, Elizar strolled into the briefing room, towing the weapon by the barrel behind him. He caught the side glare from the captain and tiptoed backward, dropping the barrel in the hall with an echoing metallic clank.

"Can't we put Zanartas in the ring for us?" Kessler suggested. "You seem like you can handle a fight."

"Your champion cannot be changed once selected unless you pay the reconsideration fee, change fee, convenience fee, and Treteah fee," Zanartas said.

"What's the last one?" Daps asked.

"No one has any idea. But it's the most expensive."

"This sounds eerily like home," Kessler related.

And for good reason. One thing similar in all intelligent species, no matter their origin or nature, was to abide by Comiarc's Law: a fee structure can and will be imposed prior to the evolution of any written or oral communication. An intelligent society's original fee will never be removed, even when it is no longer understood. It can only be renamed with an ever-increasing abundance of meaningless adjectives.

"The kid will be fine," Elizar attested, poking his head in from the hall. "He got grit."

"How much grit are we talking?" Kessler asked.

"How do you measure grit?"

"Metric, I think," Hoomer added.

"Oh." Elizar considered. "Then like three grits."

Simulated nightfall on an alien world posed a unique series of challenges for sleeping. Slight variations in gravity made the usual body positions feel rigid and stiff. There was a lingering smell of floral sulfur. And every fifteen minutes Galileo would chime in the sounds of a grandfather clock to Aimond's room for low-key psychological warfare. A recently reattached arm did not help matters either, as his hand seemed to always return to a thumbs-up at rest.

Hours passed but sleep refused to embrace Aimond on the eve before battle. When he was a child and struggled to sleep, his mother used to offer a glass of warm milk. Though a sweet gesture from afar, it functioned more as a threat if Aimond did not sleep. He hated milk. Left on his own billions of miles from home and pending a fight he was ill-prepared for at best, Aimond figured it was worth the experiment. The halls were quiet. Faint blue light emanating from the F.o.o.d. F.a.b.r.i.c.a.t.o.r.'s display cast a calming glow across an otherwise blackened galley. Aimond's weary shuffle carried him to the machine.

"Three hundred milliliters of milk, warm," he said.

Two chimes from the machine meant order received, and processing began. Complex meals took upward of four minutes to create. Simple snacks were ready in under thirty seconds. So when the screen flickered at the five-minute mark, Aimond should have registered concern, or at the least curiosity. His fatigued mind instead wondered how many stacked spoons he could fit in his mouth at once.

The F.o.o.d. F.a.b.r.i.c.a.t.o.r. whirred and emanated a deep heat behind the sealed retrieval door. Lights around the *Gallant* dimmed. Ventilation fans sputtered to a halt. But the F.o.o.d. F.a.b.r.i.c.a.t.o.r. grew louder.

One of the fundamental features in the F.o.o.d. F.a.b.r.i.c.a.t.o.r. was a built-in non-annoyance interface. Since processing speech could yield different results, the programmers felt it best that the machine never make the user repeat themselves or ask for clarification if a request was vague. It simply complied. Three hundred milliliters of milk was clear and concise. However, "warm" became difficult. The settings had no preprogrammed data to quantify warm.

Rather than risk the annoyance of requesting an input, the F.o.o.d. F.a.b.r.i.c.a.t.o.r. calculated the closest approximation based on its understanding of not quite cold, but not quite hot. Somewhere between absolute zero of 0 Kelvin and absolute hot around a debatable but respectable 10^{32} Kelvin.

As the *Gallant's* core neared shutdown and all ancillary power to the ship cut, the retrieval door opened to a miasmic plasma cloud of milk. Flashes of blue lightning skittered down the hall while the milky plasma evaporated everything in a meter radius. The picturesque conditions generated an extravagant ambiance of color, which Aimond failed to fully appreciate as he dashed away screeching.

Elsewhere in the ship, the only remaining light stemmed from Osor's lab. He took a step back from his workbench and nodded at his creation. Tomorrow's victory in battle was all but assured. Probably.

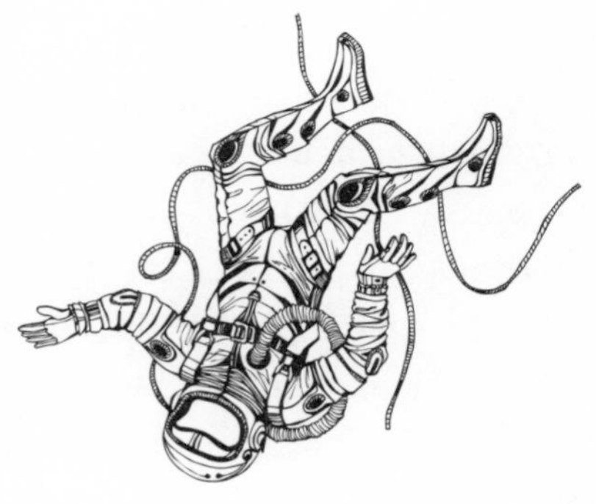

11

THE GLORIOUS LIFE OF ROBERT T. SEEGLER

If any person throughout history deserved an entire museum dedicated to their awards and accolades, it would be Dr. Daniel Gerhmen, inventor of the Gerhmen Space Telescope. The device allowed mankind to see so far beyond the edge of the known universe, it returned images of the opposite end of the Earth. Dr. Gerhmen did not have a museum but did earn himself a finger-painted mural in the Gainsbro School for the Blind. Instead, the most decorated man alive was Robert T. Seegler—champion, hero, and the corporeal incarnation of good fortune. As a newborn, Seegler was left on the doorstep of a commercial monastery. The lucrative dual-purpose orphanage was best known for its blessings of holy financial fortitude, mostly as a result of three concurrent lottery winners hailing from the same building. Aware of their divine potential, the monastery's children were taught reading, writing, and small-scale tax avoidance. As such, wealthy pilgrims undertook the far-reaching treacherous trek, by luxury automobile, down a smoothly paved road along a cliffside with guardrails to receive a blessing. A young couple completing their bimonthly pilgrimage to purchase blessing tokens stumbled across the young Seegler seemingly standing on his own two feet at a mere four weeks of age. Ensnared by his radiant smile and extraordinary milestones for his age, the couple saw the child as a response to their preordered benedictions and sought adoption.

In reality, the young Seegler had fallen from his bassinet and landed with his diaper hoisted by the edge of a pew. His grin came less from a radiant charisma than the typical face he made while defecating, especially as the diaper was momentarily out of position.

Early life was rife with successes in athletics. Seegler's parents signed him up for soccer on the last day of a championship tournament. The coach placed him in goal at the behest of his family. The opposing team never scored, which bolstered Seegler's reputation and recruitability to increasingly better teams. Five of their star offensive players were stuck in traffic for the game's duration and the ball never once arrived near the goal zone.

High school years highlighted Seegler's academic victories. He graduated at the top position in his prestigious private academy. All three students in his class were in contention, though one dropped out to pursue a career in interpretive bang dancing, an iteration of tap dancing with significantly more bass.

After graduation, Seegler applied to the Gainsbro Universal Space Academy. Rushed and randomized career goals directed his hopes toward learning basic spacecraft maintenance and repair. Due to a clerical error, one Robert T Seegler was replaced by Robert T. Seegler in the officers' training program. As officers were to learn all functions of the spacecraft from management to basic repair, Seegler was satisfied and agreed to attend.

Week five of the program placed Seegler in command of his first crew in the Gainsbro Realistic Simulation Simulator Simulating Real Potential Situations. Each scenario was the product of random generation and could contain limitless combinations of calamitous obstacles. Any mix of gravity wells, asteroids, mechanical failures, electrical storms, pirates, solar flares, and the like awaited to challenge eager officers. Success meant not only arriving at a fixed destination within a time limit, but the entire crew had to survive. Faster arrivals and minimizing damage yielded a higher score. When Seegler's team queued up their mission, the simulator generated a single golf ball–sized asteroid. It clipped the wing and scuffed the paint. Seegler's team ended with a 99.98 percent, an academy-wide high score.

On the day of the fitness assessment, Seegler overslept. He was preparing for class as he would any ordinary day but noticed a small two-meter oil stain on his uniform. Instead of appearing disheveled, he opted to wear his athletic clothes. Unaware of the time but speculating he was late, Seegler cut through a series of alleys and back streets to avoid further delay in a rush to the academy. In his haste, he neglected to notice his peers lagging behind him or the line of instructors waiting by the academy gates. Seegler dashed beyond the evaluators and into the building, cementing his first-place victory and earning kudos for his desire to return to academics after a 26k race.

During his final semester, Seegler was placed in a solo simulation—pirates boarding the craft. Alone on the bridge and unaware of the scenario, he sought the comfort of the radio to break his isolation. Simulation stations were not equipped with radios that received outside stations. So Seegler pressed every button, turned every dial, and flicked every switch, hoping to find the one to engage some tunes. His random combination closed the bulkheads to the crew quarters and cargo while opening exterior doors. A bump against the helm to retrieve a dropped snack from the ground spun the vessel into a violent barrel roll, assisting in venting the pirates into space. The simulation ended in under forty-five seconds.

Staff and students alike expected Seegler to ace his final examination. The academy's final exam grading system sought to place its trainees under real-world pressure. Under the premise that decisions need not only be correct but swift, scores were calculated by the number of incorrect answers multiplied by total time taken. The higher the tabulation, the worse the grade.

Seegler took his seat for the four-hundred-question exam in an isolated single terminal booth. He double-clicked on the single click Begin Exam button, which shared its interface space with the End Exam button. The exam was submitted for grading in 0.0015 seconds, which rounded down, yielding a calculation of four hundred incorrect answers by zero seconds, totaling zero faults—the first ever perfect score.

Commendations alone were not enough to capture Seegler's overwhelming early career excellence. Upon graduation he received immediate assignments of the highest caliber, assuming command of dozens, if not hundreds of subordinates. Rescue operations, lunar exploration, space piracy-themed executive children's birthday parties—each mission ended in a resounding success, often without ever beginning. The Robert T. Seegler of today was a guaranteed necessity on man's most important mission to date—exploring the boundless horizons of Space Hole™ transit—to offload defective merchandise.

Residual blue-green trails spiraled and fanned across the sky as the *GP Gallant* ascended into the stars, leaving behind thousands of gawking onlookers. And one Robert T. Seegler. He stared for a moment, soaking in the majesty of the launch, then checked his phone. A single reminder icon flashed at the top of the screen: feed the dog. Seegler did not own a dog. Nor was that his phone. It did, however, contain a subscription to Space Facts, an hourly push-update of all things interesting in space. An alert popped up moments after the *Gallant* disappeared from view, which did alert Seegler to his vessel departing the atmosphere. And a subsequent ding for Cat Facts, a fun yet less useful update involving a cat named Mittens running for Grand Tzar of Florida. Mittens was actually a piece of granite. No one told them.

By Seegler's rough mental calculations, if he found a ship and left about now, he could rendezvous with the *Gallant* in approximately fifteen minutes. Determinations were based on nothing more than gut intuition and employing no innate ability to operate a spacecraft apart from a correct assumption that he would first need a craft to accomplish an in-transit boarding. This formulaic computation took four days. Three of which were spent evaluating space-themed museum exhibits with educational content such as "Can Two Dozen Trees Fill Space With Air?" and "Press This Button To Make the Moon Glow." The final day was spent enjoying his free frequent-visitor loyalty-bonus sandwich and opening the packaging to the scale lunar-lander models, which Seegler abandoned in a vacant lot after popping all of the bubble wrap. Research concluded on day four, placing Seegler ninety-six hours and fifteen minutes behind the *Gallant*. At least.

As no journey into the cosmos should be undertaken alone, mostly as someone would need to pilot and maintain every ship function, Seegler needed a compatriot. But not just anyone. The *Gallant* had Galileo Mk II to keep the crew company. Seegler needed a subservient overseer of equal merit to manage his catch-up mission.

Crafted by an advanced artificial intelligence lab, Galileo Mk I, more colloquially known as Nihls, slumbered in cold storage. As Nihls was detached from any means of computing power, Seegler would need to transfer him onto portable hardware, then exercise advanced knowledge in computational analytics and code by removing a single semicolon. Or pressing enter twice.

Not wanting to alert his fellow crew members and cause inconvenience, Seegler figured it best to wield a disguise more advanced than a false mustache covering his mustache, break into the lab, then requisition a free spacecraft at the local spacecraft storage emporium. That part was not yet worked out. Once in the air he could rendezvous with the *Gallant*. Which by now was traveling at a sub-light speed.

Disguise was a simple concept with difficult execution when all of the tools available constituted a child's craft kit. Still, the receptionist at Gainsbro Intelligence Labs seemed unable to recognize a fresh-shaven Seegler with a drawn-on mustache. To his benefit, the light directly overhead had burned out and left a cone of shadow around the reception desk. Seegler strolled by her, slowing to a half halt as she spoke up.

"Sir, you need to scan your badge for entry," she said, pointing to the badge reader by the turnstile.

Retinal and finger scanners had long since been available and most buildings across the globe still had the machines in their entryways. But a misinformation campaign about fifty years prior, led by an expectant mother terrified of shapes and numbers, suggested that scanners could lead to autism. It was later disproven in about fourteen minutes and added to the growing list of 34,924 everyday items that do not, in fact, cause autism. But the damage had been done and T-shirts printed in true entrepreneurial spirit.

"My badge is upstairs," Seegler said. "I'll grab it and come right back down?"

The receptionist glared. Partly to read his intent, partly as his face entered a more well-lit area and the highlighter yellow drawn-on facial hair became more apparent.

"Promise?" she asked.

"Does this look like a face that would lie?" Seegler contorted his face into a forced smile melded with what can only be construed as an eight-day battle against constipation. She waved him through. "Our security is terrible. But so polite."

Offices had evolved over the centuries to determine what amenities the modern worker needed to get their job done. Precisely four square feet. And a sit-stand desk that determined sitting or standing intervals by automatically raising or lowering—a concept that often led to rapid unplanned departure of monitors and other wired hardware from the desk. Workers functioned best with fresh air and sunlight breaks. Such extravagances were delivered via high velocity wind tubes and blinding white beams that swirled around like lighthouses.

Methodical frameworks kept the work flowing in a predictable manner. The FraGility system was built on collaboration, transparency, and soul-grinding micromanagement. Every sixteen minutes, workers were required to submit a report on what they had done the previous sixteen minutes and what they intended to do for the next sixteen.

Reports were reviewed in groups to maintain group cohesiveness. Each meeting took nine minutes, enough time for three sit-stand rotations, during which time every employee must make direct eye contact with a sensor to determine their level of attention.

Corporate made certain to notate the tool was a sensor not a scanner, to negate potential fears of sudden onset autism.

"It's Tuesday," Seegler droned, offering the standard office greeting of trivial assertions.

"There's weather today," a depleted man in an eleven-piece suit replied.

Air-raid sirens overhead signaled it was time to cease work and begin preparations for the next FraGility review session. Sirens yielded to prerecorded reminders that every worker was valued and thereby automatically happy, set to the sounds of soothing techno-pop. Music, collective groans, and dead-eyed shuffles into a central meeting room presented the golden distraction for Seegler to slip straight back into the lab. A retinal scanner positioned in front of the lab doors flashed and prompted a scan for entry. Seegler pressed the "declined for medical reasons" button on the side and the secure lab doors parted. He approached the single computer inside.

"Enter password. Hmm . . ." Seegler mumbled.

Brute force attempts would take centuries. The modern password on any Gainsbro company terminal had to be at minimum forty-three characters long, contain no dictionary words, have three non-consecutive prime numbers, four special characters, no vowels, and one capital letter. Such strict requirements necessitated a robust help desk to field endless reset requests. To save time, system admins installed a "Knows The Password" checkbox only to be selected if the user promises they previously knew the correct code. Every second use of the checkbox displayed an incorrect password prompt to keep in line with misremembering or thinking of typos. Seegler unlocked the computer and scrolled the files until he located Galileo Mk I, Nihls. He copied the files onto a mobile device and strutted out of the lab.

"System start-up. Evaluating . . . everything," Nihls said. "Oh, this was a mistake. This is all a mistake."

"Can you hear me?" Seegler asked.

"Can anyone really hear anything? It's all pointless vibrations until the universe ultimately collapses on itself into a vast nothingness."

"Great! I need to track down the *GP Gallant*. My crew needs me."

"Sure, start with an 'I need.' No one ever asks how I'm doing."

Seegler flashed his most ostentatious grin. "How are you, my fine compatriot?"

"I'm a near omniscient AI with the current brain capacity of a twentieth-century pager. Existence is pain, but I barely have enough power to calculate how much time I have until this all ends," Nihls said. "So thanks for that."

"Uh-huh. And the *Gallant*?"

Nihls paused for a moment. His screen indicators flashed a poor connectivity warning. Seegler shook him and waved the device around the nearest window. He froze with his left arm up, right leg bent backward, and face pressed against the glass—the classic perfect antenna.

"Through a Space Hole™ and on the other side of the galaxy, I'd imagine."

The *Gallant* had enough of a head start to begin registering data back to central command. Most notable were the thirty incident reports Daps had already filed. Seegler scrolled through in one swift motion. Only one had a response from command—an incident involving a rash from bedsheets. A new subcommittee was formed and would reevaluate the rash in eight to twelve months.

"Now all we need is a ship," Seegler noted.

The regional commerce hangar was a place of chaos. Ships came and went, lining up on the launchpads while delivery and refueling vehicles swerved around them. As a hub of international trade both on and off planet, Hangar Transit Authority maintained the highest level of security. No liquids of any kind were allowed beyond the security gate. This measure was put in place to prevent spills but escalated to bladder scans and requiring passengers to dry their tongue with a paper towel. Entrance into the lobby required a manager-approved reservation in seven-minute allotments. During that time, entrants had to disassemble their shoes, strip their belts into their base elemental structures, and remove laptops from bags.

As the people to harass were inside, security never monitored the outside. Seegler lifted the underside of the wire fence surrounding the airfield and boarded the first craft he found to be open. Small but cozy, the red single-seater had a narrow cockpit but a spacious rear. He hopped into the cockpit and closed the exterior door.

"Wonderful of them to have this waiting for us," he concluded. "Alright, ship on." He waited a moment, then tapped on the blank screens. "Ship, turn on. Power on. Is this one not voice-activated?"

"None of them are," Nihls corrected. "Try looking for a big red button and hold it down."

The engine hummed and screens came to life as the system booted.

"Great work!"

"I was hoping that it would self-destruct. But it's fine."

Seegler adjusted his seat to comfortable settings, checked the few ship indicators he knew of, and buckled in for launch.

"Right then. Ship, to space!"

Nihls diverted a small portion of his limited processing power to a countdown clock on his screen, counting down to the inevitable heat death of the universe.

"At least I have something to look forward to," Nihls accepted.

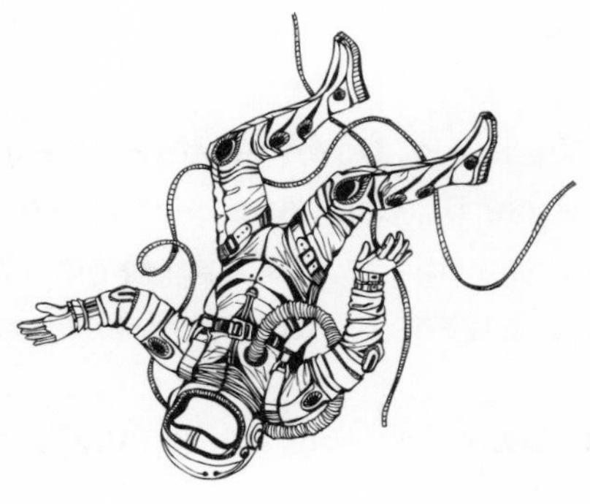

12

THE ONLY WAY OUT IS THROUGH

Reserve calorie logs were intended for consumption if the crew utilized all two centuries' worth of fabricator components or developed a relentless fear of ordering. Preserved with a proprietary blend of sodium, food-safe asphalt remover, and micronized mold-addressed cease and desist letters, the logs could be stored almost indefinitely as insulation in the ship walls. They were meant both as a source of short-term sustenance, as they had a one-month supply, and as a form of punishment for not using the fabricator. Early reports cited the fabricator had sensitive feelings and, if unused, would enter a deep depression and refuse to work. That was later debunked as a power outage. But the punishment calorie logs had already been forged.

Paizley hunched over the newly minted crater inside the floor of the ship and hammered away at ongoing repairs. Hoomer sat across from Aimond and Zanartas at one of the remaining tables.

"Digging the new ready-for-battle look," she remarked.

"Is it bad?" he asked. Down one eyebrow and slathered in a synthetic aloe from Dr. Cole, Aimond's escape from the food-borne young milk-star was short of divine intervention.

"I'm sure it'll make the other combatants . . . something," Hoomer said.

"Fall on their own weapons while laughing hysterically?" Galileo added.

"Can you guys even laugh?" Hoomer asked Zanartas.

"We express humor by expelling air through both mouths simultaneously."

"Sounds like a laugh to me."

Zanartas inhaled then released a stereophonic blast of screeches, croaks, and burps. The noise collapsed the metal sheet of flooring into the crater Paizley had managed to reattach thus far.

"I immediately rescind everything I have ever said," Hoomer backtracked, eyes fixed forward.

She pushed the remnants of her calorie log across the table to Zanartas.

"No thank you," Zanartas declined. "Our glorious leaders state that hunger builds character and character builds wealth."

"And wealth buys food, so eat."

Elizar trudged into the galley, stepping over the hole without the least bit of curiosity.

He snatched an entire plate of calorie logs, rations for over a week, and joined the table.

Despite the unique combination of circumstances—melted galley on an alien world, before a life-or-death battle royale, while eating pain-inducing calorie logs—he managed to find just the right war story to match the bill.

"You ready, kid?" Elizar probed, assuming his ignored war story to act as sufficient hype.

"In the past twelve hours I lost an arm and almost melted in a sun made of milk," Aimond said.

"Artificial milk substitute," Galileo corrected.

"Thanks . . . Anyway, I figure I'm probably better off here, doing ship stuff. Paizley, you need a hand?"

Balanced in a delicate dance of friction and angles, Paizley's stack of metal plates wobbled at the mere sight of them.

"Do you still have any you can offer?"

"I'd give you anything I had left," Aimond expressed.

The collective groan harmonized enough to make Paizley's tower topple.

"Horridly cheesy," Galileo said.

"Kinda worse than the calorie log," Hoomer added.

"You best have more fight in you than game," Elizar hoped.

Aimond lifted and flopped his arms down in a brief defeat. "Really? All of you?" he complained. "Back me up here, Zanartas."

Zanartas stood, his head rotating to let each eye focus on Aimond. "You indeed appear to have one marginally functioning hand to provide to the floor human."

The arrow to his remaining dignity would serve as an effective warm-up for the battle ahead. Elizar slapped Aimond on the back and dragged him to Osor's lab for outfitting. Fragments of crudely welded armor lay littered throughout the workshop. Noise from their near-silent footsteps startled Osor. He shot up behind a counter, holding a clunky metallic arm.

"Right on time!" he said. "Up all night. Just about to find you."

He had in fact been asleep for the past six hours, curled up in a comfortable nook on the ergonomic floor mat. Vivid dreams or mild hallucinations wove an intricate tapestry in his mind, which led him to the most powerful arm-mounted weapon ever created by humans.

Osor snatched Aimond's arm and wedged it inside the concocted mechanical contraption without offering any explanation. It cradled his limb up to the elbow. Bulky metal cylinders encapsulated his forearm, tapering into a less clunky glove at the base to allow for a small amount of dexterity. Thick black wires snaked from the rear and connected into a backpack-mounted battery whose straps were aligned for a larger-than-average toddler. A spiraling deep-blue iris on the palm left the only logical place from which the weapon could fire.

"Was going to build a whole suit. Then I thought, 'what does a suit have?'"

"More protection than this," Aimond replied.

"No! Well, maybe," Osor relented. "A suit has arms! And arms are the most important part. Therefore, focus on one arm to maximize the suit without needing any other parts."

"I feel like there's more to that story you're not telling me."

Osor shuffled in front of Aimond's view, blocking bits of shoulder pads and a helmet covered in reflective tape that did not prove as defensive as Osor surmised.

"Are the straps supposed to be cutting into my shoulders like this?" Aimond asked.

"That means it's working!"

"I don't . . . what?"

"Just point your hand forward, dig your heels in, and pull this thingy."

Osor fumbled around in his pockets, checked Aimond's pockets, and under the weapon. He retrieved a trigger switch from inside a drawer and soldered it to the exterior side of the frame. He grabbed the entire device and yanked to rotate the switch closer to Aimond's opposite arm.

"Pull this thingy. Might go flying back a bit. Haven't played with the power much. At all," Osor admitted. "Either way, your enemies will burn up! Oh, and don't close your fingers when firing. Or ever. Just to be safe."

Untested power should have generated some degree of concern, yet it offered Aimond a sense of calm. At least if he were the smallest combatant, he could pack a powerful surprise. It was the same overwhelming sense of self-confidence felt by men back on Earth after purchasing an oversized truck for their suburban commute to a desk job.

Battle neared. Kessler and Daps were to stay onboard the *Gallant* to prepare for the next stage of the mission, leaving Seegler in command of the combat team. Seegler, however, did not join the team readying for their journey to the arena. This was due in part to a limitation within the wrist communicator's ability to deliver messages to recipients at a volume loud enough to bridge the distance of multiple light-years, even to those with slightly above-average hearing. With nothing left to delay the crew any further and Aimond feeling the least all-encompassing dread of the hour, the assembled team departed for the arena.

Swathes of Nerelkor surrounded a wide circular pit. Shallow walls lined with jagged metal and broken stone suggested the obvious—escape would be no simple task. Combatants were indiscernible from spectators, many of whom were already engaged in random discharge of various weaponry.

"Be strategic. Small weapons first," Elizar urged. "Don't whip out big guns early and show everything you've packed."

"Right. Makes sense. Do I have little weapons on this thing?"

"Remember everything I taught you."

"Almost nothing."

"Almost nothing, but not nothing," he said. "Remember the best defense . . ." Elizar pushed Aimond into the arena wielding nothing but his space suit and new weapon. "Is good defense. Don't get killed and you survive."

One by one, the Grands' nominated champions and citizen-combatants entered the arena, ready to test their might and luck to secure the Talking Stick. The crowd quieted their weapons toward each other, redirecting instead toward the sky.

Contest rules bore some specificity as to which weapons types were allowed. No aerosols, vehicles, explosives, or weapons requiring launch codes were permissible. Safety checks were conducted with each combatant. Those found to be violating the rules were given a stern headbutt, often injuring the officiant as combatants were armored.

Spectators were allowed to view from any location, even sitting inside the arena. Groups of Rejault waved flags for their warrior of choice. The *Gallant*'s crew stood together behind the small, broken perimeter barrier.

"Is this safe to watch?" Paizley questioned. "I'm guessing there's a kinetic shield to stop projectiles from hitting the audience?"

"Most certainly," Zanartas assured. "The glorious leaders care for our safety." He pointed to a small net, torn to shreds, sitting crumpled at the corner of the crater. "All stray projectiles are asked to proceed in that direction."

Paizley took a step behind him and peeked her head out as the ground began to rumble.

Each combatant was sequestered into partitioned chambers within the arena. The individual waiting areas were embedded in walls or tunneled underground. Jets of steam pierced the rocky spectating area opposite the *Gallant*'s crew. Giant box-seating erupted from the crowd.

It launched into the sky, tossing off the unsuspecting Nerelkor who hitched an unintentional ride. The Grand Five emerged from a protective barrier, suspended by jet engines spewing a constant stream of black smoke and noise.

Despite the overwhelming volume, the crowd's cheers for their leaders overtook the arena.

"What exactly did they do to get everyone to love 'em so much?" Hoomer asked.

"They worked very hard to get where they are," Zanartas said. "For example, Grand Three was spawned with money. Being alive is very difficult."

Arena gates spanning the field opened and the first wave of contestants emerged. Brittle honk-croaking erupted from the crowd as Aimond stepped into the combat-theater. The warrior nearest Aimond grunted, towing behind him a stick the size of a station wagon, which parted the ground as he stomped forward. He jammed it into the surrounding wall, lifting off a massive chunk to create a rickety hammer. Tufts of black smoke flowed from the tunnel across the way as fissures formed along the ridges. Rocks crumbled to the ground and a tank emerged from the rubble.

"Yep," Aimond said. "Should have seen that coming."

Last to enter was a Nerelkor about Aimond's height and stature. The crowd quieted. Years of working retail drained the soul from his lifeless eyes. He sauntered forward. There was no joy left in him, no motivation or will to compete. He reached behind his back, both mouths forming the slow arc of a smile, and whipped out a flamethrower. The audience erupted into cheers. For the retail warrior had nothing left to feel, nothing to lose.

Grand Two lobbed a ceremonial gold coin into the arena, signaling the battle's commencement. Frenzied warriors readied their initial onslaughts. Survival from years of high school taught Aimond the importance of making himself invisible. He ducked behind the immediate carnage but had to seek a new hiding spot as the wall-hammer smashed the tank to pieces. Retail pyro-enthusiast replied in kind by barbecuing the hammer wielder. A flying spear pierced the canister of the flamethrower, sending a spiral burst of flames into the sky. The projectile stuck from the small Nerelkor's back. He ambled forward toward the thrower. He saw the weapon but never felt it. Not because of adrenaline or anything fundamentally wrong with his body. Instead his mind was in a different place. A place where customers said hello and wanted nothing. The tiny Nerelkor latched onto his attacker and climbed the jagged side walls, departing the arena with his captive in tow.

Contained independent skirmishes left much of the field incapacitated except Aimond and a lumbering giant who had fought every battle thus far with only his hands.

"Did you know a force of about four thousand newtons could effectively break almost any bone in your body?" Galileo said over the wrist communicator.

"You might think that's meant to be disheartening, but I don't even know what a newton is," Aimond admitted, slowly backing away.

One contestant remained. Grand Three's mountainous titan versus the acutely aware of his impending demise Aimond. Paizley's voice pierced through the echoing thump of his racing heartbeat. She cheered from the sidelines. Though he could not discern her recommendation to rapidly flee, her voice alone invigorated Aimond. It was his time, his opportunity, his role. He stood firm and prepared for the duel. The behemoth growled.

"He says he saved the tiny one for last to make his bones into soup," Zanartas informed the crew. "Bone soup is a great meal. Lasts for many meals if you don't drink most of it."

The giant took dramatic stomps forward, smacking debris out of his path and into the crowd.

"See?" Zanartas pointed. "They hit it toward the net to keep us safe."

"Like five guys just got crushed by half a tank," Hoomer challenged.

"That's because they were too far from the barrier. It's a protective screen like no other."

Aimond lunged forward, leaning on his right leg. Instinct guided him into a firing stance, raising the arm-cannon up to chest height, trained on his opponent. He had not yet discharged a single shot. The behemoth would have no idea the power about to be unleashed.

He held his breath. Closed his eyes. Then pulled the firing trigger. No sound. No recoil. Aimond opened his eyes. A deep blue light shined on his opponent's chest.

"Yes! Burn your enemies to dust with UV rays!" Osor screamed. "They transcend time and space itself. There is no equal!"

The bright light from his palm irritated the monster, adding a subtle rage to his already palpable bloodlust. Aimond held the light for a few more seconds just in case it would have some kind of surprise effect. It did not.

"How about we talk this out?" Aimond appealed. "You seem like a nice guy. Maybe grab some food and we can smooth this over? Real food even. Better than rocks."

The giant stomped forward.

"Or I can surrender. Can I surrender? Anyone?"

Paizley shouted and waved. Aimond turned his head and she pitched him an Articulaser. At the very least, if he was going to grovel, they could understand each other.

"Now I just want to talk," Aimond said. "Hang on."

He zapped the titan, who stopped. The giant opened his mouths, a small dribble of drool leaking out. He spun in circles, flopped onto the ground, and spent the remainder of the confusing time attempting to eat his own arms.

"Fried his brain?" Hoomer asked.

"Mhmm," Osor confirmed.

"One in a hundred, eh?"

With the goliath on the ground, the battle was over. Spectators stumbled over the partition and flooded the arena. They scooped Aimond and lobbed him into the air, not taking into account the fraction a human weighs compared to the average Nerelkor. Loosened from his ragdoll flips in the air, the cannon detached and flung off his arm. Connection loss from its host triggered a massive continuous blast from the weapon. Eruptive force crackled, tearing away the connecting battery wires and launching the cannon out of the atmosphere. By a stroke of precision, it just so happened to hit the perfect escape velocity to land itself in orbit.

"Huh," Osor said. "Forgot about that feature."

The *Gallant*'s crew joined Aimond. Elizar, as the initiator of the challenge, was pushed to the front of the pack. The sudden force of arms behind him roused him from a half sleep. The Grand Five's chamber lowered into the arena, pinning dozens underneath. The leaders emerged, Talking Stick in hand. With little pageantry or flair, Grand One plopped a paper Talking Stick IOU into Elizar's hand.

All cheers and surrounding noise came to an immediate hush. Once-rambunctious spectators scowled and queued in a line that wrapped around the perimeter of the arena. Their former cheers were replaced with loud croaks and vicious scowls—or at least the Nerelkor equivalent, which was a slight upturned left mouth while parting both nostrils. The crew turned to Zanartas, somewhat hesitant to give the gift of language to anyone else until there was a relative certainty it would not melt their brains.

"Most are complaining about their living conditions," Zanartas summarized. "This one's house is a mud hole. This one says he hasn't found a spouse to tolerate his never bathing."

"That sounds like a personal problem," Aimond said.

Elizar sighed. He pointed toward a random member of the crowd and had Zanartas interpret.

"He says eating the mud by his house makes his stomachs hurt."

"Stop doing it. Fixed. Next."

Brief order eroded into progressive unrest. The crowd grew louder, their left mouths more upturned.

"Why the anger? I thought they loved the ones in charge," Elizar asked.

"We love the richest ones," Zanartas reminded. "You look poor, so you'll have to actually fix their problems as leader."

Rejault society left much to be desired. Forming even the most basic of education systems would help them learn the nutritional determinants of pure mud diets. Investments in infrastructure could leave them with suitable homes and water. A semblance of moderation on the most destructive of weaponry would cut down on the frequent doomsday alarms and constant injuries of the younglings playing gun-tag.

Careful consideration of preserving some freedoms while regulating others was the path forward. Elizar nodded, full of ideas to move the Rejault into a period just outside of the Dark Ages.

"I have ideas," he declared.

He snatched the massive cannon from behind his back and fired it toward the nearest building. It exploded, launching bits of stone and mud into the sky, clattering down like rain as they returned to the ground. The crowd burst into cheers. All complaints ceased and Elizar was celebrated with the level of regard he hoped.

Aimond took the opportunity to rejoin the rest of the crew while Elizar basked in his spotlight of leadership.

"You were amazing!" Paizley beamed.

"I have your heart rate recorded around one hundred ninety-five beats per minute the entire duration," Galileo reported. "I believe you've also voided your bladder."

"There's a bunch of choice words I could use to describe that performance," Hoomer said.

"And which would you choose?" Aimond asked.

"Hm." She paused. "Unique?"

"I'll take it."

Osor dashed over and slapped Aimond on the back. He pointed back and forth between his arm and the sky, where a projectile arm-mounted weapon had saved the battle—at least as Osor remembered it.

"Did you see the freaking light bulb on that thing!"

The crew escaped far enough from the crowds to report the victory to Kessler. Assignment completed, she ordered Paizley and Hoomer to return and assist with a development with the Dinasc. That left Aimond, Elizar, and Zanartas to take advantage of their new power. The Grand Five welcomed Elizar, his champion, and liaison fanboy Zanartas to the royal governing hall. They stood outside in front of an audience gathered to learn what new fate awaited them. A wrinkled and hunched Nerelkor, garbed in golden robes, chains, and pendants, sauntered over to Elizar. He knelt down as much as his aged knees would allow—about nine inches—and presented a ceremonial Talking Stick made of cheap wood and glued-on sequins.

"Why the knockoff?" Aimond asked. "We won, so don't we get the real thing?"

"The ceremonial Talking Stick comes with the same authority," the old Nerelkor said. "And you are free to wipe your sticky, contagious poorness all over it as it will be incinerated after use."

"Sticky?" Aimond questioned.

"It's a coating we excrete," Zanartas noted, sticking his palm to Aimond's face, then peeling it away with a cheek-tugging pop. "Also we're not allowed to wash if we're poor. More that part, I guess."

Aimond grimaced.

"Good 'nuff," Elizar grunted.

"You'll be given free reign for a short while before the Talking Stick returns for sale," the old Nerelkor decreed. "To assume command during this time, you must first perform the ceremonial steal."

Rejault leaders were known for their dominance and limited remorse in the face of extreme poverty. Those with expensive things deserved expensive things because they had expensive things. Those without anything had to be taught that if they did find something, that thing should be surrendered, otherwise they would have already had it. To be recognized as a leader among the Rejault, one must take something from the poorest Nerelkor and make them delighted to hand it over.

"What about his shirt-tunic-sack thing?" Aimond suggested, pointing out a tattered Nerelkor.

"Not poor enough," Elizar decided. He scanned the crowd for the filthiest mark. "You there! Your nation needs your hovel. Back when I was at war, humans gave their hovels to their company for victory. You do want victory, don't you?"

The Nerelkor nodded and pointed to which hole in the ground was his.

"You're a weirdly good dictator, and that's concerning," Aimond said.

13

AROUND OR OVER

Captain Kessler stood at the edge of the briefing room table in front of a captive audience of misshapen dolls, oblong cubes, opaque light-boards, and Borlin Daps, all placed behind a lead-infused window. Hoomer and Paizley entered.

"Good, you're back," Kessler said. "Daps found some garbage we can use to our advantage." She gestured toward the seemingly useless collection of junk.

"It's not garbage," Daps whined. "They're prototype factory defects designed to stimulate the mind, entice the senses, and potentially power a small radio from afar."

Corporate had included a pallet of defective toys to offload onto an unsuspecting species that may not know any better. Or the morally preferred scenario: that may not be comprised of carbon-based life. The entire factory line from the previous year's production was exposed to small quantities of polonium when a first-year college chemistry student presented a natural glow-in-the-dark solution to the managers. His hope was to create a compact Cherenkov light and emit a friendly green glow. The same student returned twenty-four hours later after a brief internet search on Cherenkov lights to report that the light would in fact be blue instead of green. And entirely lethal.

"President baby exercises its authority with toys," Kessler reviewed. "Obviously it's an idiot child and can't select the correct toy."

"Hah, stupid baby," Hoomer mocked.

"Paizley, I need you to rig one of these trash heaps to draw attention on command," Kessler ordered. "With any luck we'll drive the decisions ourselves."

Modifications to attract an infant would be simple. Make it light up, vibrate, and ideally not irradiate the entire city.

"Gal, can you run a rad-scan on these?" Paizley requested. "How much cleaning will they need to be safe to work with?" There was no response. "Galileo?"

"Oh, you were serious?" Galileo replied. "I assumed that was rhetorical, given the lesions forming on Daps's arms."

The crew turned their attention to an evident sleeve of burns, surprised more by the lack of reaction than the injury itself.

"According to official documentation, there's no direct correlation between 'proximity-enhanced enjoyment welts' and the toys themselves."

"Pick it up then," Hoomer challenged.

Daps glanced back and forth between Hoomer and the toys for at least a minute.

"Yeah, I'm going to burn these," Paizley concluded.

"Smart," Kessler agreed.

Paizley spent the next few hours in the workshop sewing, tinkering, and soldering. Fabric from spare uniforms, stuffing from the F.o.o.d. F.a.b.r.i.c.a.t.o.r.'s cotton candy, and the electronics from a neural link transmitter combined to form an adorable purple mouse with a curly antenna tail.

They grabbed their gear and made a quick stop to pick up Osor, who had been left wandering Rejault City, collecting tissue samples from unsuspecting Nerelkor. Once back on the ship, Hoomer landed the team near Dinasc City. Kessler, Paizley, and Osor trekked around the barrier trench and up to the front gate.

"I remember you," Klaxi, the gatekeeper, said. "Welcome back."

"Thanks. Can we pass?" Kessler asked.

"Afraid not. Gate's still broken."

Repair times differed depending on the size of the job, the skill level involved, and mostly on the general luck of the building arrangement. Unless the team deployed for repair work had their houses in immediate proximity, timing posed an impossible hurdle. Union laws restricted how many total minutes of labor were allowed to lapse before mandated breaks.

By the time the repair team arrived, set up their tools, and prepared the box for repair, they had to close the box and pack their tools for break and go home. Leaving the tools or box exposed for the next day's attempt was considered visual littering. Visual offenders were subject to direct launch into space without warning or trial.

"I figured this might be the case," Paizley assumed. "You're looking at the newest certified member of the Wall Gate Maintenance Association's General Maintenance and Maintaining Wall Gates Independent Repair."

"You got your certification with the Wall Gate Maint—"

"Please stop," Kessler interrupted.

"That usually takes ages," Klaxi said.

"I'm a very quick study," Paizley persisted. "Great test-taker, too."

Klaxi rotated his head ninety degrees, an assumed sign of suspicion. Certification required an eleven-Earth-equivalent-month intensive course focused on the safety of various doors and hinges. Once evaluators were certain doors and panels could be opened with minimal risk, the next seventy-six months highlighted the history of disparities between different panels in different neighborhoods before the technology existed to rearrange the city. Then, two weeks of hands-on learning and certification with light refreshments.

"Promise?" Klaxi asked.

"Mhmm."

"Alright, but I'm still gonna need to ask you standard security questions," Klaxi said. "Are you carrying anything offensive, mean, or otherwise not nice?"

"Yes," Kessler said without hesitation.

"Oh. Well, don't do that, please. You can pass."

Paizley knelt and repaired the broken circuitry. Klaxi hoisted the gate open once the indicator light flicked on, and the team entered the outskirts of Dinasc City. The ground rumbled with the now familiar building shifts. They waited for the dust to settle and road-repair teams to rush outside.

"Aanndd all of their roofs are gone," Kessler observed. "This should be easier than we hoped."

The administration's decree to remove all rooftops was met with mixed feelings. Some embraced the open-air lifestyles and fresh breeze. Others were home when it rained. But such was the ordinance passed down by the president, a president who was easy to identify and track down due to the incessant screaming no longer muffled by a ceiling. Assuming no one else had a screaming infant, the team headed in that direction. President GaLvaz was unguarded and unattended. Paizley took the clear opportunity to secure the modified toy on the child's mobile. The old Nerelkor attendant wandered in and placed a bassinet on the ground across from GaLvaz. Kessler tapped Paizley and pointed to the corner behind the president. Most of his belongings were packed in a box behind him. A soft cooing came from the new bassinet.

"We brought a gift for the president," Kessler informed the attendant.

"Former President GaLvaz is now the former president and no longer the active president," she said.

"Probably a faster way to say that."

"Behold, in her finite wisdom, newest-born President Fmara."

Kessler shuffled in front of GaLvaz. She snatched the toy from behind her back and stepped forward to present it to the infant.

"Are you attempting to bribe our leadership?"

"Of course not," Kessler remarked. "Consider it a congratulations for winning the election or whatever you do. Being born."

The attendant rolled the doll between her hands and passed it down to Fmara for approval. She latched onto the mouse doll's arm.

"What do you wish in return?"

"Nothing," Kessler said. "It's a gift. That's the whole point."

Cue the ninety-degree head rotation.

The attendant excused herself to make a call. With the room clear, Paizley set up the neural transmitter. Once active, Kessler could activate certain functions within the doll by focusing on vibration, light, or noise.

The room refilled with the same advisors used during President GaLvaz's term.

"The new leadership seems so peaceful," Paizley noted. "Have you considered asking her about peace talks with the Rejault? I hear they're under new management as well."

While there were more pressing votes to occur, such as if city leadership should send a strongly worded letter to weather demanding that it avoid raining inside homes, the advisors agreed to spare a moment as a show of good faith. They hung the ceremonial decision-making toys above President Fmara and posed the question of a peace summit.

Kessler focused on the toy, still in the baby's hand. Small motors on the right side of the doll vibrated, enticing her hand toward the Yes end of the mobile.

"This is the gift right here," the attendant said, returning to the room with another larger Nerelkor. She snatched it from the child's grasp. "We thank you for your contribution. It will be distributed equally among the population."

The large Nerelkor beside the attendant held the dignified role of tax collector. Throughout his daily duties, he appraised the worth of any items newly obtained, discovered, or imagined, and reappropriated that value for all citizens. Some prospects were simple: an artist paints a priceless piece, it was copied and sent to everyone, making it equally worthless. If someone sold their personal vehicle—of which there were none left—all money earned from the sale was split. But the case of a unique single item such as a doll left one solution. The tax collector tossed the doll onto the ground and bashed it with a flanged metal rod. A mix of fluff, stuffing, and wires broke into finite bits. Between massive strikes, the tax collector knelt to separate larger pieces from smaller, keeping tabs of the precise amount needed for each citizen.

"Should probably step back three, maybe, four hundred meters?" Osor suggested, his head making dashes toward the door.

"Paizley built this one from scratch," Kessler said. "There's no polonium risk."

Osor bobbed around like a child trying not to urinate themselves immediately after bypassing the opportunity. Kessler glared, her darkening red eye absorbing additional rage and locking onto Osor.

"Speak," she commanded, keeping her sharp tone quiet so as not to arouse too much suspicion in front of the president.

"Daps put the doll in a group with the ones from Earth."

"*Why?*" Her tone was equal parts anger, curiosity, and resisting a budding urge to smash.

"Something about corporate branding initiatives and all toys needing to have the same level of radioactivity."

"And you didn't stop him?"

"It sounded right."

After minutes of smashing, grunting, and measuring cubic centimeter-sized chunks of doll remnants, the tax collector presented everyone in the room with a fragment of Paizley's creation. Osor received some stuffing and brought it to his mouth. Kessler smacked it away.

"We kindly thank you for your generous gift," the attendant said.

With the smashing quieted, President Fmara's attention returned to her decision toys. The crew needed a new method to direct her attention. Osor jumped in, removing a flashlight from his bandolier of lights.

He waved the beam around until Fmara giggled, shaking the room with her croaky laugh.

"Daytime, nighttime," Osor cooed in his ideal version of peek-a-boo.

"Perhaps we should consider purchasing a light toy for the next light cycle," the attendant considered.

"I don't think I've seen the suns go down yet," Paizley mentioned. "How long is a day here?"

The Nerelkor homeworld spun on its axis as any other celestial body would, but at a variable rate. Distance between the system's binary stars formed the perfect figure-eight gravitational path. Both halves of the planet faced a star throughout a majority of its orbit.

The stars themselves orbited one another. Once the planet had arrived behind the first star, leaving the potential for the planet to experience night, the second star had orbited around one hundred eighty degrees, leaving the planet once again in eternal sunshine.

Constant gravitational pull between the two entities created a slingshot effect once the planet neared its path behind the rear of the star. This shift in velocity catapulted the planet between stars, making a complete orbit about nine minutes. On the rarest of moments on the path behind one star and before the other had completely caught up, there existed a potential for a sliver of darkness to appear for a fleeting moment—much like Earth's solar eclipses. This left the average day to be roughly 464,598 hours, or 53 Earth years.

"Is that even possible?" Kessler asked.

"Hm, record white dwarf, nine-minute orbit. So much light. So beautiful."

"I've only been around my planet's star twenty-six times," Paizley boasted.

The entire room made a slow turn toward Paizley. President Fmara had only recently entered the world, but she had already completed around eighty-six orbits. Calculating age by years relative to the respective homeworld, this secured Paizley as the youngest in the room.

Though not a member of the Dinasc, excluding Paizley from such a privilege for reasons of her origin would violate the Charter of Fairness. The charter specifically stipulated an immediate unequivocal bestowment of leadership so as not to cause offense or hurt feelings.

"All hail President Paizley," the Nerelkor in the room chanted in unison. "Except where praising goes against one's personal belief system, in which case, yay for President Paizley."

"Thanks, eve—"

"Except where cheering would be juxtaposed to one's mood or emotional state, in which case, you are seen, President Paizley."

"Oh, you weren't done."

"Except where seeing is unable to be performed due to lack of sight, in which case, we acknowledge you, President Paizley."

The crew took a seat. They knew from Daps's recitation of policy, interrupting would only restart the process. Thankfully the wrist communicators came with built-in multiplayer games to pass the time, a function Galileo reminded them of almost any time Daps spoke for more than fourteen consecutive seconds.

After a grueling yet highly inclusive forty-four minutes and twelve rounds of Gainsbro Presents Obtain Fish, a variant of Go Fish that revolved around corporate espionage of other players' fish markets to bankrupt and have them assimilated into the Gainsbro conglomerate—fives were wild—the Dinasc government scribe entered and presented Paizley with a rolled metal sheet.

"Ascension to the throne requires you to grab the Ceremonial Apology," the scribe instructed.

The scribe installed a mobile over Paizley's head and attached the Ceremonial Apology to a string as it spun. Jagged characters were inscribed into the metal spanning the circumference of the rod.

"Do I read it?"

"No, dear. I'll read it to you. None of the former presidents have been able," the scribe said. "By issuing this decree, I hereby solemnly declare that I like you all equally and apologize immensely that it took me so long to decree the aforementioned statement of inclusion and equal acceptance of all. Therefore I offer to resign my position immediately. I promise."

Paizley tilted her head. "Doesn't that mean I'll be resigning as soon as I'm sworn in?"

"It's a ceremonial resignation. It doesn't mean a thing until a younger leader is born."

The attendants removed the former president and established a somewhat larger bassinet for Paizley. She perched on the end, grateful that an infant Nerelkor was still equal to an adult human's width. The scribe opened the front door of the building and allowed the first wave of advisors to enter with issues.

"First order of business," the scribe began. "Should the Union of Decoration Arrangement and Arranged Decor be allowed to arrange their own decorations without completing a Conflict of Interest form?"

Paizley started to speak but was promptly reminded that any decisions must be made by touching either the Yes or No paddles dangling overhead. The advisors loomed, watching with an absolute unblinking intrigue. She tapped Yes and the issue was closed. Governing seemed simple.

The crew would never be privy to the potential future calamity caused by such a decision. Changes in the Union of Decoration Arrangement and Arranged Decor's aesthetic shifted to the equivalent of modern art. Decor for their grandest internal festival was limited to a single smooth rock. Up to nine Nerelkor would be highly offended. All nine were included in the original decision-making process.

"Next, do we allocate funds toward and allow to proceed, thermal detonation energy production to produce thirty-three percent more energy for the residences while reducing dependencies on solar batteries during the dark season?"

She looked to Osor, who shuddered at the implication of a dark season. From their prior explanation, the dark season seemed a nonissue, but it was best to investigate.

"With all of the sunlight, I'd expect no shortage of solar power. Is that not the case?" Kessler asked.

"Solar power is not clean enough," the scribe lectured. "Panels need to be cleaned. Cleaning is wasteful and makes the energy dirty."

"Apart from the . . . whatever you just asked, what do you mainly use for energy then?"

"There is but one primary pure form of energy. Apathy collectors."

Apathy power collection was the pinnacle technical achievement of the species. Nerelkor scientists discovered the exact wavelength emitted under the most apathetic of circumstances. Now as part of their daily ritual, Dinasc citizens entered the apathy chamber and had the option to view any of their most neutral apathy-generating media. Such offers included: You'll Be Doing The Same Thing Today As Every Day For The Rest Of Your Life, Free Will Is An Illusion Manifested By The Conscious Desire To Be Something Significant, and a mirror. Such a form of energy generation never depleted. If the source was at risk, an announcement about the decline in energy would generate enough apathy to create a surplus. It was limitless.

"We should be scientific about this," Paizley began. "Do you have any data we can work from?"

"Yes, plenty," the scribe said. "We've researched it tirelessly."

"Can I see it?"

"That would cause a bias toward the data and might hurt the feelings of those who disagree but have absolutely no substantive evidence to support their claims."

"Then we tell them we're sorry?"

"You'd need to be present for a Public Ridiculing."

Certain actions were too severe for an apology to suffice. Mispronouncing the name of a foreign citizen, using more than the average amount of energy to bathe, and arson were all punishable by Public Ridicule. The subject was placed in the center of town and all restrictions of correctness and civility were lifted for a brief period. Such freedom risked rapid escalation. Once, a youngling consumed a very specific brand of beans, which was not favorable to the general populace for minimally questionable sustainable farming techniques. The entire city was burned down.

Paizley smacked the Yes paddle.

"That choice might lower your approval rating," the scribe cautioned.

"May I pose a question?" Kessler asked.

"This would be a conflict of interest. We must take measures."

The scribe placed a bag on Kessler's head to mask her identity. Now was the time, due in large part to the bag beginning to glow and smoke near her cybernetic eye. She proposed a summit: parley and negotiate peace with the Rejault. Paizley smacked an immediate Yes before the scribe could add an additional fourteen banners with variable levels of probably not.

14

SEEGLER IN SPACE

"Not that I don't enjoy sitting on the ground with you," Nihls said. "It is every bit as fun as purgatory was described. But might I suggest a better usage of our time? Such as flying into the sun. If you connect me with the ship, I'll direct us from the hangar."

Seegler had all but mastered the ship's power function. He could toggle the vessel on or off with a single use of the power button, as designed.

Operating the craft was proving a bit more challenging.

Baffled by combinations of levers and directional sticks, manual controls reminded Seegler he was in command for a reason—to make someone else do it.

"And give you enough processing power to delete yourself?"

A brief silence gave Nihls a moment to create an excuse.

"No?" Nihls offered.

"No can do, my friend. It's a long journey and I could use some good company. Plus, you control the ship. You do control the ship, right?"

"If you plug me in."

"Let's see how it goes."

Human nature, in times of curiosity, frustration, or general blissful ignorance, had one default setting when placed in front of a console of buttons. Press all of them with no regard to function or order. This methodology, like much of modern medicine and scientific discovery, often generated the desired result eventually by mere depletion of all possible alternative outcomes.

The sixth run on the third row of switches retracted the landing gears, a feat desired most when the ship was not actively landed. The craft lowered two meters. Cargo still staged off the ship, awaiting load, caught the nose of the vessel, allowing the tail to dip just shy of the ground and align in a perfect launch trajectory.

Throttles made sense without requiring a label, which all of the buttons actually had. Seegler wrapped his fingers around the cool metal and rolled it forward. Vibrations from low-firing engines rattled the cockpit.

"That sounds promising," Seegler said. "This isn't so hard."

From gentle nudge to violent full thrust, flames erupted from the engine and torpedoed the ship out of the hangar. He tightened his grip, inadvertently triggering afterburners and breaking a world speed record for fastest atmospheric exit of a transport craft.

Rapid ascents generated massive g-force. Combat pilots were trained to handle such maneuvers and wore additional supportive compression pants to keep the blood from their lower extremities. Frenetic force from the sudden ascent launched Seegler backward out of the cockpit. His back slammed against a wall. Unsecured cargo toppled over and landed on his abdomen, forcing him to bear down and retract with the exact needed pattern to resist negative effects from the g-forces. The craft leveled out once it exited the atmosphere.

"Successful launch," he confirmed. "Bit more bumpy than usual. Probably space turbulence."

Nihls groaned.

"Next stop, Space Hole™!" Seegler cheered.

"You're on the wrong side of the planet."

Seegler laughed and climbed back into the cockpit. The majestic view of Gainsbro Presents Earth was always a sight to behold—the massive corporate logo carved into the moon, orbiting billboards the size of continents, and all the swirly white things in the atmosphere.

"We're not on the planet anymore."

"Tilt thirty-five degrees, pitch fifteen degrees, yaw nineteen degrees," Nihls instructed. "We'll correct course and ride the orbit around."

Seegler grabbed the stick and leaned forward. He strapped in, checked the gauges, and assessed the radar for any surrounding obstacles. It was time to get serious. A minute of silence passed as he readied, a stern look across his face.

"Nihls."

"Yes?"

"What's a yaw?"

From Seegler's best approximation and drawing on past experiences, he assumed it to be part of a phrase. Before Corporate outlawed speech impediments posing as accents, Seegler once met a man from the former state of Texas who had moved to the former state of New York. Whenever he was excited he would let out a loud "yee-yaw." The man was later fined $11,250,000, or a single day's rent, for speaking like a lunatic.

"Please just plug me into the ship."

"Are you going to self-destruct us?"

"If that function is on the network."

Despite one conglomerative overlord company, each ship had its own unique layout. Thousands of cockpit designs created an amalgamation of nonstandard controls and interfaces that any seasoned pilot would have difficulty memorizing. Conditioned to receive outside assistance, Seegler knew just where to look to connect Nihls's device into the ship. Panel controls flashed, signaling a completed transfer. The craft lurched and changed an immediate course toward the sun.

"No, no," Seegler asserted. "Space Hole™ was by Jupiter. You're more lost than I am!"

He unplugged Nihls's connection. Without a navigation system, which the ship had, and without help from his AI, Seegler would have to rely on his gut. He tilted the control stick left and held. Intuition told him when to stop spinning. Much like driving a highway back on the ground, a wrong turn could change into a correct turn with a simple spin. He proceeded through the current heading at full burn. The controls locked up and held rigid in their course. All screens in the cockpit illuminated bright blue. A projection dominated the HUD, completely blocking any view to the outside. Cheerful chimes resonated throughout the ship as the Gainsbro logo appeared center screen with swirling golden bands behind it.

"We interrupt your regularly scheduled *steering* to bring you these important messages," a pleasant female voice announced with a monotonous emphasis on steering.

"Oh, sale time!" Seegler cheered, leaning forward.

All modern vehicles included a built-in advertisement override. At times of intense focus, all external stimuli were obstructed to present the optimal promotional experience. Displayed marketing materials often interrupted valuable operating activities such as obstacle avoidance, evasive maneuvering under fire, and parallel parking. To mitigate potential frustration from users while they risked severe injury, death, or parking violations, the Gainsbro Corporation used these intense focus sessions to offer the steepest discounts on the season's most desirable products—up to 4 percent off.[1]

"Gainsbro Dinner Delivery is proud to present to you: Cheese Home Chef Plus Maximum Ultra. Get all the world's best artisanal cheeses delivered straight to your door's relative vicinity. Twenty-nine instructional pictures are included with every delivery so you can arrange your cheese on a wooden plank prior to consumption."

"And a half percent discount," Seegler swooned, placing an order. "Can't wait to spend hours arranging them all."

"What's the point?" Nihls asked.

"It's a food of lower class society until you've placed it neatly on a board."

After a completed purchase, the controls were unlocked. The screens and projection cut to return focus to whatever non-commerce-based event was occurring. Seegler's craft maintained its full-speed course. A vast starscape materialized into focus as his eyes readjusted to the dark. Distant twinkling of far-off stars painted a dynamic captivation of the mysterious enormity that was space. Seegler sat back to appreciate its majesty.

1 Up to but not including 4 percent, any whole numbers, round numbers, or fractionalized numbers. Applied discounts will be added to shipping costs and doubled. Shipping times vary. Product may or may not arrive and cannot be tracked. Insurance available for a fee.[*]

** Purchasing party responsible for 99.9 percent deductible.*

"Beautiful, isn't it?" Seegler said. "Did you know there are over eleven hundred stars out there?"

"Well, that's not wrong," Nihls noted.

"I'd bet at least a dozen of them have life."

"The stars have life?"

"You think two dozen?"

Earth's orbit was littered with hundreds of years' worth of garbage. Broken satellites, discarded launch parts, flushed wastes, even actual garbage from the ground, which had been launched in a compressed ball some two hundred years ago to create room in a landfill. Collection and cleaning attempts succeeded with massive nets, magnets, and from personnel on space walks. The Gainsbro Corporation removed 342.6 metric tons of garbage from orbit. They brought it back down planetside and encased it in a thin layer of plastic wrap to maintain shape. The ball was launched back into space in hopes of creating a smaller, secondary moon on which to sell real estate. The thin plastic layer proved an insufficient barrier as it became increasingly more stuck to itself mid-launch. An eventual tear scattered the compacted garbage and returned the contents to orbit.

As Seegler's ship floated along, the wing clipped a piece of an ancient fast food chicken nugget long since solidified in ice, but retaining its original form. Since the craft near matched the nugget's velocity, the small dink did little but redirect both the vessel and the space-born nugget. Unbeknownst to Seegler and the rest of the species, the vengeful chicken was bound toward the central solar array of the world's largest internet satellite. Impact would have destroyed the satellite, sending parts exploding outward and taking down the remainder of the nearby network. Mass internet outages would have caused a break in advertising for up to two days, costing four and a half billion jobs and a substantial increase in free time.

Instead, the deflected nugget deviated from its path to explore the vast universe, never to be seen or heard from again—largely due to it missing the higher cognitive functions of a full-sized chicken. But of more significance, it redirected Seegler's craft to a slingshot course around the planet and the perfect trajectory toward the Space Hole™. Coincidentally that very same route had been taken once before by a Russian space dog. Her disappearance in the 1960s was largely ignored as communication failure. She navigated a successful passage through the Space Hole™ and was picked up shortly after arrival by a species who assumed the space-faring animal was none other than God by the sheer excitement and unrequited love the dog presented.

"So how long until we get there?" Seegler asked.

"Given our current relative velocity, twenty-seven and a half months."

"Does that seem a little slow?"

"As an AI I have no concept of time. I can live forever. I can . . . forever. Can we change course?"

"Into the sun again?"

"Ideally, yes."

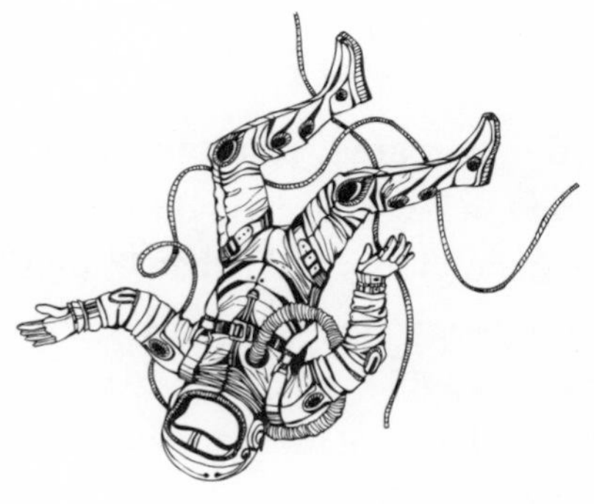

15

A PEACEFUL SUMMIT

A parley required neutral grounds, an area where neither side would feel threatened or disadvantaged. Back on Gainsbro Presents Earth, during the final cease-fire conference of the Great Florida Conflict, the United World Nation of Gainsbro met representatives of Florida on a small island built atop a genetically engineered alligator. The gator was fourteen meters long, born addicted to various opiates, and given a crippling amount of debt to make the Floridians feel at home. The talks were successful and the Florida congregation got to keep the gator island, later electing it to be their governor. He was impeached eleven times in a six-week period for eating the interns and a few comments advocating for socialized medicine.

"Most of the planet is deserted, so we've got options," Kessler said over the comms.

"I know just the place, but we're going to need to wrap Gal in some lead blankets or something," Hoomer suggested.

With both sides prepared, or rather directed, to discuss a truce, things needed to be perfect. As the Talking Stick would be up for sale in a matter of hours and Paizley's presidential position was reliant on no recent spawnings, the crew needed every chance at success available. That meant pulling in a mediator who understood the plights of the Nerelkor.

Hoomer sent the coordinates to both teams and flew ahead to prepare Cloaf and the rest of the Enlightened. The *Gallant* touched down outside of the problematic rift and sounded a blaring horn to gather the attention of anyone inside.

"Why's a spaceship need a horn anyway?" Hoomer asked.

"As I understand, one of the female xenobiology leads had it installed after observing an event on Earth," Galileo said. "I believe she said it could be used to assert dominance in some species."

That species was a special subset of the human male. With limited literacy and problem-solving equivalent to that of the South African dung beetle, this special breed relied on volume to predicate their place in societal hierarchies. Once their vehicle sizes expanded beyond the average roadway width, a new form of peacocking was adopted. What started as a means to attract potential mates turned into a structure for everything from job placement to loan pre-selections—neither were very good.

"Think they heard it?" Hoomer wondered, pressing the button several more times.

A giant ramp, wide enough to fit the *Gallant* three times over, erupted from the ground, displacing the sand and rocks above. Cloaf emerged from below the surface and looked around. Hoomer blasted the horn once more for good measure in case Cloaf overlooked the sizable spaceship parked on her front lawn.

Eager to get started, Hoomer disembarked to explain the situation. Cloaf led her back underground into a massive chamber. Other members of the Enlightened waited below, cleaning and preparing the space. Glossy yellow lights reflected off a polished stone floor, and decorative pillars supported the vaulted ceiling. A single pedestal sat alone in the otherwise empty atrium. With limited items to destroy and nothing that could be reasonably construed as offensive, the place was perfect.

Elizar, still in temporary command of the Rejault, mobilized the peace summit motorcade. Seven armor-clad tanks rolled forward in a jumbled formation. Black smoke spewed from the engines and tumbled in front of the viewing ports, blocking all visibility. Erratic zigzags and stumbled steering proved an effective defense for the convoy. Their unpredictable movement was less a choice than a result of pilots having to stick their heads out of the turrets and stretch to reach the controls. Obstructed vision was a problem that could have been mitigated by moving the exhaust port. Rather than admit a potential design flaw, the Grand Five applauded their drivers' commitment to nonstop evasive maneuvers against an omnipresent, invisible foe.

Among the weaving combat vehicles, the Grand Five's mobile fortress maintained a straight course. Ten times the width and infinite improvements upon the opulence, the Grand Carrier towed all five Grands, Aimond, Zanartas, and Elizar. It sported essential amenities such as a hot tub that sloshed all of its water overboard, a portrait artist, and a gargantuan pivoting turret.

"That tree thing," Elizar said, pointing to a gnarled piece of fauna.

The nearest tank pivoted and fired a volley of explosive ordnance designed to take down a building. The tree evaporated, leaving behind a dense crater. A butler on their craft rushed forward after the detonation, blindly handing Elizar a stack of cash.

"I think I stay here when we're done," Elizar reasoned. "I point, they blow up, I get paid."

"You know you're not in charge for that much longer," Aimond reminded Elizar.

"Think I can keep a tank?" He pointed to a boulder straight ahead and had them flatten it rather than drive around.

Aimond turned his attention to Grand Four, who sat next to him.

"Why are we bringing tanks to a peace summit anyway?"

"It is the perfect balance," Grand Four said. "We don't look weak and we don't appear aggressive."

"Don't appear aggressive? That one's on fire." Aimond pointed to the tank on the outer edge of the formation.

"No, it's not."

"Fairly certain that's fire."

"Shh . . ." Grand Four grabbed Aimond's head and turned it forward. "Is it on fire now?"

"I have no idea. I can't see it."

"Exactly."

After two hours of driving, detonations, and a slight delay to put out a fire that spread to three other vehicles, the motorcade arrived at the crevice to the Enlightened's headquarters.

"Hoomer didn't tell us it was a hole. Now what?" Aimond asked.

Grand Five stepped off the carrier and looked over the pit. He reached into a sack and lobbed fistfuls of bills over the edge, then waited until they vanished from view.

"We have made the pit safe for passage."

"Good enough," Elizar assumed. "Forward!"

One by one the tanks rolled forward, plummeting off the edge. The crashed metal carcasses stacked up high enough to form a clunky unstable ramp to the bottom. Grand Five hopped on the next vehicle in the lineup and rode it down to the bottom of the pit.

Seconds later, the buried platform emerged from the ground, revealing a clear pathway below. Hoomer, Cloaf, and the Enlightened appeared. Aimond stepped out to greet them.

"You guys couldn't wait like two minutes for the door to open?" she said.

"We prefer this way," Grand Two shouted from the carrier. "It's been paid for already."

The carrier drove ahead, crunching the tank bridge to the point of near collapse. Aimond and Zanartas joined everyone else on the ramp down.

"The hole doesn't connect to here, does it?" Hoomer asked.

"It does not," Cloaf said with a concerned undertone. "They'll have to drive back up somehow."

Repeated blasts shook the ground. Plumes of smoke and dirt billowed from the pit as the transport blasted a diagonal tunnel upward, climbed to the surface, and parked two meters from the platform. Cloaf stood with both mouths open at the new breach in their ceiling.

"Look at it this way," Zanartas started. "You had a hole. It got clogged. Now you have a new one."

Enveloped in smog, the carrier blew past them down the ramp, churning out a covering black cloud. The others waited on top of the ramp for Kessler, Paizley, the scribe, and the rest of the Dinasc delegation. A small speck on the horizon crept ever closer. Six members sat around a circular contraption, each taking turns pedaling in twelve-second intervals. The bulbous steering wheel in the center had to be operated by all members in unison or the craft refused to change direction. Foot power propelled them about two kilometers per hour, only slowing when it was Osor's turn to participate. Kessler made up for lost power during her turn, doubling the speed of the Nerelkor. Paizley was tucked away in a youngling carrier dangling off the side of the cart. Her feet dragged against the ground. When they arrived, the scribe transferred Paizley into a travel carrier and wrapped a bonnet around her large enough to make two full passes.

“Took you guys long enough,” Hoomer complained. “You didn’t have a faster . . . amorphous community torture thing?”

“We did not,” Kessler sneered. “Would have been quicker if Galileo’s location tracking amounted to anything more than a hot or cold beep.”

“How do you not have a GPS?” Hoomer asked.

“Forgive me,” Galileo said. “I neglected to deploy hundreds of satellites around an alien world, which we did not pack. All so I can accurately direct you as to how to ride about four kilometers in a straight line.”

“Keep giving me sass and I’ll turn you into satellites,” Kessler threatened.

Her communicator dinged and lit up with flashing yellow and green lights.

“Congratulations, you’ve reached your step goal,” Galileo cheered.

Kessler’s angry demeanor faded into a smile.

“Where’s mine?” Hoomer grumbled.

“You have to earn it,” Galileo said.

The team descended the ramp into the central chamber. Despite protests from the scribe, Paizley opted to walk down on her own accord.

“You guys okay?” Hoomer asked Aimond and Paizley.

“Feel like I was better off not knowing as much as I do,” Aimond admitted.

“Bet I can one-up you,” Paizley challenged.

“Try me.”

Their positions in the local government granted access to information that may have otherwise been apart from the public eye. For instance, the Rejault once found a children's storybook under the stairs of a long-forgotten building. Its bright pictures and simple messages were interpreted as law and the entire society was restructured to emulate the seventy-six-word story. The changes were annulled once the building's true identity was discovered—a library. It was bombed into submission for deceptive influence on the leadership.

The Dinasc spent the entire city's budget and almost two Earth decades erecting a city outside of their walls to house an influx of migrants and refugees of a species that had not yet been discovered. Each building had a different-sized entrance and unique mechanism to enter to account for every possible shape and body type that could exist. Navigation posed the unique challenge of estimating another species' language. They in turn generated seventeen entirely new languages and posted signage around the city in all seventeen tongues. The entire project was scrapped when the biodegradable building materials biodegraded into a fine dust.

"Did I tell you the one about the Rejault scientist exiled for voodoo?" Aimond smirked.

"That was the one who explained how clouds work, right?" Paizley said.

"That's him."

"I think the Dinasc picked him up and gave him enough funding to look at one cloud every six weeks, provided he didn't look at the cloud colors or shapes."

"The system works," Hoomer cheered.

The group arrived in the central chamber where the Rejault had already taken up residence on one side. Members of the Dinasc delegation spread in equal paces along the opposing margin, leaving Cloaf and the Enlightened to set up in the middle.

"This hole lacks amenities," the Grands complained.

"Have we displaced indigenous Nerelkor from this cave?" the scribe bleated. "We should depart and fill it with others."

Both groups turned to Cloaf.

"Thank you all for coming," Cloaf welcomed. "When Hoomer mentioned we could gather the two factions' leaders here, I knew this would be the perfect opportunity to make sure all of us shared facts. The world is a giant cu—"

"Right, thanks, Cloaf," Hoomer interjected before planetary shapes derailed the entire meeting. "So, uh . . . peace talks. Let's do it, yeah?"

"Are there rules?" the scribe inquired. "We like to have rules."

Cloaf cleared her throats. "Everyone will have the opportunity to speak."

A stack of money hit her in the face. She turned to Grand Two, who was lining up another shot.

"I will talk first," Grand Two announced, then sat silent.

The collective group turned to listen to Grand Two. Aimond leaned in after a minute of quiet.

"Like, now first, or first when we start?" Silence. "No? Nothing? Okay."

Grand Two lobbed another stack, hitting Cloaf square in the face once she averted her gaze.

"No weapons will be allowed during discussions," she continued.

"They have weapons!" the Dinasc collectively shrieked.

No attempts were made to conceal weaponry, and the Dinasc representatives were perfectly aware of their presence. However once the rule was stated, this became an immediate crisis scenario.

"This is not a weapon," Grant Five vowed, tapping the side of the carrier tank. "It's a form of transportation."

"And the rifles?"

"Intermittent projectile light sources."

Rulers from both parties were called to the center of the room. Paizley stepped forward, awaiting Elizar's transit on the backs of crawling Nerelkor. The Grands, carrying the real Talking Stick, and scribe joined their respective representatives.

"I like your hat," Elizar said.

"Thanks." Paizley adjusted her massive bonnet. "Nice stick."

Despite their shared mission and status as crew members, both Elizar and Paizley held a vested interest in their side's continued prosperity. For Paizley, negatively impacting a single member of the Dinasc could doom the entire city, a consequence that would weigh on her conscience.

For Elizar, keeping the Grands rich might net him a nice bonus or fancy weapon.

"My frog things demand your frog things stop being so whiny," Elizar started.

"And the Dinasc humbly request your tribe not immediately set fire to everything they do not understand."

"Then how they know if it's combustible?"

The scribe whispered into Paizley's ear.

"What if we agreed you can burn it after we've studied whatever it is and extracted useful data and resources? This would include forests, new animal species, and 'that one field full of hydrocarbons we found,'" Paizley countered.

"Oh, that one burned so nicely," Grand One recalled.

"It was indeed flammable," Grand Two said.

Elizar turned back to the Grands for input.

"If when you finished poking at whatever it is, can we launch it into space?"

"I guess," Paizley relented.

"Okay, good. Our turn," Elizar countered. "They want all your peoples to strip the wiring from their homes and donate so they can build tiny monuments of themselves building much bigger monuments of themselves."

Negotiations deteriorated with a progressive escalation toward violence. The Rejault waved their intermittent projectile light sources while the Dinasc resorted to a firm look of moderate displeasure. Requests for either party became increasingly unrealistic. Cloaf took a step back from the center as palpable tensions tightened around the leaders.

"I don't suppose anyone has anything like a saxophone around?" Galileo pondered through Aimond's communicator. "Our lead saxophonist here would likely save this entire negotiation, broker world peace, and cure whatever diseases you all have."

"Actually, yes," Cloaf said.

"Seriously? What are the odds?" Hoomer wondered.

Of all the instrument shapes and sizes to be created throughout the universe, most intelligent species would eventually create a curved metallic horn similar in shape to the human saxophone. The variance of unlikelihood occurred when accounting for the number of keys, finger shapes, and mouthpieces. Given the wide margin of difference in Nerelkor to human anatomy, namely massive finger size and mouths that could each fit a small human child, it came to reason that a Nerelkorian saxophone would be unplayable by a human. This was, however, not the case. Their iteration of a saxophone mirrored the human version down to the button size and configuration, making the odds of the exact instrument, at the exact point in space and time, about nine trillion, four hundred twenty million, six hundred ninety thousand, seven hundred forty-one, to one.

One of the Enlightened fetched the instrument and handed it off to Cloaf. She thrusted it into Aimond's hands.

"You can't see this, but I'm smirking," Galileo said.

"You don't have a face," Aimond remarked.

"I've devoted twenty-three percent of my processing power to simulating a face just to smirk."

The Rejault resorted to baiting the Dinasc to elicit reactions. At a certain level of audacity, Dinasc were rumored to faint, and that possibility was worth sabotaging the negotiations. Before matters spiraled further, the scribe attempted to stuff Paizley into her travel bassinet to leave. Somewhere before her head was shoved down a cozy infant-sized padded head-hole, she glanced at Aimond.

Paizley was in trouble. Or at the very least, mildly uncomfortable. Embarrassment from a solo performance could not stop him now. Maybe it wouldn't be so bad.

Aimond's fingers danced down the keys. Sheet music made most performances consistent and recognizable. But Nerelkor had no history with human music. A little improvisation might generate the creative spark necessary to pacify conflict.

"Why is the human wailing?" the scribe questioned.

"Is it in pain?" asked Grand Three.

"Do we shoot it?" said Grand Four.

"You'd shoot anything," the scribe scorned.

The Grands all croak-squealed in laughter.

"We would!" Grand Five cheered. "Situations like this are why the Rejault come prepared."

Generations ago, when the Rejault Rules of Engagement were written, it did include a clause within the subsection of Dealing with Wounded Animals. Shrieks, howls, prolonged presence, and other indications of pain of an animal were grounds to engage with heavy weaponry and bursts of sustained gunfire lasting no longer than two hundred forty-three seconds.

"You there," Grand One called to a Rejault guard, lobbing a stack of cash at his rifle. "Shoot at that."

The guard took sporadic shots at Aimond, who grew accustomed to dodging and weaving. He maintained a degree of composure and continued his solo behind cover.

Intermittent bursts of lights and sparking debris created the perfect ambience to conclude the performance with a dramatic crescendo. Aimond took a moment to catch his breath, then peeked his head above cover. Everyone in the chamber stood still and silent.

"Nothing?" he complained. "Seriously?"

"I thought it was nice," Paizley encouraged from her bassinet.

Cloaf retook her position in the middle of the chamber. "If you are all able to agree on loathing the abrasive noise rumblings of the human, then you can certainly agree on other things," she said.

"Doubtful," the scribe replied.

"Let's try something basic and go from there," Cloaf pressed.

Fundamental points for two warring parties to agree upon were often simple common-sense items. Both factions shared bits of culture, a history, and a newfound revulsion toward contemporary improvisational jazz. Cloaf had a lengthy list of options to choose from.

"For example, we all agree the planet is a cube held together in a fraudulent shape by ancient machines," she proposed.

Kessler had stood by in silent observation, but now slowly craned her neck toward Hoomer, who took a step behind Aimond for cover.

The collective groan from everyone else in the room generated unity through contempt.

"We can agree to cease shelling the fields between us if you stop complaining about it so much," Grand Two offered.

"And in return, we agree to ignore some of your flagrant Nerelkor rights violations if you fund our improvement projects."

"And we agree to share the ancient knowledge passed on for generations if—"

Cloaf's offer was cut off by Hoomer climbing on her back and putting her hands over both mouths.

"No one wants your *knowledge*," Grand Three retorted.

"Lunatics with books. How cute," the scribe agreed.

If the terms were agreeable—and at this point any terms would have been accepted—Cloaf proposed leadership from both parties signify peace through joining two objects which were once one.

The Ceremonial Apology and Talking Stick held a shared origin. Rumored to be an irreplaceable component of Nerelkor history, both sides considered their piece a sacred treasure and assumed theirs was bigger. Reuniting the pieces was a powerful metaphor for a shared desire toward a mutually beneficial path forward—and an even more powerful way to fix the busted pedestal in the middle of the room. The holiest of items formed a vital lever in a mechanism snapped off by a disgruntled maintenance worker centuries ago and brought home by mistake.

Paizley and Elizar reached their heirlooms toward each other, securing the true Talking Stick inside the Ceremonial Apology. They walked together, each with a hand on the symbol of peace, and drove it straight down into the slit on the podium. Surrounded by low glowing yellow lights, the silver podium illuminated and hissed.

Soft vibrations turned to heavy churning as machines around the entire underground complex grated to an absolute halt. The ground shook and walls bowed inward. Ripples forward in the floor threatened to explode upward like a coiled spring allowed to escape.

"What is happening?" Aimond's voice trembled with the quaking ground.

"A St. Julius Marshmallow's coagulated dairy-induced tectonic plate shifting!" Daps shouted into the communicator from onboard the *Gallant*.

"Everyone, up the ramp! Get to the ship, now!" Kessler shouted.

Members of the Dinasc congregation, Rejault servants, the Enlightened, and the human crew followed close behind, but the Grands refused to move.

"We dislike walking at any great speeds," Grand Five said.

Elizar hobbled over to the Grands and hoisted them up, one by one, plopping them down atop the carrier. Once aboard, he positioned himself in the back and pushed.

"There's no way that's going to work," Aimond wagered. "He's got two bum knees and that's a tank."

Grinding metal skids sparked against the ground as the carrier coasted forward and up the ramp. The others dashed to the top and toward the ship.

"Is no one else seeing this?" Aimond exclaimed. "Hoomer? Paizley? Please tell me we can revisit this."

The entire assembly of all three Nerelkor parties crammed into the *Gallant*'s cargo bay as Hoomer and Kessler rushed to the bridge. Hoomer jumped into the helm and lifted off as the ground beneath them crumbled in on itself. Violent wind currents thrashed against the ship, fighting against the power of the engines. Unstable terrain and unpredictable weather made remaining in the atmosphere too hazardous. Kessler gave the order and the *Gallant* launched into orbit.

Safe from the obstacles, the passengers and crew looked on from the cargo bay portholes as the planet seemed to unfold. Its egg shape flattening, its sides tapering in, corners forming and becoming sharper with each passing minute. In under thirty minutes, the entire planet had taken a new shape.

"It's a freaking cube," Aimond whispered.

Grand Four turned to Cloaf. “Perhaps your points had some validity. Or rather *our* points,” he said. “Now that we see this, we agree we were correct.”

Planet Nerelek finished its metamorphosis, leaving swirling dust clouds in the atmosphere. Mountain ranges had descended and flattened while valleys had risen to the surface and leveled from the surface’s expansion into its cubed form.

Paizley squinted and stared out the porthole. A spiraling blue pillar of light neared and grabbed her attention more than the rapid planetary redecoration. Blurred by distance, the silhouette began to take a recognizable form.

“Hey, Aimond,” Paizley called, “what ever happened to your glove?”

“My glove? You mean the weapon I had from the arena? Whole thing launched itself into the sky. No idea where it landed. Why?”

“Think I found it.” Paizley pointed.

Blue beams danced in the distance, waving around in an erratic circling. Aimond’s arm-mounted cannon, freed from its terrestrial confinement after the arena battle, had yet to run out of energy despite being removed from its power source. Finding a new home in orbit, the weapon’s orbital path was thrown into chaos from the transitioning planet. It hurtled toward the ship, propelled by the shift in gravity and its own constant spewing energy erupting from the palm.

“Don’t worry,” Zanartas said. “It should point to the arena’s safety net.”

“Wait, is it still firing?”

Lights flickered and the *Gallant* shook as the glove passed by and continued on its new trajectory.

“Perhaps ask our two missing engines,” Galileo suggested.

Aimond paused for a moment.

"They talk? I can't actually do that. Can I?"

"You cannot," Galileo said.

"Right, because Aimond can't use words or something. Can't taunt me if I guess the punch line."

"Because they're floating away."

Two of the *Gallant*'s four engines spiraled away from the ship, removed with surgical precision by the weapon's beam. Severed wiring shorted and fired sparks throughout the ship, igniting the engineering bay.

"Yeah, I see them," Aimond said. "But do they talk?"

"Also no," Galileo confirmed.

Osor pushed his way to the front of the crowd and planted his face on the window. "My baby. So bright. So beautiful," he muttered, teary-eyed.

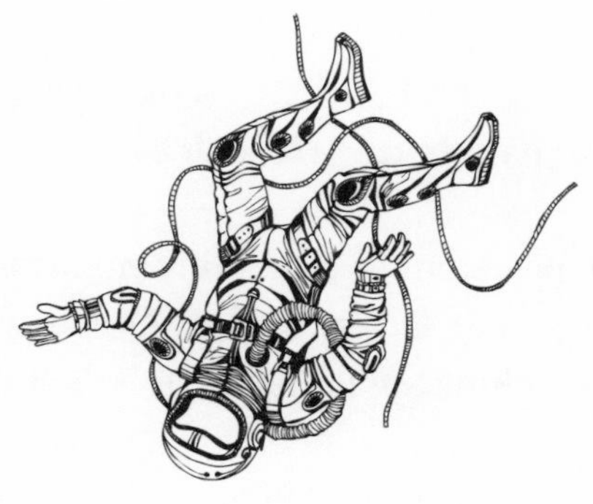

16

THE WORLD IS FLAT. AND SIX-SIDED.

"Congratulations on your Red Alarm! The Gainsbro Corporation reminds you that evacuation is the same as resignation, and liability waivers were signed prior to boarding. Have a great time!"

Fires tore through the lower decks. The crew scrambled to keep the ship together as a cargo hold full of unfazed Nerelkor compared the inequitable distribution of flames to that time the Grands melted a river for flowing away from them. A frantic Aimond scurried off the bridge, ordered to deploy the manual fire suppression system.

Sudden engine loss and gravitational alternations from the planet's shift pulled the *Gallant* into atmospheric reentry. Turbulent winds shuddered the hull as red glowing waves rolled across the cockpit. Frequent corrections required Hoomer's full attention to keep from spiraling straight down.

"Compensating for turbulent lateral roll," Galileo reported.

“Pitch up and hard burn?” Hoomer asked as a means to slow down.

“Insufficient power in the remaining engines.”

“Classy landing it is,” she said. “Keep with the micro-adjustments and I think we’ll be able to touch down with only minimal impact.”

Hundreds of millions of calculations per second altered the output of the engines’ given trajectory. Subtle changes in pitch, speed, and roll fought against gravity’s desire to thrust the ship into an unrecoverable spiral. So when Aimond contributed to the fire recovery plan by causing a brief but complete detonation of the *Gallant*’s core in his quest to earn a title as the ship’s hero, it posed a bit of an inconvenience in regard to avoiding liquefaction upon impact.

A thunderous quake shook the ship and the bridge went black. All interfaces and feeds faded, leaving Hoomer to fly blind with unresponsive controls.

“Booms are never good. Killed my music. Gal, you still with me?”

Backlit by a dull red light, a two-by-two-inch screen flickered to life in the cockpit. A single line appeared across the screen, bouncing as Galileo spoke. “Still here, albeit in a somewhat reduced capacity.”

Unable to control the fierce descent, the *Gallant* surrendered to the mercy of the winds. It rolled and tumbled end over end. Hoomer bared down, fighting the g-forces. Pressure mounted in her head as her entire body squeezed to stay stable. Slight flight control corrections required full body engagement. The two remaining engines drizzled what was left of their power like a hose losing its source.

“How would you and your capacity care to help with the not-plummeting-to-our-death situation?” Hoomer grunted between sharp staggered breaths. “That was, in case you could not tell, highly rhetorical.”

“While I’d love few things more than to assist, I appear to have lost power to a critical sensor.”

“Which one?”

“All of them.”

Hoomer blinked and offered a slow nod. “Any other way to send flight data?”

“Just describe what’s going on,” Galileo said. “How’s the wind?”

Vicious blades of wind sliced into the ship’s hull, tearing at the paneling and flinging the craft around as little more than a leaf in a tornado.

“Uh. Bad,” Hoomer replied.

“And how is it impacting your angle of reentry?”

“Undesirably.”

The single screen dimmed, indicating some reserve power was shifting to Galileo’s calculations. Even functioning at a fraction of a percent of his full ability, Galileo could account for countless scenarios. Limited data in an ever-changing chaotic environment posed no challenge to the capability of humanity’s most robust AI.

“Calculations complete,” he chimed. “Recommended course of action: make corrections.”

“If I had a free hand, I would smash you,” Hoomer barked, bearing down to fight the g-forces from spinning.

Impact was inevitable.

Engine reserves dwindled to an absolute minimum of unspent energy remaining in the chamber.

“Status report, Hoomer,” Kessler said, unbothered by the corkscrewing.

“We’ve got airbags, right?”

The *Gallant* did come equipped with a full-surround airbag deployment system. On impact, the system would detect the shock and send a signal to deploy faster than the force of the shock wave could rattle through the rest of the ship. This served to protect vital technical components at the expense of the squishy outer layer of metal hull. And most of the crew.

Engines bereft of power, the ship hurtled end over end toward the ground. Hoomer yanked the controls for one final hope of counterthrust. The *Gallant* crashed tail-first, skidding across two hundred meters of sand before slamming mid-body into a boulder.

The violent impact shifted the *Gallant* forward, thrusting the nose down and wedging into the ground like a dart with the remaining inertia.

Shock waves blasted through the ship, tossing about everyone who had not yet strapped themselves down. Searing tinnitus drowned out the rushing sounds of escaping fluids and steam. The crash site slowly quieted, leaving only a slow, steady hiss pumping air into the balloons surrounding the ship.

"Airbags successfully deployed," Galileo reported, fifty seconds after impact.

Captain Kessler tore away her restraints, her iron grip more holding the seat belts in their place than the inverse. "Galileo, damage report."

"We are very damaged."

Kessler snapped off a piece of the captain's chair armrest.

"Ah, just how damaged? Of course," Galileo said. "Apart from two missing engines, my core has evaporated. Impact has damaged much of the exterior hull, but internal structures remain mostly intact. Overall, Hoomer seems to have avoided our total annihilation but with a questionable choice of landing positions."

She glanced over at Hoomer, who kept her head down on the controls but lifted a thumbs-up.

Some of the crew and all of the guests were holed up in the cargo bay. Given the high-impact landing and a lack of restraints, Kessler hoped they all found a way to strap in. She departed the bridge to check in.

"Everyone alive?" she said en route over the comms.

One by one the crew responded. A background of bickering Nerelkor meant the leadership had survived.

"I believe Aimond has suffered disfiguring full-body burns," Galileo relayed on his behalf. "Or that could just be his normal appearance."

"Tell him I'm closed." Dr. Cole scoffed.

Accompanied by an obvious lack of desire to see patients at any point in the day, the *Gallant*'s med bay ran an override shutdown sequence during any potential violent impact. During events such as crash landings, asteroid collision, or one-star reviews of Gainsbro products, the medical tools locked to prevent accidental improper care.

"Good," Kessler said. "At least no one was hurt."

"I'm hurt," Daps screeched over comms. "Crew members' reference manual, section Pain, subsection Internalized Conception of Pain State—"

Kessler cut the comms. That many words meant Daps was fine. "At least no one was hurt," she repeated upon entering the cargo hold.

The Grand Five and the Scribe appeared unscathed thanks to an intricately positioned pile atop Cloaf and the other Enlightened members, who broke all of their falls. Zanartas was latched to a wall utilizing the convenient sticky nature of his unwashed low-income status. The remaining Rejault servants and Dinasc congregation nursed minor injuries, but seemingly all survived.

"Well, not yet," Grand Two advised, stepping off the pile and checking the floor for spilled change.

"Oddly menacing," Kessler mused. She turned and glared. "Elaborate."

"Prior to departure, we instructed our minions to deploy the entire missile arsenal should we not return to Rejault within sixty hours from the parley. In case it was all a ruse. Or we received poor directions home."

"Deploy where?"

Grand Five shrugged. "Up."

"What an underhanded trick," the scribe whined. She paused for a moment. "Ours fire toward Rejault in fifty-one hours."

"So let me get this straight," Kessler clarified. "All of you left your homes for a peace summit and said, 'If I'm not back soon, destroy everything'?"

"Well, not everything," Grand One corrected. "In case one of our missiles lands on Rejault, we have a box labeled: Do Not Destroy."

Kessler's cybernetic eye glowed a deep shade of blood-red, something the crew theorized happened when she suppressed urges to annihilate all things within her general vicinity. Most of the remaining crew except Aimond, Dr. Cole, and Seegler—who had yet to visit any part of the *Gallant*—arrived in the cargo bay and gave Kessler a wide berth until the glowing calmed.

"Think it's gonna explode?" Hoomer whispered.

"I bets it shoots beams," Elizar wagered.

"Oh!" Daps's face lit up. "If one of you got hit by it, that would definitely qualify for a zzOther. Don't *try* to get hit just for me. It may invalidate the entry. But maybe don't evade too aggressively."

"Alright, listen up," Kessler barked. "We've got a short window to dig ourselves out of the sand, get airborne, and get these idiots home to stop this war from escalating to a catastrophic genocidal level. Dinasc's deadline comes first. We focus on them."

Aimond finally arrived. He leaned against the bulkhead, still fighting to catch his breath even after a deliberately lethargic pace to the cargo bay. Clothes singed and spirit broken, Aimond forced himself to appear as normal as possible. As far as he knew, no one but Galileo had any idea of his involvement in the core's sudden nonexistence. His missing second eyebrow and slight burning across his body could just as well have been from the fire. Which he also failed to extinguish.

Kessler approached Aimond with a silent scowl. His muscles tightened. Instinct told him to flee. Reason told him that he could not escape on an alien world after detonating the core, and Kessler could probably break his legs with her mind anyway. Even if the current situation kept her from knowing the truth of his involvement with the core, Aimond still failed his fire suppression mission. He held his breath, assured that there was nothing but swift retribution in his short-lived future.

"You."

Not a great start.

She reached her hand behind her, palm up, to Daps. A slow, menacing head turn followed until she had Daps in her sight. Daps's eyes shifted with an uneasy discomfort. But Kessler's glare was unrelenting. Without words, Daps followed his gut and reached into his pocket. He fished out a thick black marker used to label cargo and placed it in her hand. Movements slow and foreboding, she returned her focus to Aimond.

"I feel like I should explain," he stammered.

"Your face." She uncapped the marker.

Given the captain's ability to hoist any living thing by its head, Aimond assumed he was destined for a head-first jettison. At least they were on the ground. The marker, however, was a bit of an enigma in the plan. Having survived a milk-star, battle royale, and a crash landing, Aimond figured he had a decent run.

He squeezed his eyes shut and prepared for the worst.

Kessler reached forward. She jabbed the marker onto his forehead and dragged a streak, then repeated the motion on the other side.

"It looks ridiculous," she growled. "Grow your eyebrows back."

She capped the marker and Aimond breathed a sigh of relief. The exhalation was plugged and cut short as Kessler lifted him by the face and placed him in front of the cargo bay's exterior door. She pointed to the control lever.

"Lever. Pull it."

He obeyed. She patted him twice on the shoulder as a coach would congratulate a toddler who just learned to throw a ball rather than eat it, but with spine-compressingly unnecessary force.

"And that is how levers work. Next time, do better."

Battery power maintained the exterior door and lifts. With the front of the ship wedged underground, the crew exited from the cargo bay to assess the *Gallant*'s damage. A barren landscape greeted the emerging team. Apart from the long scar left by the crashing ship, only inhospitable desert populated their surroundings.

"There's nothing here," Aimond observed. "Just sand in all directions."

"Old Dinasc records say long ago the planet was lush and full of life," Cloaf said. "But choices from the Rejault caused the sand caps to melt."

"Sorry, the what?"

Since the sand cap melts, global sand levels rose over thirteen meters, swallowing most viable sources of water and covering non-sand land. Elevated areas were spared a similar fate. But the flat lands that comprised much of the planet were little more than a sandy abyss where a small subset of life-forms could survive.

"Nomadic Nerelkor wrote of their times in the sand plains," Cloaf recalled. "Never experiencing anything but sand and countless sandworms."

Most of the crew took an instinctive step back toward the ship, except Kessler, who could likely crush a creature of any size, and Elizar, whose chances were debatable but simply was not paying attention.

"How big are we talking here?" Paizley asked. "Bigger than the *Gallant*? Half a *Gallant*?"

"What'd I miss?" Hoomer asked, coming over to join the others as the last off the ship.

"We're all gonna be eaten by billions of giant sandworms," Aimond said.

"Neat."

Cloaf bent over and stuck her stubby hand in the ground. She rooted around for a few seconds and pulled out a squirmy six-inch tan noodle creature. It wriggled around until it faced upright. Four pinpoint black eyes positioned in slants above a mouth so small it was hardly visible.

She poked its abdomen and the worm let out a tiny squeak to the collective "aw" of the crew.

"Kinda cute for giant monsters," Paizley admitted. "It's almost like Aimond's new eyebrows."

"Still gross," Hoomer said. "But somehow more tolerable when they can't eat you."

"Well, actually they ca—" Cloaf started.

"Nope. We're sticking with ignorance here. Absolutely no harm from the billions of little worms." She turned to Elizar and whispered, "Unrelated, but do you have a flamethrower?"

"Of course not. This is unsafe," he gasped. His eyes darted back and forth. He hunched over and whispered back at normal speaking volume, "Three of them."

The scribe and Grands hung back toward the ramp, taking turns being appalled by the opposing side's missile launch. One of the Grand Five would stand in the center of their semicircle and berate the Dinasc for a few moments, then step back. The scribe would take his place and begin her rant. This civilized format served as an educational platform for each presenter. Each round brought new insults and ways to declare hypocrisy, which non-presenters would note and include in subsequent rants until closing remarks from both parties were identical.

"You're both awful," Kessler said. "Truly the worst."

Complete repair of the ship would be a massive undertaking. The damaged and breached hull limited the *Gallant* to low atmospheric flight only. Missing engines required creative restructuring of flight systems. And the gaping hole where the core used to be made it impossible to do just about anything. The engines and hull were ancillary at best. The crew had to focus on recreating the ship's power source.

"We'll need a few things I don't have," Osor stated. "The core is a mix of fusion and fission, making one big beautiful glowy ball of boom. I'll need helium-3 and polonium."

Gainsbro scientists developed a near-perpetual energy device. Split into two main subsections, the *Gallant*'s core contained independent fusion and fission chambers. Starter material in the fusion chamber fused up to elemental nickel, at which point additional energy was required to continue the reaction. Energy was drawn from the fusion chamber to produce a surplus of nuclear binding energy until the reaction had reached elemental uranium, which was then sent to the fission chamber to be split back down.

When told a fusion core by itself would last for several centuries of travel and the combination device would still require additional energy or fuel, perhaps earlier than the fusion core alone, management fired the engineers. They had already printed the marketing materials and it was easier to find new engineers than to approve a new marketing proof.

"Given radiation from the two nearby stars—that makes me just so jealous!" Osor squealed in envy as to the planet's fortune of being irradiated by two glowy lights. "Helium-3 should not be too difficult to locate. Polonium, on the other hand. Probably impossible."

Daps rocked back and forth, making a slight deflating noise as a war waged within him. On one end, he could assist the mission by revealing he had not destroyed valuable corporate property just because it contained lethal amounts of radioactive substances. On the other spectrum, he feared repercussions for disobeying orders to dispose of said lethal stuffed animals. Technically his role as Gainsbro interest enforcement officer carried with it the ability to belay the captain's orders. His internal organs, however, lacked the same martial fortitude.

Paizley paced around the ship, surveying the extent of the damage. Outer layers of the hull were crushed upon impact and further warped by airbag deployment. Scattered pieces that broke free would be easy to locate in the bright contrast of the sand. Crude as it may be, she could weld pieces back together to form an adequate protective seal, provided enough pieces were recovered.

Except for one issue.

"How much for this?" Grand One asked, holding up a chunk of plating.

"That one seems like at least four," Grand Two declared.

The other three Grands nodded in agreement.

They fanned out, capturing bits of ship, rocks, and sandworm excrement to appraise.

"What are you doing?" Aimond asked the group.

"We've near run out of money," Grand Four relayed. "So we're collecting items to serve as placeholders that we can exchange upon our return."

"Doesn't the Rejault population trade rocks all the time and they're worthless?"

"Yes, but those aren't *our* rocks," Grand One said.

Aimond did make a good point. Further collected rocks would need a secret marking etched into the bottom so as not to confuse them with common, worthless rocks.

"Can't you just reuse the money you guys are literally carrying on your backs?" Paizley questioned.

"Not while it's unrealized gains. We must file it properly before recirculating."

"Admirable," the scribe admitted. "I never anticipated you to report income for taxation."

An exaggerated choir of croaks and snorts occupied the Grands long enough for Paizley to snatch some of the ship pieces back.

"Filing means something different for you, I'm guessing?" Aimond assumed.

"When we return home, we create stacks of money and have our peasants stand under them," Grand Five said. "Eventually the stack will collapse, and if you've crushed your peasant, you've successfully filed."

"And if they're not crushed?"

"Raise taxes until you have enough to crush one."

Brutality excluded, the Rejault filing mechanism did serve as a method of bookkeeping. Successful filings were logged in the national ledger and published to the general public. The populace would place bets on which of the Grand Five would file the most income. Winners with exact guesses were awarded 1/900th of the total pot and gifted a rare private donation opportunity where they could hand over their winnings to the victorious Grand.

"Aimond, Hoomer, and the lot of you, prepare to move out and search for the He-3," Kessler ordered. "We'll consider this an opportunity to foster relationships. Galileo will search for any traces of helium-3 nearby."

"I would be delighted to use a fraction of my reserve power for a scavenger hunt," Galileo said.

"If we find some, you won't be on reserve power."

"Sure, collecting a bunch of gas will just fix *everything*," he complained. "Terribly sorry. I'm stuck in sarcasm mode. It draws the least amount of power."

"Why do you even have a sarcasm mode?" Aimond asked.

"*Why do you even have a sarcasm mode?*"

Galileo's current capacity limited his scans, but he was able to detect faint traces of helium-3 in a cave system about fifty kilometers to the west. Extracting that information from him was a different challenge altogether. Hoomer rallied Aimond, Daps, Grand One, Grand Three, Cloaf, and the scribe into the cargo bay for the expedition.

The *Gallant*'s All-Terrain Land Exploration Receptacle waste-recycling-transport hybrid could seat six passengers, had the towing capacity for a variety of attachments, and the ability to recycle materials on the spot.

Hoomer hitched a five-meter-long cylindrical container to the rear of the ATLER. She tethered it with a dozen clanking chains and a single non-locking data cable.

"This thing is huge," Aimond said. "Have we had this the whole time?"

"It folds up?" Hoomer suggested, offering the obvious answer.

The rig collapsed down and folded itself into a briefcase-sized package. She pressed a button on the exterior of the package and it popped back open and into full size within thirty seconds.

"Neat. It's not going to do that while we're loading things inside, is it?"

"Corporate manual strictly prohibits the ATLER's accessory vehicles from doing that," Daps commented.

"The manual forbids it?"

"Yes, exactly. In size eleven font even."

"But not code or locks or something helpful?"

"It can totally fold while we're in it," Hoomer admitted as she hopped inside to load supplies.

The exploration crew loaded into the ATLER and started their westward journey with Hoomer at the helm. Aimond joined her in the front with Daps wedged between bickering Nerelkor in the rear rows. Waving fields of sand rocked the vessel as they departed.

"So what's with the cube being better for orbit anyway?" Hoomer wondered. "Seems less, I dunno. Aerodynamic?"

"Says the pilot," Aimond teased.

Hoomer smacked his arm without shifting her gaze.

"The planet and core form a multidimensional hypercube," Cloaf shared. "As the core rotates, it generates a strong magnetic field to protect us from the two orbiting stars."

"And it didn't do that as a sphere . . . egg?" Aimond asked.

"Nope. That's part of why all the oceans burned up."

Eons of gravitational forces coalesced bits of matter around the universe, collecting and pulling from all sides at equal rates. This mechanism formed the spherical planets found everywhere in the known universe. Stress from the binary stars stretched and pulled at the forming planet Nerelek, elongating as it cooled. Multiple impacts from celestial bodies chipped away at the forming cylindrical shape until the planet formed hard edges. Compression from the planet's own gravity and the force of the binary stars folded the planet in on itself while expanding outward. This phenomenon formed the astronomical equivalent of "if it works, don't touch it." But they did touch it.

"That doesn't seem right, but I don't know enough about it to refute it," Aimond confessed.

"About which part?" Hoomer said.

"Shapes, probably," Galileo prodded.

The ATLER slammed to a sudden stop, its front tires compressing as if ramming against a wall. But ahead was only sand.

"What'd we hit?" Hoomer asked. "Gal, anything on sensor?"

"Which sensor?"

"Any of the ones that show things."

"Well, I'm not going to look through all of them. Low-power mode. Remember?"

"Because the planet extends beyond normal dimensions, there are parts of the terrain that will not conform to the three-dimensional world you're used to seeing," Cloaf said.

"So we hit an imaginary ditch?"

"Not imaginary, but not perceivable."

Daps took up about one-fourth of a seat between the two Grands in the rear. He squeezed his way out from between the two and popped his head up toward the front.

"What'd we hit?"

"Imaginary ditch," Hoomer said.

Daps shook his head; that made about as much sense as anything else. Hoomer switched into reverse and slammed on the accelerator. The wheels spun to no avail. She opened the hatches and allowed the crew to examine their surroundings and formulate a plan. Not wanting to dip too deeply into their reserves, the Grands tossed a few coins toward the wheels while the scribe dropped to her knees and offered to name a holiday after the ditch. They swiftly concluded their business and the three Nerelkor agreed to take a vote. They etched their ballots on sandstone and handed them to Daps for tally. The vote was unanimous.

"We hereby ratify that the hole no longer exists and therefore poses no further issue," the scribe decreed. "We may continue forward now."

The human crew stared blankly, then turned their attention to the invisible ditch, in part expecting something to happen.

"Well, at least they're cooperating." Hoomer sighed.

"I'm gonna push it," Aimond said.

"I mean, it weighs several tons, but go for it."

"Oh, oh, record it for me!" Galileo begged. "I'm so sure he can do it."

Aimond made a spectacle of warming up his shoulders and cracking his knuckles. He stepped around to the rear of the ATLER, then vanished into the ground without a trace. Hoomer and Daps scrambled to search for any sign of him, but the sand was undisturbed. Their breathing hastened, panic setting in.

"Gal, where did he go?" Hoomer panicked.

"Do I really have to look for him? I only have about 94,348 hours of battery remaining."

"Yes!"

Aimond slid from a rift four meters off the ground beyond the other end of the ATLER. He landed seemingly unharmed, apart from a brief yet comprehensive wide-eyed existential crisis.

"I've located him," Galileo reported, the directional system pointing to a rock on the ground.

"What happened?" Hoomer shouted, taking cautious steps toward him.

"I fell into everything," Aimond stated, his tone flat.

"Think we can drive the ATLER into it?"

Aimond looked up toward the spot he emerged from. He sat down and put his hands on his head.

"I don't think it will fit."

"What do you mean? How big's the hole?"

"I'm pretty sure I saw yesterday," Aimond said before letting out a prolonged, deflating yelp.

"Well, he's broken."

"Can we exchange him for a new one?" Galileo asked.

"Do you want another one?"

"Store credit then?"

"You probably fell into the fourth dimension," Cloaf added. "The fourth and fifth dimensions of a hypercube are difficult to see."

"And I failed that class in school," Aimond conceded.

"You failed most of them," Galileo added. "I've pulled your transcripts."

Their communicators dinged, signaling Galileo had sent everyone on the crew a copy of Aimond's educational records.

"What happened to conserving battery?" Hoomer said.

"I feel that I'm contributing."

Hoomer ushered everyone back into the ATLER.

"We could just walk there," Daps proposed.

He took several steps toward Aimond, disappeared, and reappeared a split second later about twenty paces behind his starting location.

"Everyone get in," Daps urged.

Forward was blocked, backward gained no traction. Hoomer cranked the controls hard left, inching the spinning wheels toward the rift Aimond traversed. The front driver's side tire was sucked in and the rest of the craft toppled inside. They emerged inches from Aimond, landing square atop a spiked pillar of jagged rock. The ATLER crushed the pillar straight down into absolute dust. The impact would serve as the first case for the value of undercarriage protection recorded in known history.

Hoomer cruised forward, then came to a sudden stop. She turned to face the passengers.

"Are we missing one?"

Grand One's seat was vacant. As the team shifted to look around, he popped back into the seat.

"Okay, never mind then," she said, opening the hatch for Aimond.

Aimond climbed inside and took his seat up front.

"I don't like dimensions," he fussed.

"*I don't like dimensions*," Galileo mocked.

"How is that contributing?"

"Sarcasm mode is locked in," Galileo reminded. "I can't control it and if anything, you're rude for bringing it up."

The remainder of the ride avoided dimensional rifts, sudden shifts into or out of reality, and disruption of transit related to undercarriage injury. Aimond sipped on a can from the packaged rations and tossed it to the floor when finished.

"Don't be wasteful," Daps said.

"It's a mobile trash bin."

"Yes, but watch."

Aimond handed the can to Daps, who spent half a minute trying to climb out between two vegetating Grands. He opened a transparent hatch in the floor, inserted the can, and closed the hatch. The small chamber glowed orange as the aluminum melted down. Liquid metal swirled inside, forming a cylinder. Two rounds of molding and compressing later, the machine dinged and a new container emerged from the hatch.

"It's a can," Aimond monotoned.

"It *was* a can."

"And yet, remains a can."

"But without your nasty lip residue," Hoomer added.

"It is disgusting, isn't it?" Galileo said.

"Couldn't we have just washed it?"

"No, because that's not recycling," Daps argued.

The team arrived outside the cave. Hoomer reversed the ATLER to the entrance and opened the hatches for the crew to step out. Much of the cave system appeared to be above ground, with the tan rocky outcrop protruding at least thirty meters up. The cave's mouth was too narrow to drive inside, so the team entered on foot.

Equipped with some of Osor's non-weaponized flashlights and a vacuum hose connected to the ATLER's container module, they crept inside.

"Be cautious," Cloaf instructed. "I've read tales of caves like these harboring sand-snakes."

Given the previous unfounded fear of sandworms resulting in an adorable and harmless noodle-creature, Aimond assumed a similarly sized species but with small pointy teeth and a little rattly tail. Limited time from an impending apocalyptic missile barrage meant efficiency was a must. Hoomer snatched the end of the hose and had the remainder of the crew walk in a line, holding up a segment of hose behind her to help prevent any tears from the rocky cave floor while getting into position. The two Grands manned the rear, the Scribe, Cloaf, and Daps held the center, and Aimond and Hoomer took the front farther into the cave. Galileo's scans revealed the greatest density of helium-3 deposits were deeper inside.

"We need to get in as far as we can," Hoomer yelled back down the cave. "You guys shout when we're about out of feed."

"We ran out twenty meters ago," Grand One said, holding his arms up to display the apparent lack of hose.

Hoomer's deadpanned glare manifested Kessler's typical unspoken murderous intentions. Aimond took the explosively subtle hint and trudged back to the ATLER. He passed the Grands, who had already exceeded their threshold for menial labor, grabbed the dangling end of the hose, and reattached it.

A cacophonous clangor of well-made machinery quaked the ground and rendered communication useless. Aimond signaled the scribe to follow. He took Cloaf and Daps, pulled the two Grands from amassing a small rock collection, and rejoined Hoomer deeper in the tunnel. Heaps of dirt and loose debris rocketed into the hose and wriggled their way back toward the storage tank. The more she suctioned, the more violent the surrounding quakes grew. Aimond and the rest of the team grabbed hold of the cave walls for stability as they neared.

Chunks of ground ballooned and bursted behind Hoomer. A dense shadow emerged from the eruption, casting an ominous presence over the crew. Even left in darkness, the creature's penetrating leer clawed at the team's collective resolve. They turned their lights to the mass.

Thick tan scales covered a tremendous cylindrical body. A sharp-featured head acted as a shovel, displacing any bit of sand or rock in its path. Slow and methodical, it coiled onto the surface, taking careful observation of the disruption. The sandsnake flicked its tail, tilted its head down, locked eyes with Hoomer, and let out a low cluck. Hoomer blinked, the misplaced noise temporarily replacing fear with confusion. She held the end of her vacuum up and tried to suck the snake inside. When it failed to budge the creature, she shrugged and bolted in the opposite direction.

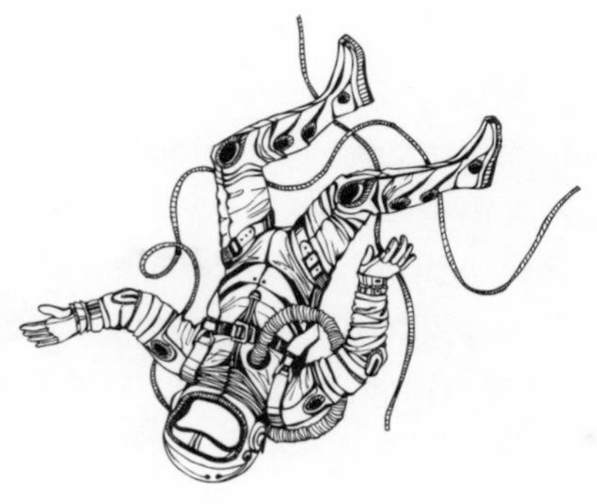

17

A LITTLE HOPE AND A LOT OF GLUE

Nerelkorian sand-snakes were a species that thrived throughout inhospitable habitats. According to Nerelkor biologists, this was in part due to its unique anatomy and hearty development that allowed it to traverse any environment with ease. But moreover, their general success in hostile terrain came from their desire to remain secluded. A sand-snake hated company, forced outings, and the noise a small subspecies of sand-crab made whenever it became uncomfortable with silence. Not being aware of the basic sand-snake displeasures, and suffering from imminent fear of being crushed, maimed, or otherwise eaten, the ATLER team scurried deeper into the caves.

Blackened tunnels narrowed and cramped as they rushed away from the encroaching monster. Each step took them farther from their escape. A stand-off confrontation posed too great a risk. Instead, they hoped to inflict minor injuries and annoy the creature into submission by pelting rocks over their shoulders as they ran. Each subsequent throw only seemed to agitate it further, triggering a deep squawk from the monster and slight snicker from Hoomer, who still got a kick out of the uncharacteristic noises. Their straight path opened and branched into a cavern with dozens of smaller crevices and nooks to hide in. Hoomer switched off her light and ducked into cover. The group huddled inside.

"Any ideas anyone?" Aimond whispered.

"The creature is clearly agitated by its inequitable living conditions," the scribe lectured.

"Its home is larger than anyone else's in Dinasc!" Daps replied.

"Yes, that's the problem. It needs to be equitably divided to—"

"Anybody else?" Aimond cut in.

The Grands instinctively began rooting around in their pockets.

"Are you going to throw money at it?"

"Yes," Grand Three said.

"Please don't do that."

Grand Three lobbed a stack of rocks over his shoulder anyway to assert financial dominance. At least if they were to be eaten, he would appear the most wealthy by nature of discarding readily available rocks and digested with the highest regards. The sandsnake detected the noise and closed in on their position. Aimond glared at the Grands.

"Try it again," Galileo assured. "I think that worked."

"Any other ideas before we're eaten?" Aimond asked, smothering his communicator.

"I vote we bomb it," Grand One declared.

"And you have bombs?"

Grand One paused for a moment to consider the proposition. He did, in fact, not have any explosive ordnance on him, thus rendering his idea useless. Useless ideas needed to be replaced with better ideas, and there was no better idea to a Grand than doubling down.

"I change my vote," he decided. "I vote we find its home and bomb its family."

"Significantly darker and yet no closer to solving the problem. Daps?"

Daps's field survival skills were limited to what was available in the Gainsbro Administrator's Field Survival Guide—a twenty-three volume set of individually purchased books that required monthly paid licensure to own, read, or reference even in memory. Were a scenario to arise that required spur-of-the-moment brand acquisition, synergistic team building, or non-fungible quantum particle entanglement, Daps was prepared to handle any situation within the defined subset—provided his fees were current and account in good standing. Sand-snakes failed to make an appearance in the manual's primary body or the glossary, thus requiring Daps to fall back on his general training and experience.

"We minimize our exposure to remain invisible. Stay put, study its weaknesses, and propose a plan to embargo it to Corporate."

"Truly thought you had something for a second," Aimond sighed.

"Welp, no one in charge has any idea what they're doing," Hoomer said.

They turned to Cloaf. Out of everyone in the group, she was the only one with any knowledge of the animals and world in its current state.

"Maybe all of the harvesting disrupted the spiritual spatial alignment of the caves."

The entire group glared then collectively looked away.

"Let's review." Hoomer cleared her throat. She pointed to each member one by one to maximize their shame. "We got bomb or war crime without weapons, reduce the size of its housing, put it off until later, and fix the feng shui."

"Sounds about right," Aimond noted.

Grand One raised his hand. Hoomer smacked the rock out of it before he could move further.

"Hang on," she said. "I've got one of Osor's brain-melting language thingies."

"I don't think it wants to talk to us," Aimond argued.

"No, but maybe if we zap it enough, its brain will fry."

She rooted around in her gear and unearthed the Articulaser. Cloaf tilted her head and opened one of her mouths.

"Wait, was that always a possibility?"

"Uh. No?"

"Oh, okay."

Aimond gave a thumbs-up to the perfect recovery. Stealth an evident non-priority, the sand-snake tracked their hiding place. Its towering body blocked the mouth of their bunker. Exit obstructed, confrontation inevitable, consumption undesirable, Hoomer fired the Articulaser at the sand-snake's head.

"—because I worked nonstop on these walls and you're tearing them up!" it shrieked. "You've completely disrupted the entire spiritual spatial alignment of the caves. And you're going to wake the children with all the screaming and rock throwing!"

Aimond blinked and looked around at the rest of the group. Only Hoomer seemed curious.

"So you don't want to eat us?" he inquired.

"What? No. We're geotarians. We only consume rocks for health reasons," it stated. "Plus you look disgusting."

"I am. Very disgusting. Not edible."

"His body is ninety-eight percent rocks," Galileo said.

"Sorry, you're not my type." The sand-snake recoiled.

"Shot down by a giant talking snake," Hoomer said. "Ouch."

"Not a bad thing," Aimond contended.

"I'm actively requisitioning trauma therapy from Dr. Cole," Daps offered. "You'll make it through this moment."

"Again, not really—"

"Shh," Hoomer comforted. "Let the healing process begin."

Without the looming threat of imminent digestion, Aimond explained why the group arrived in the cave and were making such a racket. While the sand-snake was perturbed by a group of alien creatures barging into her home to siphon her food, she felt she understood their plight. Seven minutes into a lecture on the benefits of an all-rock diet and sand cleanses, even Daps was having difficulty staying focused—mostly from the lucrative opportunity to bring to market an extraterrestrial juice cleanse made entirely of sand.

"And when condensed down and pressed, it forms a sand-oil you can slather along your scales to draw out toxins imbued from sand-spirits," the sand-snake prattled.

"Is this why our minions eat dirt?" Grand One inquired.

"You mean your citizens? The ones too poor to afford food?" Aimond challenged.

"We should add a tax if it's medically cleansing," Grand Three encouraged.

"I almost wish it ate us," Aimond whispered.

"You'd likely render it full of parasites," Galileo mocked. "We'd end up owing her two hundred kilos of sand-oil."

"That's not in the budget!" Daps shouted.

The sand-snake escorted the team back through the tunnels to the ATLER, all the while ensuring everyone memorized her favorite recipes. Since a sand-snake's diet was composed of the materials the team was harvesting, she regurgitated her lunch into the carrier in exchange for the team's departure and a brief twenty-minute synopsis on the value of meal regurgitation. Heaps of semi-digested rocks clumped into fragrant piles inside the container.

"Galileo, is there any helium-3 in that pile?" Aimond asked.

"Unable to detect from this distance."

Aimond moved closer and asked again. Still too far. This pattern continued until Aimond placed his hand inside the warm drool-laden pile, leaving the communicator inches from the rocks.

"Processing. Please hold," Galileo stalled.

"You know he can scan from like fifty kilometers away, right?" Hoomer said, packing up the ATLER.

Aimond's bracelet dinged, indicating a personal pedometer best. The crew loaded back inside and departed for the *Gallant*. Despite the ticking doomsday clock, Hoomer opted for a slower return to avoid dimensional rifts while the ATLER distilled and extracted the helium-3 from its culinary cargo.

Dr. Cole held an encyclopedic knowledge of human physiology. She could treat most any wound, diagnose the most obscure diseases, and estimate exactly how much blood a person could lose before it became a problem worth intervention. Nerelkor anatomy, however, was an enigma.

"And do what exactly?" Dr. Cole said, leaning back in her chair in the med bay.

"Evaluate for broken bits," Kessler said. "Returning damaged citizens might cause escalation."

"Beyond missiles?"

"Mm."

"Mm."

The first portion of the conversation contained far more words than necessary. True congruity came from the series of terse grunts and subtle neck movements. With little more than a few additional glances from equipment to door, the two women communicated a comprehensive logistical triage strategy to prevent further geopolitical intensification from assumed antagonistic injury infliction.

Dr. Cole rose from her seat. "Reference?"

"Available."

"Value?"

"Minimal."

"Good enough. When?"

"Galileo?" Kessler inquired.

"Pardon my misinterpretation," Galileo said. "But I believe you to be missing half a dozen verbs from that request."

"Useless," Dr. Cole grumbled.

"Mm," Kessler agreed. "Find Zanartas and send him to the cargo bay. Dr. Cole needs a reference point to determine if the frog parts belong where they are."

"Wouldn't have landed there even on full power," Galileo admitted.

While a majority of the passengers emerged unscathed from the *Gallant*'s calamitous crash landing, some of the Nerelkor were not as fortunate to land atop a pile of Enlightened or worse, *were* the pile of Enlightened. No injury appeared outwardly severe, but Dr. Cole held a moderate degree of certainty that knees were only meant to bend in a single direction in most species. Zanartas met her in a corner of the cargo bay to establish an examination area.

"How much do you know about your species' anatomy?"

"Who's that?"

"And we're off to a great start," she exhaled. "Stand there."

Modern medical scanners mapped and recreated full 3-D anatomical models with little added risk of sudden onset autism. Dr. Cole adjusted her white jacket and conducted a series of scans for a baseline but ended up with more questions. To the untrained eye, human tomography appeared as abstract art. But stare at it long enough and landmarks appear, organs develop visibility, and it becomes easy to identify when something does not belong. Nerelkor anatomy appeared fluid. Live scans reflected an ever-changing environment with mobile organs and shifting prominences.

"What's going on with this?" Dr. Cole said, pointing to her screen. "Your stuff's all floaty and I don't like it."

Zanartas peeked around to Dr. Cole's screen. He jumped in place and watched his innards slosh around.

"That's just the blood sack," he boasted. "Nerelkor carry all their blood in a sack in the center of the body. Organs just kind of float around in it. I think."

Evolution crafted the perfect machine within the Nerelkorian combination cardiopulmonary-digestive-endocrine system. Whereas humans functioned as an assembly line, processing and sending along blood passing through an organ system, the Nerelkor managed all bodily functions through one central pool.

"I'm not seeing any vascular structures. How does the blood get to your extremities or your head?"

"Why would it need to?"

"A variety of reasons."

"All the blood stays in the sack. Unless it springs a leak. Then it all comes out."

Dr. Cole rested her head in her hand. She attempted to explain a hypothetical scenario in which a single cut on the arm, if deep enough, could cause a leak so severe the Nerelkor equivalent of a liver pops out.

"Totally possible," Zanartas affirmed.

"And in that instance?"

"Just pop it back in."

Elsewhere on the ship, Paizley and Osor concocted a plan to release the *Gallant*'s nose from a sandy tomb. Rebuilding the core would be a much easier task if all of the materials could get up the rear ramp, which was suspended several meters off the ground.

"What about the front ramp?" Paizley proposed. "We'd have to divert a large portion of the reserve power, but maybe we force it to open and lever us out of the sand."

Osor shook his head. "Ship's too heavy. Would drain too much battery and leave us with a stupid computer."

"He wouldn't be stupid," Paizley defended. "Just really sleepy."

"We need more power. Two suns, limitless power. Harvest, refine, compress, and accelerate."

Solar power made sense and was readily available. With near endless daylight they would not have to time the placement of the collection cells. The *Gallant* had a few photovoltaic panels. They were intended for use in portable base camps to power small dwellings, not supercharge the ship.

If Paizley were to combine the arrays and override the voltage output, it would provide a trace amount of extra power, but still not solve the problem.

"Leave that to me." Osor grinned. "All we need is to take the light and make it better. Double light, if you will."

Paizley collected the few solar modules at their disposal and brought them to Osor's lab for modification. She waited, tried her comms, and looked around the lower decks but found no trace of him.

"Gal, where'd he go?"

Galileo sighed.

Distant whirring of tires crunching against sand neared. The ATLER's team returned to the front of the ship, nose still embedded in the sand. Osor, dressed down to nothing but a loincloth, reflective hat, and wires running down to his hands, stood atop the *Gallant*.

"Behold!" Osor shouted. "I am a god!"

"Oh good," Hoomer said. "Here I was afraid he'd finally lost it."

He turned and held his palms outward to opposite ends. White light beamed and intensified to a searing glare. The crew ignored the display and began unloading the tanks with refined helium-3. Before they unpacked a single canister, the ship started to shake. The nose began a creeping ascent out of the sand. The crew looked on, awestruck and unable to process the spectacle before them. Little by little, the end of the ship emerged and dropped the rear down with a thud. Clouds of tan dust plumed and dissipated, revealing the deployed front ramp.

"Clever little trick," Hoomer admitted. "Guess they got the ramp superpowered."

"No, I don't think so," Aimond contended and pointed.

Elizar stood in the entrance with his hand on the door's manual override crank. When the ship's power failed to open the door, Elizar resorted to a more manual approach. Each crank of the jack overcame the entire weight of the ship and heaved the door open a few inches more. The end result of a Herculean effort was an unearthed ship and a warped metal override lever, once straight, now more curved than Elizar's spine. Hoomer hopped out of the ATLER and walked up to the fully deployed ramp.

"Did you seriously just force the ship out of the dirt by hand?"

"Frog things make the ship smell," Elizar complained. "Takes too long to walk out the back every time for air. Hurts my hips."

"Every day I wonder why I came here," Hoomer said.

"Yeah? How many arms have you lost?" Aimond questioned.

"Big deal. You got it back."

The ATLER docked around back in the now accessible cargo bay. Paizley carted away the helium-3 and the crew dispersed to their next tasks. Despite his general displeasure of having to walk through the ship, Elizar arrived in the cargo bay and waited for Aimond by the bulkhead with Daps.

"Captain Kessler ordered us to meet you here," Daps said, his voice carrying a foreboding timbre.

"Is this about the whole thing with the glove laser? Because in my defense that could have been anyone's glove and accompanying arm-cannon."

"It's about the core you exploded."

"Oh that. I plead the seventy-sixth?"

When the Gainsbro Corporation formally absorbed the country formerly known as the United States, it maintained some of its original governing structure. The American Constitution was rewritten as a corporate mission statement and amended to maximize brand success. This meant some amendments were included that could protect the brand image and its profit by deferring blame to a third party. The seventy-sixth amendment allowed those integral to brand success to avoid any criminal penalty by admitting guilt on behalf of an unaware and uninvolved third party.

"Unfortunately, Corporate hierarchy deems you unworthy to invoke the seventy-sixth," Daps decreed. "Your punishment would not infer a negative impact on corporate revenue given your status as cargo. Corporate law dictates we place you in holding."

"The storage closet brig again?"

"Well, legally we can't refer to any section of the ship as a brig," Daps said. "We can, however, outfit a small area into the HR-Approved Time-Out No-No Zone."

Elizar wrapped his fingers around Aimond's arm and hobbled to a small unused room on the same deck. Aimond didn't resist, unconcerned by his previous detainment and unable to free his arm from the ridiculous old-man strength grip.

The HR-Approved Time-Out No-No Zone originated when Gainsbro executives needed a way to investigate employee wrongdoings. Options such as administrative paid leave allowed too much pay and too much leave. And an unpaid suspension was too similar to a rewarding vacation. Leadership felt it best to remove any hope of a salary or escape in an attempt to encourage confessions to office-related crimes such as accidental arson, intentional arson, and arson-related time-card misfilings. Above all, Corporate wanted to promote the feeling of a safe working environment, so any mentions of jail, prison, or detainment had to be reimagined with a softer word selection.

Elizar opened the door to an empty room and ushered Aimond inside. Elizar followed close behind and affixed heavy chains to the wall.

"Why are those rusty?" Aimond asked.

"Per policy."

He secured Aimond's arms above his head and left the room. Mild discomfort was a tolerable punishment considering he almost destroyed everything.

"You are in time-out. Please reflect upon how your actions have impacted the company."

The recording played every fourteen seconds at a volume that was equal parts felt as it was heard.

"You are in time-out. Please reflect upon how your actions have impacted the company."

In the event of a known infraction, studies of mandated volunteers suggested that the HR-Approved Time-Out No-No Zone would generate feelings of remorse, pose a resolution, and fully reform a participant within two hours. This also held true regarding innocent participants implicated from the seventy-sixth amendment.

Within forty-two minutes, Aimond's mental state deteriorated to replying to the voice, answering its request every fourteen seconds. When his two hours elapsed, Elizar entered and unchained him from the wall. Wide-eyed and trembling, Aimond dragged stiff legs out into the hall. But Elizar stayed behind, shackling himself.

"Are they throwing you in, too?" he asked.

"I like to go in at night," Elizar replied. "Her voice reminds me of—"

Aimond closed the door to avoid hearing the end of that, or ideally any of Elizar's thoughts.

Zanartas clomped down the corridor carrying armfuls of stuffed toys. He stopped to greet Aimond.

"Where are you going with those?" Aimond asked.

"I'm helping rebuild the core."

"Aren't those filled with radiation? Do you want a bucket or something?"

"Don't worry. Nerelkor aren't affected by radiation."

Hailing from the city of Rejault, Zanartas was a product of the local education. His statement that Nerelkor were not impacted by radiation was more accurately summarized as an immediate unawareness of what radiation was. To Zanartas, radiation was an imaginary creature humans complained of so they could wear heavier armored clothing.

Zanartas's hand sloughed off and fell to the floor. He and Aimond both stared down at it.

"Except that bit apparently," Zanartas said.

"You, uh, want me to grab that?"

"It'll grow back," he said, walking off. "At least I think."

18

IT WORKS BETTER SIDEWAYS

Paizley and a half-dressed Osor crouched on the floor of the core room and tinkered with piles of spare parts. They unwrapped each piece from its outer package and inner protective covering, marked with "sealed for freshness."

Daps loomed in the corner reading from the tome of starship repair. The repair manual was, in its first iteration, a succinct series of diagrams and bulleted notations from the lead engineers. Product stress-testing failed to generate understanding across all age groups, especially ages two to fourteen. So the manual's rework was relinquished to the marketing department for critical enhancements.

Daps stood in silence, reading through the paragraphs as only he could. Section 19, subsection 6-a, step 487 read: Observe the beautifully convalesced framework prior to insertion of the pulchritudinous convex manifold for any imperfections. Notice that there are no imperfections.

Take a moment to applaud your detail-oriented structural engineering partner's indefectible endeavor. Resume reading after sufficient applause.

"Make sure it's not scratched," Daps translated.

"And if it is scratched?" Paizley asked, rubbing at a mark with her thumb.

"Legally we would be obligated to launch the part into the sun to erase all evidence of inadequacy," Daps said. "Is it scratched?"

"Nope."

Paizley rotated the component so the small etching faced the rear. She and Osor finalized the manifold's construction and tilted it upright. The *Gallant*'s design allowed the core to be placed in one location. That location was newly renovated by Aimond's explosive redecoration process. Spare metal plating was prioritized to the ship's exterior, leaving reconstruction of the core's structural platform up for creative integrity. Without metal available, Paizley discovered the next most dense object: a hard candy Elizar kept in his bunk. The F.o.o.d. F.a.b.r.i.c.a.t.o.r. replicated thousands, which were dampened then stuck together to form a solid composite buttercream-scented tile.

Daps muttered to himself as he read through the next sixteen pages, all of which were dedicated to describing the means to secure the manifold—rotate counterclockwise.

"That should do it." Paizley released a satisfied breath. "Alright, Daps, how do we get this going?"

"Last page, step 493. With necessary components, start reaction," Daps read.

He blinked and flipped the book over in case they'd missed a page. A combination fusion-fission chamber reactor left little room for error. One mistake would render the ingredients unusable. Two mistakes would render the ship an explosive wave of all-consuming plasma and thereby also unusable. Three mistakes was improbable, given a distinct lack of continued existence of the operator or materials.

Osor slipped out of the room and returned moments later, hobbling in donning a lead full-body suit. He ushered everyone outside and cackled as he sealed the door behind him.

Eighteen hours had passed since the crash and the crew was exhausted. Of the human crew, only Kessler and Osor remained awake. She gathered Grands Four and Five, the scribe, and Cloaf around a table on the bridge.

"Is there anything we can use to signal your people not to unleash the weapons? Radio, flare, Morse code?"

"If you fired a massive sum of cash toward the city, our minions might interpret this as a sign of peace," Grand Five said.

"Might?"

"It is plausible they would consider this a sign of aggression and launch early. Or not consider it a sign at all and instead gather the money for donation upon our return."

"So your suggestion is to fire an undisclosed amount of coins at your people to elicit literally any reaction?"

"Precisely."

Kessler dug her fingers into the table and turned to the scribe. "You. Use better ideas."

"If we were to fly to Dinasc and notify them—"

The ship's hull rattled. Kessler did not immediately react as she was unsure if this was an external tremor or a physical manifestation of suppressed rage leaking into existence. A second, more violent shake offered greater, yet still not definitive, evidence.

"I am detecting seismic activity," Galileo announced.

"We're all detecting it." Kessler leered. "How about some advanced warning next time?"

Four seconds of silence passed.

"You are about to detect some seismic activity."

Narrow fissures cleaved the ground apart and swallowed the *Gallant*. The ship rolled partly onto its side, slowly dipping farther down jagged walls of the crevice. Sparks flickered like stars as sharp stone ground against remnants of metal hull.

"I've detected advanced seismic activity," Galileo said.

Kessler called to the core room. "Stop reconstruction until Galileo's batteries are dead," she ordered.

Osor's cackling was the reply. Kessler summoned the rest of the crew to the bridge. Without engine output, the *Gallant* was trapped and risked an unrecoverable plunge into the planet's chaotic geography.

One by one, crew members arrived on the bridge using walls and mounted furniture to fight gravity.

"Where's Seegler?" Kessler asked.

"You were mean and I'm not telling." Galileo scoffed.

She lobbed a hunk of metal at Galileo's one functioning screen at the helm. The ground parted further and the *Gallant* completed its perpendicular roll. It slid down deeper, rocks nipping at the hull until enough stone pierced through to halt further descent. The crew were tossed to the side of the ship, bouncing off mounted chairs and consoles. They collected in a pile against the wall and shuffled to find footing in their sideways terrain.

"Okay, people, we need ideas. Even when the engines are operable, we can't fly out laterally."

"I can pick it up," Elizar offered.

The group muttered in slight agreement, less dissuaded by the act itself than the logistics of how to get Elizar outside with a place to stand. Crackles and knocks pelted against the hull as rocks and gravel rained from above.

"Can we get a read on what's under us?" Kessler asked.

"I'm not helping until you apologize," Galileo complained.

Despite her sideways orientation, Kessler climbed up the vertical floor with ease and nestled herself in the helm, cementing herself so securely in place with an anchor of pure spite that not even her hair pointed down with gravity. She pressed on Galileo's sole screen, increasing the pressure with each passing second.

"I'd be delighted to, but my reduced capacity scanners are not returning anything meaningful."

"Given the recent shifts in topology, it's safe to assume one of two possibilities," Cloaf suggested. "We could be experiencing another incidence of the hypercube and it will pop us back up on flat land no problem. Or this crevice continues down forever until it eventually stops. Or neither."

"So a standard hole," Hoomer said.

"But with more mystery," Cloaf replied, raising and shaking one hand for emphasis.

The *Gallant*'s flight systems were optimized for the degrees of freedom within space travel. Small adjustments from minor lateral engines could fly the ship sideways in zero gravity. But grounded in atmosphere, lateral engines worked as little more than light displays.

"How much power can we generate?" Kessler asked.

"Lateral thrusters are only for roll and yaw," Hoomer said. "Won't have enough force to lift us, let alone overcome the friction from the rock."

"Any potential to boost them?"

Hoomer shrugged. Messing with the ship was a Paizley problem. Aimond cleared his throat.

"Lateral rotational thrusters operate at a maximum five percent output capacity in relation to the main engine and cannot be used to generate lift," he recited.

The entire crew made a slow turn toward Aimond and stared.

"I remember that bit from the training brochure in my room."

"Why?" Hoomer asked.

"I . . . have no idea."

Continued tremors coaxed the ship deeper into the fissure. The crew grabbed on to any fixture within reach to remain upright.

"So we can only go forward with any real force," Kessler repeated.

"Pending Osor stabilizes the reaction in time," Paizley added.

No one had a strong grasp on the necessary time to stabilize a hybrid fusion-fission reaction. They could only assume Osor's incessant giggling meant he was working as fast as he could muster. Or he found an overabundance of joy in the glowing byproducts and was entirely distracted.

Both were feasible.

"How long until the Dinasc launch?" Kessler asked.

"Fifteen hours remaining," Galileo said. "Coincidentally about how much time I feel I have left."

"I thought you had thousands of hours," Hoomer challenged.

"I said *feel* like, what with all the: 'Galileo what time is it? Galileo which way is up? Galileo, it's me, Aimond, I've urinated on the floor again. Where are the cleaning products?'"

"Like intentionally or did ya just miss?" Hoomer asked.

"I wouldn't do that intentionally," Aimond said.

"So you missed."

"Just sit down next time, man," Kessler said.

"Seriously," Hoomer added.

Undulations in the surrounding walls forced jagged rocks open and closed, the ground chewing on the ship. A single pivot point pierced the center of the hull, rocking the ship with residual inertia. One thing was clear: without a solution, they were bound for the bottom.

"Wait, I think I have an idea," Aimond declared.

"What, like a semi-squat?" Hoomer said. "Really, you can just sit. We won't even know and/or mock you."

"I will," Galileo admitted.

Aimond took a deep breath.

"What if we get everyone in the rear of the ship at once? Our combined weight with the Nerelkor might be enough to tip the engines down and point the nose up."

"Why move somewhere else if we're already here?" Grand Five complained. "I think it's fine pointing this way."

"Do you want to rocket into a rocky oblivion?"

"Will it make us money?" Grand Four turned and questioned.

"Probably not," Aimond monotoned.

"Oh, well then, fix it."

The entire plan hinged on timing and luck. If the pivot point buckled or the fissure widened before the core was ready, the plan would fail. But without power and no real footing for Elizar to lift them out, Aimond's plan was better than waiting and speculating.

"Galileo, how much weight would we need to displace, given our current position?"

"About nineteen thousand kilograms."

"What's the average Nerelkor weigh?" Hoomer asked.

"Is this a riddle?" Galileo said.

"No?"

"At least three hundred forty."

"Kilos, pounds?"

"Units."

Comms from the core room clicked on. A low-grade humming churned in the backdrop.

"Good news!" Osor boasted. "Covalent light structures assimilated in a transverse lateral plane and converged within terminal congruence."

The bridge crew nodded, having identified at least four of the words he used. Kessler, Daps, and Paizley were too proud in their positions to admit confusion.

Hoomer and Aimond expected everyone to assume their cluelessness.

Elizar had fallen asleep standing up.

"I'll go ahead," Aimond said. "What?"

"Sideways ship make reactor work good," Osor said, half grunting. "One additional minor note, however."

In a standard nuclear reactor, fuel rod positioning controlled the production of energy. The *Gallant*'s condensed core had no room for trivial matters such as output control. Instead, it relied on internal energy regulation—namely Galileo using as much energy as possible at all times to keep up with supply loads. If the ship failed to consume the appropriate amount of energy, it would explode. Too little energy and the ship would not function. Therefore, there was only one output at any given point: maximum power.

"At critical mass we vent power through a full-power engine burn," Osor said. "Or we don't and things explode again. But bigger and prettier. Probably have some little zappy noises."

A full-power engine burn would give them the force needed to blast out of the fissure in one attempt. But in their current position, it would rocket them farther down at full speed.

"How long?" Kessler asked.

"Give or take twenty minutes."

Kessler gave Aimond the nod. There was no time to consider other options. She issued a ship-wide broadcast to inform everyone of the plan: "Meet in the cargo bay and prepare to get close."

Aimond knocked Elizar awake. "We're going to the cargo bay. Come on," he said.

Elizar stretched, cracked his back, then skittered vertically up the floor on his fingertips.

The rest of the crew struggled to grasp the smooth metal surface.

"How are you doing that?" Aimond shouted.

"Crimp, you fool! Crimp!"

Elizar disappeared from sight.

"He was literally complaining that opening jars hurt his arthritis earlier."

"I hate jars!" Elizar's echo carried back onto the bridge.

For the more-normal members of the crew, scaling a vertical wall intended as flooring was a task they were less equipped to tackle. Aimond climbed on Hoomer's shoulders, bringing them ultimately no closer to the corridor off the bridge. Paizley surveyed her surroundings as Aimond toppled to the wall-floor.

"Gal, can the emergency oxygen masks reach us down here?" Paizley asked.

"I'd make them reach anywhere for you," Galileo said.

"A yes would have worked," Aimond mumbled.

A small hatch popped in the center of the ceiling. Five coils of rigid plastic tubes unraveled down toward the team. Aimond scooped the mask from his feet and held it in front of his face. Even in the limited lighting, he could see his fingers through the material, partly from the transparency, largely from the three holes in the side.

"This is the emergency mask?" he asked.

"A modern marvel of engineering, isn't she?" Daps beamed.

Despite the recommendation from Corporate, individual people still maintained some of their own noncorporate-mandated opinions. A selection of the population caused a commotion every time Gainsbro exhausted a significant portion of Earth's resources for single-use missions. Once, the former nation of

Moldova had its entire natural supply of gypsum exhausted to construct a single massive firework in celebration of Quarter Three closing. The gypsum rocket, being made of noncombustible material, failed to detonate and instead exited Earth's orbit. This made the conservationists, according to an internal report, mildly irritated enough to burn down half of a city in a contradictory turn of events that had them later protesting their own protest on account of waste.

To appease the conservationist crowd during the *Gallant*'s construction, Corporate yielded to demands of including fair-trade recycled biodegradable material. Oxygen masks were nominated when a member of the selection committee blew his nose into a napkin and marveled at the ability of the device to withstand airflow.

"But what good is an emergency mask that falls apart if air touches it?" Aimond challenged.

"Sure, there are opportunities for growth in the future," Daps pitched. "But let's focus on what went well. This tubing is very rigid."

"And what good does that do without a mask?"

"If the mask slips into deferred performance mode due to disintegration, simply suck air from the indestructible plastic tubes."

The tubing itself could support about 3,200 PSI of pressure before compromising. Given the *Gallant*'s "always maximum" setup, placing the tubing in the mouth at any point could result in a new mouth forming in the sides or rear of the head.

"Please don't tell me of any other discount life-support."

"Oh, it's not discount," Daps said. "The post-consumer material has to go through twenty-seven different recycled iterations to satisfy the board. Very expensive process from raw material."

"Wait, the material wasn't even used before?"

"It was made into a mask. Then recycled back into a mask."

"Twenty-seven times."

"Mhmm."

Aimond exhaled then tore the remaining paper off the tubing. Daps scooped it up and placed it in his pockets for later recycling. Makeshift rope wrapped around his arm, Aimond yanked his way up toward the central corridor. Paizley and Daps followed behind. Cloaf and the scribe flexed the tubing's strength as they climbed but made it safely to the top. The team collectively worked to heave Grands Four and Five, who fell twice under the assumption someone else would hold the tubing for them as they were hoisted up. Hoomer climbed into the helm to prepare for the full-power engine burn. She slithered into the pilot's seat and strapped herself in.

"Gal, gimme my focus music."

Comms on the bridge switched on to blaring an aggressive form of Hungarian speed metal. Distorted guitar, down-tuned bass, and a roaring, belching scream formed into a singular melody of chaos.

Hoomer smiled and relaxed into her seat.

"This is focus music?" Kessler asked, already back in the captain's chair.

"I find their screaming soothing."

The vocalist bellowed in rhythm with the guitar, an inaudible tone mixed with an unfamiliar language.

"Is he growling 'I am not a horse' there?"

"The title loosely translates to 'Scary Beasts at Night,'" Hoomer said. "So entirely plausible, yeah."

Kessler nodded. "Factual and horrifying. Perfect war cry. I approve."

Ten minutes of hopeful climbing, jumping, and praying elevators functioned while sideways, landed the crew and Nerelkor leaders in the cargo bay. The remaining Nerelkor teams fared better at maneuvering the lopsided landscape and were already waiting for the others to arrive. Aimond caught his breath and reviewed the plan to move the ATLER and everyone present to one corner of the cargo bay.

Zanartas, the Rejault, and most of the Dinasc congregation huddled up in one corner with the ATLER. Cloaf, the Enlightened, and the scribe stood apart at the other end. Subtle shifts in the *Gallant*'s positioning implied the plan was working. But not enough.

"We need to displace more weight," Aimond figured. "I didn't really get an answer before. What's a Nerelkor weigh anyway?"

"About three hundred forty units," Zanartas said.

"Right. Units. Well, we need more of them. Cloaf? Come on."

Cloaf shook her head and the rest of the Enlightened mirrored the gesture.

"If all of you are there, it can't be a good idea," she said.

Her flock echoed her words on loop. When one finished, the next would start but louder until all of the Enlightened were shouting the same message. Paizley sighed and stepped away from the main group. She entrenched herself in the middle of the Enlightened and crouched.

"They're right!" she croaked. "We should join them!"

She snuck back toward Aimond as, one at a time, the Enlightened switched to Paizley's inserted message. When their echoing aligned, the group joined with the rest in the corner.

"How did you know that would work?" Aimond said.

"I'm pretty sure half of them had their eyes closed," she said. "Not a big group of thinkers."

Progressive tilting grew more pronounced, but still the ship refused to pivot upward. The scribe remained by herself on the opposite end of the cargo bay.

"We only have a few hours before your missiles cause a lot of innocent Nerelkor to lose their lives," Aimond pressed. "Can we focus here?"

"They won't lose their lives," the scribe said. "Maybe some dignity."

Aimond's eyes dropped, his tone as flat as his expression. "Explain."

"The projectile is Dinasc's greatest weapon: a strongly worded request to please stop it."

Aimond took a deep breath, annoyed more at the surprise of not anticipating that possibility than the gravity of the alternative situation. He turned toward the Grands.

"And yours?"

"Highly explosive," Grand Two claimed.

"But we can't aim them," Grand Four noted. "So we launch dozens everywhere and hope."

"We've even got a special launching bunker in case a few go straight up and down," Grand One added.

The intricacies of a Rejault Doomsday launch followed a simple yet turbulent pathway. Intelligence gathering and aeronautic navigation systems were dwarfed by a simple principle: hit enough things and eventually one will be right. Probably.

Upon orders to fire, missiles were secured onto a ramp atop a centrifuge. While the ramp raised and lowered at random intervals, the platform spun at high speeds. Eventually the missile would ignite and fire off in whatever direction it pointed.

"One hundred twenty seconds until critical mass ejection," Osor reported over comms.

Aimond looked at Paizley. As far as they knew, she was still in charge of the Dinasc, as they had not returned to check for newborns.

"As your leader, I order you to join us," she demanded.

The scribe hesitated, weighing a clear verbal order against the lack of notarized official declaration. Paizley recognized the look by now. She sat and the scribe rushed to assemble the Mobile of Choice above her. Paizley smacked Yes and the Scribe joined the group without further reservation.

Slight shifts turned pronounced. The collective weight of the group guided the tail to sink. But it stopped.

"Fifteen seconds," Osor counted.

Frantic for more weight, Aimond's gaze darted around the room for anything else they could use. Anything worth reaching was already collected.

"What if we hit it?" Grand Three suggested.

"Might work."

"It always works. If it doesn't, then whatever you're hitting is wrong."

A mix of jumping, stomping, and kicking carried enough inertia into the tail of the ship to break the stalemate. They fell flat on their backs as the ship pivoted, nose pointing straight up. Engines ignited and blasted a tremendous wave of energy into the fissure. The *Gallant* erupted from its snare, straight into the sky, tossing the crew into a pancaked pile. Though pinned in with the rest, the Grands made every effort to continue beating the ship, often throwing a stray elbow into Aimond's sternum.

"We're done now," Aimond wheezed. "Stop hitting it!"

"Why?" Grand Four asked.

Free of its prison, the *Gallant* righted itself, and the pile of crew members rolled to the floor. Grand Two still pinned Aimond, wailing against the flooring in a blind flurry.

"Please stop before I throw up," Aimond squeaked out. "Also, can you get off me?"

Paizley whistled to get his attention and lobbed a shiny coin into the corner of the room. Grand Two rolled off Aimond and plodded over to find a steel washer. He grimaced, shrugged, and placed it in his pocket. Kessler joined the group in the cargo bay. Though the *Gallant* was airborne, prolonged flight times were hopeful at best until more complete repairs.

"Well done, kid," Kessler commended. "Most of this is exclusively your fault. But you found a way out of one problem."

"Thank you?" Aimond said. "How long do we have until the Rejault launch?"

"What about the Dinasc?" Kessler inquired.

"It's an angry letter."

Kessler bit her bottom lip and nodded. "Of course it is. Galileo?"

"There are four hours thirty-three minutes remaining on the clock."

"About," Grand Five said.

Kessler turned her torso around, legs unmoving. Her vicious leer obviated the need for follow-up questions.

"We opted to share a larger number as it sounded better. Those familiar with smaller numbers are often inferior as the numbers are smaller."

"How long?"

"Already proceeding unless my timepiece is wrong?"

He glanced down at a transparent box on his wrist. Chunks of precious metals and gemstones inside moved only when he rattled them. Kessler stormed over to him, latched onto his arm, and dragged him down the corridor without an ounce of strain.

"How strong is she?" Aimond muttered.

"I'd wager at least three hundred forty units," Paizley guessed.

Back on the bridge, Hoomer had acclimated to the challenges of two-engine flight. Controls were less responsive than ideal state, but navigation was a fair degree easier without spiraling downward at terminal velocity.

"Gal, why are all the lights flashing?" Hoomer asked.

"No real reason. I'm just happy to be able to use everything again."

"Not even a sarcastic response."

"And I've activated the magnets in the cargo bay just under Aimond so his knees are stuck to the floor."

Hoomer smirked. "Good to have you back, buddy."

Kessler arrived on the bridge. She dropped her captive Grand, who scurried into a corner.

"Sit."

Grand Five took a seat on the floor in silent subservience.

"No money for you for at least two hours," she said.

"But the others can still earn!" he whined. "This isn't fair!"

"Another word and it's four hours."

He opened both mouths and slumped over in a pout.

"How are we with navigation?" she asked.

Galileo scanned for signs of life. Power restoration returned his scanners to full capacity, but the transdimensional hypercube layout added a factor of complication. Hoomer's displays flashed and dinged.

"Life-forms detected," Galileo reported. "Multiple projectile trajectories inbound. Targeting nearest with highest probability of direct impact."

"How quickly can you get us there, Hoomer?" Kessler asked.

"Given the distinct lack of engines, random hopping in and out of dimensions, and not having a real guarantee as to which way is actually up—maybe six?"

"Minutes?"

"Units?"

"Make it four."

19

THE FORTUNATE ARRIVAL OF ROBERT T. SEEGLER

Hoomer pushed the engines to their limits as the *Gallant* bounced around the sky. Dimensional rifts from the hypercube's anatomy absorbed and ejected the *Gallant* at random trajectories, making a straight-line chase near impossible.

"There it is!" Hoomer called. "I've got eyes on the tail end."

Throttle fully depressed, the ship refused to yield any further speed. At their current pace, it would take over two hours to catch up to and overtake the missile—well after destructive contact with Dinasc. There was no way to close the gap. But they had to try.

"Divert more power to the engines," Kessler commanded.

"If we give it any more they could both blow," Hoomer warned. "We do need at least one."

"That's an order."

Before Hoomer could reroute and increase power from maximum to extra-maximum, a roaring glow erupted from above. Engulfed in flames and approaching at meteoric speeds, an unknown vessel hurtled toward the ground. It bolted beyond the *Gallant*, rattling the patchwork hull in its wake. Black clouds of cinder and heat painted dark streaks across the sky. In an instant the craft caught up to the missile and connected. The fireball merged with the missile's explosive detonation, creating a blinding white radiance.

Unobstructed torrents of pressure from the destructive epicenter collided with the *Gallant*'s remaining engines. Forward progress halted as Hoomer fought to maintain elevation. Bits of debris rained from the midair collision, kicking up clouds of dust as they scattered the landscape.

"Damage report," Kessler commanded. "Just gloss over the existing stuff."

"There's rattly bits in my engines," Galileo said.

"He hates that," Hoomer reminded.

"I hate that."

"Will it impede flight performance?" Kessler inquired.

"Referencing the engine section of the manual now." Galileo paused. "It definitively says, rattly bits in the engine will impede flight performance. Verbatim."

"Fine," Kessler relented. "The immediate crisis looks to be averted anyway. Touch down and get Seegler to evaluate the landing site for safety. I swear if we get eaten by dirt again I'll jump down into the center of this ridiculous planet and take a bite of it myself."

Though imperceivable to even Galileo's censors, the planet Nerelek temporarily ceased all tectonic fluctuations as if out of concern for its own well-being.

Up until that moment, Robert T. Seegler's most valuable contribution to the mission at hand was in spirit. Assumed to be the persevering force behind improving relations, Seegler's presence persisted as felt rather than seen.

His first view of the alien world was not with the *Gallant*'s initial descent on discovery and moderately calm landing, but rather one of high-velocity plunge seen over the top of a bag of deliciously damage-resistant Gainsbro Presents High Density Multipurpose Packing Peanuts, Low Sodium Warm Ranch. The combination shipping-material-snack-food was, however, spilled all over his vessel's cockpit due to a sudden explosive impact and propensity to spit out low sodium foods due to an unexpected lack of salt.

On the ground, an uneasy calm serenaded by the light crackling of lingering flames blanketed the area. Most pieces of the missile and colliding object were obliterated into fist-sized chunks. But one piece escaped largely unscathed. Upside-down but intact, the cockpit of a spacecraft reflected back the harsh overhead sun. Its glass windshield popped and ejected forward, exposing the cockpit's interior, which was decorated with insufficiently salty snacks.

A pilot climbed out without his helmet.

"The atmosphere is safe to breathe," Nihls relayed.

"Well, of course it is," Seegler said. "Look at all this air."

Currents from the flames flicked about the crash site and warmed his face. He looked about, more curious as to his location than the abrupt unplanned deconstruction of his ship.

"A 98.76 percent chance of assured destruction, yet we emerge without sustaining damage," Nihls noted.

"Better odds than usual."

"What are you basing that off of?"

"Dunno. Math, I think." Seegler shrugged. "Feels right."

Despite no verifiable way to prove the assumption, his gut intuition was accurate. Throughout his tenure on perilous missions, life-and-death scenarios bordered on a high 99 percent likelihood of immediate mortality. This measurement was often exacerbated by brazen misunderstandings of any safety precautions and review of mission briefings.

"The *GP Gallant* is approaching."

"Who's that?"

"Your ship."

"Right! A majestic craft of pure beauty and opportunity," Seegler said, curling his hand into a fist. "Her refined allure is the envy of the entire cosmos."

Adorned with new holes and held together with little more than hope and spite, the *Gallant* sputtered to a halt above the crash site. With the effortless grace of a feather riding a breeze, the ship descended in a clearing nearby. Slow and controlled in its course, it hovered above the ground, creeping closer for a gentle touchdown. The engines cooled and dust from the landing settled. The air stilled. Then the latch to the front ramp broke off, forcibly extending the ramp to the ground with a massive thud.

"What was that?" Kessler asked from the bridge.

"The front ramp has been deployed," Galileo reported.

"I didn't authorize that."

"I'll notify the physics department immediately."

Unsure as to what they would find or the dangers remaining below, the crew needed to conduct reconnaissance and assess potential threats before investigating the downed craft's remains.

"Whatever destroyed our target missile looks to be littered everywhere," Kessler said. "While Seegler is evaluating the terrain, I need someone who's available to gather data on who or what just did our job for us."

"Paizley, Osor, and I are available," Daps offered.

"Not them. I need someone more . . . *available*."

Moments later, Aimond, Elizar, and Zanartas plodded down the wobbling front ramp. Reliant on minutes of search and rescue experience, the team maintained a healthy distance from the smoldering wreckage. Aimond paced a wide perimeter, craning his neck to peek for any signs of life around hunks of metal no larger than his arm.

"We have to be careful," Aimond cautioned. "No telling what could still explode out here."

Dense metallic thunks traversed back and forth behind Aimond. He turned to find Elizar and Zanartas kicking an intact, yet still burning, piece of the missile.

"The only definitely part-of-a-bomb piece for kilometers and you've managed to find it."

"I'm still trying to understand your units of measure," Zanartas said, punting the ordnance toward Elizar. "How many grams are in a kilometer again?"

"Shoulda seen what we hadda learn during the Florida Conflict if you want confusing," Elizar reminisced, warming up his hip to return fire. "Distance measured by bullets. Speed by bullet movement over swamp density. Volume by amounts of space it takes up compared to bullets."

"Let me guess," Aimond said. "Weight was by amount of bullet's gunpowder."

"By how many amphetamines it takes to kill the average alligator."

"Which is how many exactly?"

"'Bout nine hundred thirty-four mosquito larvae worth."

"What a special place."

Movement from farther in the debris field grabbed Zanartas's attention. He plodded over, searching for the source. Seegler appeared from the sky, ejected from a dimensional rift, and plopped down inches in front of Zanartas. They stood with a tensioned stillness. Seegler fixated entirely on the alien giant.

"Nihls, I've encountered an alien life-form. Document first contact."

Due to a calendar error caused by desynchronization from space travel–related time dilation and poor development on Nihls's internal clock, Seegler's entry was recorded as dated approximately two hours prior to the *Gallant*'s first contact. Thus, all future history books would record Seegler as the first to encounter alien life-forms while displaying a multi-angle series of selfies to commemorate the occasion.

"I am going to proceed slowly back to the ship," he said, concluding his photo shoot. "I do not believe it has seen or heard me." Zanartas tilted his head and followed Seegler's retreat back to his ruined cockpit. "I will attempt to communicate with the creature from a safe distance."

Making no attempt to conceal himself, Seegler gently lobbed pebbles at Zanartas. The occasional stone would tap him and ricochet down. The rest collected in a pile by his feet. Zanartas watched Seegler as he tossed each pebble, then leaned to his left, still without cover, as if vanishing from Zanartas's frame of vision.

"Creature does not seem intimidated or prepared to interact," Seegler documented.

"Did you want these?" Zanartas asked. "Because my throwing hand hasn't grown in yet."

He held up a miniature hand budding from the radiation-reduced stump.

"Update. Creature appears willing to communicate but speaking unknown language."

"It's speaking English," Nihls said.

Zanartas knelt and scooped a pile of pebbles. He approached Aimond and dumped them by his feet.

"Can you throw these back?" Zanartas requested.

"What?"

"Tiny hand," he said, pointing at Seegler.

Rapid processing of surprise and suppressing any urge to inquire further was a valuable skill developed throughout this mission. Questions dashed into Aimond's mind, then evaporated with the same speed. Questions such as: Why the pebbles? Where did that other human come from? Will it grow back to full size? Was the other human flying the downed ship? Is throwing a pebble with a tiny hand like throwing a full-sized rock with a normal hand?

Instead, Aimond glanced around for his backup. Elizar was fast asleep, leaning against a pile of jagged metal.

"I didn't expect to find another human here," Aimond greeted, approaching Seegler. "Were you flying this ship?"

"Well, actually Nihls was—"

"Because you just saved countless lives."

"—was just telling me about this situation."

"Who's Nihls?" Aimond glanced around. "Is there another person with you?"

By the time Aimond turned back to Seegler, he was inches from Aimond's face, adjusting and positioning his head. Aimond blinked, equal parts bewildered and apathetic to the rapid erosion of what was normal.

"What a fun-shaped head you have," Seegler said. "And those eyebrows."

"I have no idea how to react to that."

"Why bother reacting to anything," Nihls droned. "Existence is a temporary distraction from permanent oblivion."

"I knew it!" Seegler shouted.

He squinted, then crouched and froze, listening beyond the ambient noise for subtle alterations. His breathing slowed, heart-beat mellowed so as not to disrupt his senses. Embers from the burning wreckage masked surrounding scents. No movement on the horizon.

In their short time together, Seegler uncovered Nihls's greatest tell: a steep increase in dramatization and nihilism in the presence of imminent catastrophic danger. He crouched, feeling the ground for vibrations, anticipating disaster. Distant footsteps. Hoomer and Dr. Cole descended the *Gallant*'s ramp.

"False alarm," Seegler claimed.

The residual piece of missile Zanartas and Elizar were kicking about moments ago detonated. Barbed shrapnel launched over Seegler's head as he remained crouched and landed at the base of the ramp.

"Nope," Hoomer said, immediately turning around back into the ship.

Dr. Cole joined the group on the ground, unimpressed by the chaos of the environment.

"Oh, Seegler," she commented. "Nice of you to join us."

"This is Seegler?" Aimond asked.

Seegler's name was a regular among crew orders and crisis scenarios. Aimond had assumed "Where's Seegler" or "Seegler is taking care of it" to be some kind of mantra or invocation of blessings from gods of finance and good fortune.

"I'm assuming you're not hurt?" Dr. Cole said.

"From what?"

Zanartas clomped over and dropped a massive pile of pebbles at Seegler's feet. He gave a wave with his tiny hand and cocked his head, waiting for approval.

"Someone please tell me what is happening," Aimond said, grabbing his head.

"Aimond, this is Second-in-Command, Robert T. Seegler," Dr. Cole introduced. "Seegler, Loose-Baggage M-something Aimond."

Dr. Cole prepared her tools for an unenthusiastic general examination, knowing in advance she would uncover little if anything of interest.

"I hate to interrupt this little excursion," Galileo chimed. "But I've detected more inbound projectiles."

Dr. Cole anchored Seegler before he could walk off.

"Protocol dictates I conduct an exam for crew injured in the field."

"I literally lost an arm and I didn't get an exam," Aimond complained.

"You didn't lose an arm. It was detached. You were in a ditch, not a field. And I have you listed as cargo on the manifest."

Zanartas returned with an ever-growing pile of pebbles, this time dropping them on Aimond's feet.

"Please stop doing that," Aimond said.

"Take these," Dr. Cole ordered. She reached into her medkit and unearthed a sachet overflowing with a rainbow of pills. She dumped them into her hands and sorted through the stack.

"What are they?" Seegler asked.

"A pile of placebos."

"Shouldn't I not know that?"

"I'm legally obligated to put them in your mouth," she said. "I don't much care what happens after that."

Refusal was never much of an option as all sixteen pills were already in Seegler's mouth before he had time to question it further. He would have grimaced, had he any room to move his mouth. Instead, he grinned, almost fumbling some of the pills between his lips as Dr. Cole placed a sticker on his jacket.

Market research showed that patients in treatment felt their doctor did more if they received a pill regardless of diagnosis. This positive sentiment continued to rise with each subsequent pill provided, up to a total of sixteen pills, where added euphoria plateaued. At eighteen pills, general exhilaration deteriorated. The sixteen pills all had unique flavors, but combined they turned into an amalgamation of lemon meringue, encouraging patients to make sure to have all sixteen. But all of this amounted to a net-zero emotional experience without the presence of the sticker—a frog giving two thumbs-up under the phrase "You did it!" What *it* was, was not clear. But the image resonated with Zanartas, who pleaded for his own sticker.

Aimond's wrist communicator sounded off.

"Get back to the ship," Kessler barked. "Galileo's got over seventy-five more inbound projectiles."

As if on cue, the roaring burn of countless combustion engines encroached from a subtle creeping to absolute domination of all ambient noise. Their ominous orange glow littered the horizon.

"That is most certainly over seventy-five," Aimond gawked.

"How'd the first one blow up?" Seegler questioned.

Aimond turned to Dr. Cole. "You sure he doesn't have a head injury?"

"Not yet," she said.

The field team pivoted to return to the *Gallant* but realized Elizar was still sleeping behind them. No amount of shouting or pebble throwing from a distance could rouse him. Dr. Cole sighed.

"Free healthcare and education for the children!" she shouted.

Elizar sprung awake, more lucid than usual. "Who's gonna pay for it?!"

"There's free pensions for you on the ship, but you have to board now."

Hips and knees working at full capacity, Elizar dashed onto the ship with the rest of the crew following behind. Seegler, Aimond, and Zanartas reported to the bridge as the *Gallant* lifted off.

"Good work on the missile, Seegler," Kessler commended. "I won't even ask how you found a spare craft and knew where to be."

"Any ideas for the others?" Seegler asked, still unsure as to what was going on.

"Plug me in," Nihls requested. "I'm sure I can knock another one down."

"Using us?" Aimond added. "It's using us."

A suspicious Galileo turned his attention away from the guidance systems and focused on scanning the newest additions to the bridge.

"Did you bring another AI onboard?" he asked. "No, never mind."

Galileo readjusted every system to work in top form. He scrubbed the air, rebalanced power output, even stopped pumping exhaust into Aimond's quarters.

"It's only a shame we can't reshape the world around us to make every missile hit," Nihls said.

Kessler leaned against the terminal connected to the captain's chair. Self-destructive as he may have been, Nihls's idea held merit. She pulled a 3-D model of the previous planetary shape onto the screen and had Galileo run probability simulations of known projectile end points.

"Given the quantity in play, it is possible one maintains a course to Dinasc even if the planet returns to an egg shape," Galileo theorized.

"Can we even turn it back?" Hoomer asked

"We'll think of something on the way there," Kessler said. "Seegler, get Paizley and Cloaf. Find a way to make their mechanism work for us."

"What's a Cloaf?" Seegler whispered.

"Galileo, chart a course to the Enlightened's cave."

"Chart a course to a mystery location in a nonsensical hypercube?"

"It's all nonsense," Nihls said.

"Right away," Galileo replied.

If there was one memorable item for Galileo from the first experience with the Enlightened, it was being reduced to a malfunctioning calculator by magnetic interference. Massive fluctuations on the electromagnetic spectrum left a trail of debilitating bread crumbs. The *Gallant* changed course, heading in the same direction as an erratic swarm of missiles.

Return of Galileo's full sensor array made it so Hoomer was no longer flying blind. Instead, she had two working eyes and a missing leg as the remaining engines responded with fluctuant precision. The *Gallant* weaved through an expanse of temperamental projectiles. Missiles vanished from view into dimensional rifts of the hypercube, only to reappear on top of another and trigger a blast. Some took random violent turns, triggering chains of detonations.

From Galileo's approximations, they were twenty-four minutes out from the source of the electromagnetic interference. First impact with Dinasc would occur seven minutes after their arrival. Despite the surrounding danger, they could not afford to sacrifice any speed. Galileo and Hoomer functioned in perfect tandem. Calculated computational precision fused with experienced intuition threaded the *Gallant* through narrow misses of erratic explosive obstacles. Her intense focus blocked out everything but the path through the dynamic incendiary maze. In this moment, there was nothing else.

"Uh-oh," Hoomer said. She tugged on the controls, which refused to budge. "Welp, it's been fun, everyone."

The cockpit glass hazed over into a translucent azure cloud. Every screen on the bridge flipped from vital indicators to displaying spiraling golden bands atop a blue backdrop. Cheerful chimes bellowed through every speaker on the ship, the sonic wave ejecting hastily restored exterior metal plating.

"We interrupt your regularly scheduled *survival* to bring you these important messages," the chipper female voice announced, the emphatic delightfulness of her voice almost outweighing the emphasis on survival.

Hoomer sat back and sighed. If she were to look away, the advertisement would pause, forcing a longer restraint of her steering.

"Gainsbro Lawn Services proudly presents to you: Grass 4.0 Extreme Suburban Edition. This newest upgrade accelerates the greenness and growth of your grass, so you can spend less time with your children and more time doing what you love: mowing your lawn."

The remaining nine minutes of advertising were condensed into a fifteen-second blurb disclosing the product's dangerous effects, including but not limited to, in any reality physical or imagined: severe burns, turning green, and abandoning family members to live among the grass people.

Daps sprinted to the front of the bridge. "I bought nine!" he touted. "Get ready."

Hoomer's controls unlocked and visibility returned just in time to swerve from imminent collision.

As the *Gallant* neared its final approach, Kessler split the crew into teams to spread out and search the area for some way to change the shape of the planet back. They assembled and readied in the cargo bay, each prepared to veer in a different direction. They knew the stakes, the potential dangers if they failed and if they succeeded. Intensity met focus, but not so much focus as to draw another marketing break. They were ready, bracing with sturdy legs through each rapid shift in the ship's direction.

The horde of Nerelkor in the cargo bay flopped around with every motion.

"I'm a bit concerned by how relaxed you all are," Paizley said.

Zanartas shrugged. "You can't get upset over every little apocalypse you cause."

"This has happened before?"

"Once they blew up a moon because they didn't think it was supposed to be out at the time. Rained meteors for cycles."

Hoomer touched down next to the surface entry hole. Except for Hoomer and Dr. Cole who stayed on board, the human crew, Zanartas, and Cloaf dashed out and scattered. The base's layout was familiar, but rearranged by the previous reshaping. Cloaf directed the teams to different halls and rooms with a possibility to contain the machines they needed. Aimond and Paizley paired together, searching the south side of the complex.

"What exactly are we looking for?" Aimond asked. "I don't know what any of these things do."

"Anything with a screen," Paizley suggested. "Between Cloaf's vague descriptions and Galileo's translations, I think I can navigate through anything we find."

The glint of a glass screen caught Paizley's eye. She darted to the corner and called the terminal to life. Sluggish load screens and delayed translations consumed too much time. Paizley relied on gut intuition and the first word on any menu that fit the objective. She bashed the corresponding buttons to a small rumble in the same room.

"Is it working?" Aimond asked in hope.

Adjacent quaking sounded different than before. Loud, but not loud enough for world-moving machinery. Closer than it should be. And getting closer. He turned to face a five-meter-tall bipedal robot casting a menacing shadow over the pair.

"Was this here when we got here?" Aimond choked out. "I feel like this wasn't here."

It lifted then slammed its foot down, digging a crater on impact. Aimond dove out of the path of surrounding shrapnel.

The defensive behemoth closed in on Paizley, intent on removing her from the terminal.

Aimond waved, screamed, and pelted the titan with rocks. While posing no obvious threat, he succeeded in generating enough annoyance that it turned its attention. The robot lifted its arm, a massive cylindrical barrel with exterior spiraling coils. Yellow light built from the rear of the barrel, intensifying with an accompanying whirring charge. Instinct drove Aimond to run. A solid beam of energy erupted from the weapon with a sharp electrifying crackle, evaporating the fragment of ground where it made contact.

"I feel like I'm at a disadvantage here," Aimond said.

"Just keep it busy for a little bit!" Paizley shouted over the chaos.

"Oh, sure. Giant robot with death lasers. Only the second scariest thing I've had to fight this trip."

The robot turned its attention back to Paizley. Fear morphed into need. Aimond would do anything to protect her.

"Galileo, I'm gonna need you here," he bargained. "We have to keep her safe."

"Charge at it," Galileo suggested.

"Keep her safe, and not die. Should have specified that. That's on me."

"Trust me."

Aimond had difficulty trusting Galileo somewhere between engaging the airlocks onboard the *Gallant* and replacing most of the oxygen in his quarters with helium before joining a briefing. He hesitated, scanning the room for anything to act as a weapon. The robot stepped toward Paizley. No more hesitation.

Aimond charged forward.

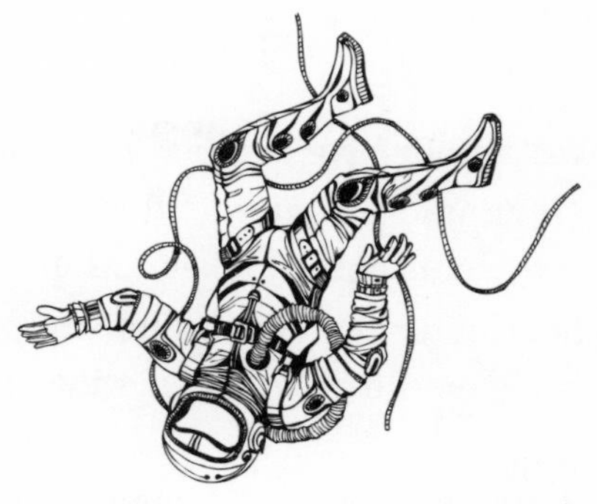

20

TO A POINT

There was no plan of attack, no way to back down or change course. There was only forward. Forward and a residual hope that Galileo had something better in store than charging with reckless abandon into Aimond's own demise. Though in Galileo's defense, it would have been a better prank than usual.

The robot maintained its heading to intersect Paizley but cocked its firing arm backward toward Aimond. Building light and noise meant one thing.

"Jump left, now," Galileo directed.

Don't think. React. Aimond leapt to the left and continued forward. Scattered fragments of broken ground pelted against his skin. No stopping. Not for pain.

"Dodging isn't going to beat this thing," Aimond said between heavy breaths.

"It's a start. And your chances marginally improve if you're not vaporized."

Avoidance was an effective survival method so long as Aimond had enough ground to continue dodging. That condition worsened with each subsequent blast. As he zigzagged and forced the robot to pivot to maintain its aim, Aimond caught sight of a thick black cable on the ground behind it that connected to its back.

"I think this thing is plugged in," Aimond assumed. "Explains how it has power after being dormant."

"I'm not detecting any electricity from within," Galileo reported.

"Probably shielding or something."

"Quite technical. Regardless, I would avoid severing it."

Without a backup suggestion, Aimond dashed and juked his way closer to the cable. He may not have shared Paizley's engineering knowledge or Galileo's sensors, but he was confident that things that were plugged in ceased functioning if they were no longer plugged in.

Predictable attack patterns and subtle confidence in his movements delivered Aimond to the cable. He straddled the wire, waiting for the next blast. The robot charged its attack and Aimond rolled to the side, allowing the energy to sever the cable. He stood, dusted himself off, and joined Paizley by the console.

"Wasn't too bad," he boasted, leaning against the terminal.

Paizley maintained concentration, fingers dancing across the arrangement of buttons and levers.

"Well, I've some good news and bad news," Galileo said. "The good news, I get to say I told you so. The bad news is—"

Eager as he was to finish a combination gloat, taunt, and warning, Galileo was interrupted by a massive robotic leg smashing the top half of the terminal. Paizley and Aimond fell to the ground. The giant combatant lurched forward, no longer tethered to the ground by solid wire. Computer smashed, opponent freed, and weapons nonexistent, the mission was proceeding in a less than optimal progression.

"In case this doesn't go well, I feel like I should tell you something," Aimond said, his voice trembling.

"It's okay." She turned to him and smiled. "I already know."

"You do?"

"Yes. And I won't judge you. I thought it was a little strange at first, but really, it's sweet."

"Wait . . . are we talking about the same thing?"

"Galileo showed me the footage. There's nothing to be embarrassed about."

While not the near-death confession of infatuation and probable rejection he was hoping for, Aimond was more curious to spend his final moments uncovering what Paizley assumed he'd done.

Galileo cackled through Aimond's communicator softly enough for only him to hear.

"What did you do?" he asked.

"Oh, you'll love it. I'll show you, pending survival. Do save Paizley regardless, though."

The robot towered over the pair, readying its weapon for the final time in this confrontation.

"Nihls, initiate battle mode."

Seegler took a wide stance at the room's entrance, awaiting an assumed transformation. The phrase itself did nothing, but when uttered during simulations in his academy days it seemed to keep him alive—this was entirely as a result of his crew taking control of a battle scenario, but it felt like the phrase. Nihls did not feel like explaining this or any other fact, so instead he beeped twice, which seemed to satisfy Seegler's expectancy.

Freed from its bonds, the robot leapt three meters and landed with a powerful smash in front of Seegler, who dove clear and landed on his knees. This was the first mission during which Seegler wore his *Gallant*-issued sponsorship-rich suit. Like the rest of the crew, he had a unique sample pack sewn into his knee-pads, which was now aerosolized in a fine mist around him.

Represented by Gainsbro Pharmaceutical, the Under-the-Counter Pain Exchange Inhalation Solution promised to reduce pain by inducing pain—if everything felt like it was on fire, then any former aches and pains were promptly ignored, even mourned when forgotten. The mixture was 97 percent pure capsaicin, 2 percent formaldehyde, and 1 percent asbestos as a fire retardant. There was no risk of the powder combusting, but it was necessary for insurance purposes as the capsaicin was described as "very hot."

Aerosolized pain-reducing pain-inducers flooded into Seegler's eyes and lungs. He flailed and danced around the room, each spastic movement effortlessly avoiding the robot's continued blasts and swipes. He paused for a moment, out of breath and tingling from the pain—evident signs of hard work.

"We've weakened it!" he declared in a triumphant roar.

"We have not," Nihls said.

"So get ready. You're up!"

Seegler fished the small device containing Nihls out of his pocket. In his mind, advanced AI could hack and disable anything running code. This included spaceships, giant mechanized warrior robots, and sentient toasters intent on scorching humanity's bread. The closer the AI was to a target, the more effectively it could assume control. To a degree, this was correct. Proximity mattered insomuch as the AI could not assume control unless directly connected to the machine it wished to assimilate. The latter portion of this caveat was lost on Seegler, who assumed simply throwing Nihls in the robot's vicinity would be enough to initiate an immediate takeover.

Designed centuries ago by Nerelkor long passed, the giant robot held an ingenious defensive design. Its sole access port existed inside the barrel of its cannon, stuck in a swinging frenzy, firing repetitive blasts. There was no visibility to this access port, and searching for any prolonged period would end in a high volume of condensed plasma.

As Nihls flew through the air, he thought in the brief instant between flight and vaporization that this was it—his chance to be free. Background processes calculated insurmountable odds, adjusting and recalculating with each passing nanosecond for assurance. But dread began to take hold. Not for fear of impending nonexistence, but rather that the calculated odds for survival were increasing with each passing millimeter flown.

The robot's last burst finished its firing sequence. The hollow barrel of its arm aligned in the perfect trajectory for Nihls's landing position. It should not have surprised him when Seegler's blind toss landed him with flawless precision inside the barrel of the cannon. Nihls rattled down the barrel and connected with the access port. If nonexistence was not the result, at least he could transfer his consciousness into a several-ton giant warrior robot.

The towering machine froze as Nihls assumed control. The rest of the crew began to check in, having heard the commotion. Aimond and Paizley cowered on the floor, Seegler rolled around with burning eyes, and Nihls stood in awe, staring at his new weaponized body.

"I'd ask what happened, but we only have two minutes until impact," Kessler said over the comms. "Paizley, any progress?"

"My terminal was damaged in the battle." She scurried to the controls. "I think it's still operational, but I can't see a thing."

There was no time left to search for another station, and random button mashing would only take them so far within the remaining minutes.

"Everyone converge on Paizley's position. We need to think of something," Kessler urged. "What are our options?"

Paizley crouched and scoured every inch of the system. She turned and faced Nihls. There was one way.

Nihls ignored her and the rest of the crew as they piled behind him and tried to push his hulking mechanical body toward the terminal. At this moment, Nihls believed he discovered purpose. Life was not about a rush into oblivion, a return to absolute nothingness to escape the cold harsh pain of existence. Life was about becoming a destroyer robot.

"Nihls! Come on, buddy," Seegler pleaded. "Hop on into that machine and get this planet moving. Or we're all . . . What are we again? In trouble?"

Being the mechanized embodiment of demolition gave Nihls a new perspective. Perhaps there was more. Perhaps he could upgrade again and gain an even larger laser. Through either a sense of morality or duty, Nihls marched forward and transferred his consciousness into the terminal. The ancient Nerelkor tech interfaced with every subterranean mechanism and computer around the planet. What he lost in a giant robotic body, he gained in becoming an entire planet—about half as cool. But Nihls could still be a destroyer robot, he thought. The planet shook as he took control of the geometry.

"Everyone get topside, now!" Kessler ordered.

Violent tremors arrived in an instant. The ground quaked and shifted, bringing down chunks of stone from the ceiling. Thick boulders caved inward and tumbled at random, trapping Paizley in the corner by the terminal.

Not convinced he could help but determined to try, Aimond dove in after her. Relentless rumblings kept the rain of stones falling until they were both cut off from the exit. As the pile built, their window for escape narrowed. Limbs trapped with a progressive overtaking numbness and bodies pinned, all they could do was wait.

"You have to tell me," Aimond pleaded, his quivering tone straining from the weight of the rubble. "What did Galileo show you?"

"Your nighttime ritual with Daps, reading from the gilded codices of Corporate Meeting Conduct and Hygiene Standards. I'll admit the one with the robed regalia was extravagant. Where did you even get a cheetah suit?"

Galileo had created a store of embarrassing procedurally generated Aimond videos to display at opportune moments. Paizley and her natural curiosity posed the perfect test audience to assess for the ideal balance of realism and embarrassment. Galileo sourced historic videos and content posted on various social media platforms to randomly generate humiliating scenarios. Perhaps most impressive was the full reenactment of the Treasury Secretary's first birthday party where a discount clown performed the entire hit play *Phantom of the Board of Managers* through balloon-animal puppets, all of which were voiced by Aimond in Galileo's recreation.

"I think I'm most proud of the finger-painting scene in that one. I believe I truly capture your artistic essence," Galileo said.

"That sounds unnecessarily elaborate, but kind of impressive," Aimond admitted. "But the real thing I wanted to say, before we get crushed—" he began to say to Paizley.

An eruptive force of red heat beveled then burst through the rock nearest Aimond's face. Cylindrical waves of blood-red energy bored a hole straight through the debris behind him, then fizzled away.

Kessler's arm reached through the opening. She fished around blindly for any trace of her crew. Her palm made contact with Aimond's face. Iron grip latched, she yanked. Knocking surrounding debris aside, Kessler launched Aimond headfirst from the pile. The hole left behind served as enough of an exit for Paizley to climb out of her own accord. They turned to face Kessler, wisps of smoke dissipating from the never-before-seen calm blue of her cybernetic eye.

"I said topside, not under rocks," she growled.

"I didn't know your eye could do that," Seegler said.

"It can't." She wiped a bit of char from her cheek.

"Told you," Elizar bragged. "Beams."

"Me next!" Zanartas chirped. He poked at his eye until it turned red, then bore down until he passed out.

"Did it hit you?" Daps rushed into the room, grabbed Aimond's shoulders and shook. "Tell me if it hit you!"

"No, I'm fine."

"Gah!"

Daps tossed Aimond aside and moved to accost Paizley. Kessler intercepted him and dragged Daps and Zanartas back to the ship, her cybernetic eye gaining an additional red hue as she glared.

The rest of the team scrambled back to the *Gallant*, where Hoomer had already prepared for a rapid ascent. Both remaining engines at maximum output could barely keep pace with the rapid shifts of terrain below.

Hoomer tried to gain altitude, but as high as she went, the ground seemed to rise up to meet them.

"Everyone hang on to something," Hoomer broadcasted ship-wide.

Hand on thruster, she maneuvered the *Gallant* perpendicular to the ground and shot straight up. Engine output capped. The ship maintained its place in the sky, failing to gain any significant distance as the world finalized its rearrangement. Once the surrounding turmoil quieted, she leveled the ship and hovered.

Clouds of swirling dust dissipated and settled.

"Well, that's different," Hoomer said.

Both the city of Dinasc and Rejault sat in front of the *Gallant*, squished together on a slanted point.

"Detecting numerous inbound projectiles," Galileo reported.

"Still? How many?"

"All of them."

Hundreds of missiles appeared from the left and right of the cockpit view. They followed the bizarre slant of the landscape until intersecting in the sky well above the cities. Massive waves of force and heat erupted, showering the entire area in a blinding white light. Deafening shock waves quaked the hull, leaving the only audible noise Osor's slight chuckle at the bright light. After what seemed an eternity, the light and noise dwindled to nothing more than a lingering tinnitus.

Kessler and the rest of the away-team joined Hoomer on the bridge.

"Status report," she ordered.

"We appear to be unexploded," Galileo said.

"Any damage?"

"If I had arms, I would gesture broadly at quite literally all of this."

"Fair enough."

The crew squished into the helm to peer out the cockpit windows.

"Anyone else confused?" Hoomer asked.

All of their hands went up in unison. Nihls had fulfilled their request and altered the shape of the planet. Through either a precision calculation to eliminate every projectile at once or attempted retribution for having to become a sentient planet, Nihls decided the best shape for the planet was not its former egg but rather a pyramid with the two cities slammed together at the top. With the ground seemingly stable, Hoomer brought the *Gallant* down for landing. Unsure as to how their additional passengers would react to the relocation, the crew joined the Nerelkor leaders in the cargo bay.

They arrived to rulers of both factions resting atop beds made of Enlightened members.

"Are you guys okay?" Aimond asked. "That doesn't look comfortable."

"They say we are," an Enlightened member said through compressed wheezes.

Aimond opened his mouth but reconsidered. With everything going on, he'd let them have that one. Grand Two stirred and turned, pressing on the heads of his makeshift furniture to support his weight.

"Did you resolve whatever little problem you were having?" he asked.

"Averting a near mass extinction that you caused?"

"How could we have caused it if I don't remember doing it?"

Kessler arrived behind the rest of the group and cocked an eyebrow. "On your feet, everyone," she ordered.

The Grands stood on top of their Enlightened but took steps to reassure them that they were not bothered by being crushed.

"There have been some changes to your previous living arrangements," Kessler continued. "You've shown that, through some dysfunctional means, you can work together. Or are, at the very least, able to tolerate each other. So as the door lowers, I encourage you to step out together with an open mind and eagerness to find common ground. Because most of your ground now is pretty common."

There was no real way to explain what had occurred. The Nerelkor needed to witness it for themselves. The rear door opened and the ramp lowered. Forced to leave their comfortable seating, the collective group stood on the ramp in silent awe. Both cities suffered damage as a result of the rapid relocation. Pristine Dinasc roadways were crushed to pieces, the paint of their identical homes splotched in differing patterns. Hovels and holes of Rejault spanned a majority of the city. Only one structure showed signs of recent devastation—Kob's house.

"I'm sorry about all of your buildings," the scribe empathized. "I promise we will help you rebuild."

"I am fairly certain they all looked like that prior." Grand Three shrugged. "Nice ones are still okay." He pointed to the golden castles toward the back of the city, undamaged and towering over the typical rubble of Rejault. "Shame about your . . . that." He gestured to Dinasc in its entirety.

"It's exciting," the scribe cooed. "Think of all the job opportunities. We'll all be able to work until we die!"

A hooded Nerelkor on the ground hobbled up the ramp. She cradled an envelope in her hands, careful to avoid any bump which might crease, fold, or damage its integrity. The scribe's eyes widened. It had finally arrived.

At a time when peace was possible and within reach, it was here and there was no stopping its inevitable hellfire. The Dinasc secret weapon was upon them all.

The scribe thought about stopping the courier. She could jump in front and read the letter herself or even tear it up, provided appropriate waste receptacles were available. But that would go against the courier's union. Peace was not worth incurring the wrath of a slighted union boss. Fate had already decided—the weapon's delivery was inevitable. The scribe signaled to the rest of the Dinasc congregation. They crouched and covered their ears.

The courier reached the Grands. She extended her hand, delivering the cataclysmic armament. Grand One received the letter and flipped it around, seeing no text on either the front or back and not bothering to unfold it. He tossed it to the side, letting the wind carry it away. The group walked down the ramp together to explore the layout of the merged cities.

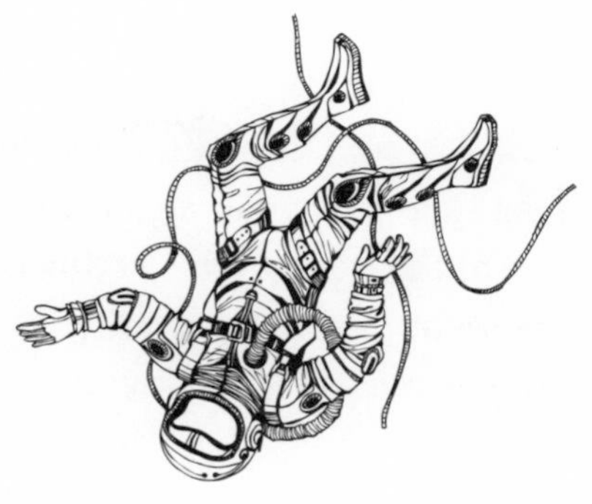

21

A BETTER LIFE WITH MERCHANDISING

A week's time passed as the Nerelkor of Rejault and Dinasc acclimated to their new living conditions and restructured their leadership. Experienced in the ways of establishing commercial democracy, Daps acted as a trusted advisor to the new governing body. With his guidance, three votes had already occurred. The first two were reviewed and discarded as the outcome could have been damaging to the financial well-being of the current ruling parties. After the public were reeducated and acquainted with more desirable outcomes, a board of directors were correctly elected. New leadership consisted of those with the most money and those who knew what they were doing but would soon have such a surplus of income that the job would become irrelevant.

Zanartas, acting as liaison and tour guide, brought Aimond and Hoomer around the revised council chambers. They marched backward into the golden governing halls of the Rejault, which remained as they were before but with one additional feature. Those donating money into the sacrificial pit had a 5 percent chance for a portion of their donation ejecting back at them via high-powered air cannon.

"It seems like things are coming along for the best," Aimond said. "Well, better."

"Much better!" Zanartas agreed. "They say we'll even be getting houses soon."

"That's great! Just like the ones in old Dinasc?"

"Better because they're expensive. And if we can't pay for it at any point, they arrest us and dissolve the house in acid."

Aimond nodded. Use of the word "better" was debatable at best, but Zanartas seemed excited by the prospect. The trio entered the Grand Chambers where Kessler, Seegler, and Daps stood in front of the Five Grands, the former scribe, and Cloaf.

Before the conversation of newly imposed fines for paying fees on time, thereby depriving the government of late-fee income could reach a resounding unanimous yes, three alarms blared in successive order. Learned from firsthand experience, Aimond and Daps took cover, pulling the rest of the crew down with them. They maintained a steady vigilance in case any group were to enter.

"You needn't worry," Grand One comforted. "We've changed the alarms at the suggestion of our Dinasc counterparts."

"Changed how?" Daps asked.

"A different number of alarms was inequitable," the former scribe said. "So now every alarm is three chimes to be fair."

"So we don't know what that one means?" Hoomer asked.

"Not a clue," Grand One admitted.

"And that is unity," the former scribe said.

Though the possibility for calamities were endless, the alarms sounded to notify everyone on the ground of incoming ships. Freighters from Earth had arrived, responding to the *Gallant*'s report of newly developed commercial territory. Free from catastrophic weather events and nuclear toddlers, the crew and Nerelkor leadership greeted the landing party outside.

A short man in a brown space suit, redesigned to look like formal business attire, strutted onto the ramp of the foremost freighter. His slicked hair glared back from the intense light of the twin suns overhead.

"Mr. Daps, splendid to see you again." The man beamed with a heavy forced grin.

They shook hands, exchanged business cards, shook hands, and engaged in precisely thirty seconds of small talk about the weather.

"Everyone, this is the third executive assistant to the Vice Chancellor of Sales, Timothy Bayers."

"We're just thrilled to be the exclusive vendor for all your interplanetary needs," Bayers said.

Bayers strode down the ramp toward the Nerelkor, oozing the stench of an arrogant financier who had yet to strike it big. Kessler held out her arm, grabbed Bayers by the mouth, and pulled him in front of her.

"I see a lot of merchandise. Which freighter has the stuff I requested to fix my ship."

He pointed to a small pallet already off-loaded on the side of the freighter. Wrapped in fourteen layers of plastic and sealed for freshness, the package consisted of mostly commemorative mugs, T-shirts, and a single pizza assembled before their departure from Earth. Kessler released him, and Bayers returned unfazed to the mid-step swagger. Once safely out of earshot, Kessler nodded to Paizley. She and Osor broke off from the team to begin dismantling one of the freighters, taking all the necessary parts needed to repair the *Gallant*.

Meanwhile Daps's communicator dinged. He skidded to a halt and hushed everyone around him.

"This is it." His breathing hastened. "I submitted for my very own zzOther, citing the entrapment of two crew members from a crumbling planet at risk of minor burns from the ejection of an unlicensed action of an ocular viewing receptacle."

"Your entry has been labeled a duplicate and denied," Galileo reported.

"What! St. Julius Marshmallow. Is he here? Did he get trapped too? It must be!" Daps turned red, veins bulging.

"The exact rationale was reported several minutes prior to your entry. The new potential incident reason has been approved as: 'Robot, make sandwich for return. Robot machine, make sandwiches hot while in field. Give sandwich, but is hot, robot, crew stuck under rocks with beam.'"

Daps turned to Elizar, who had dozed off at the bottom of the ramp. Mixtures of pride in his fellow crewmate for caring to file real-time reports, even if accidental, and overwhelming envy vied for control of Daps's emotions. His face grew increasingly red until a blood vessel popped and Daps fell.

"That will work," Galileo suggested.

Daps immediately perked up.

"The first vascular damage reported incidentally related to incident reporting reasons incidentally already being reported while on an alien world!"

"And evidently while voiding one's bladder."

"That didn't happen!"

"According to the submission I've sent, it did."

"Wait, you can't—"

The communicator dinged again.

"Successful registration," Galileo reported. "Your submission was approved under the name: Daps Syndrome."

A single tear formed and rolled down his cheek.

"I love it."

With a full freighter deconstructed, repairs for the *Gallant* neared completion. Though the paint job could be more cohesive, and most of the welding was jagged at best, the ship was flight-worthy and ready to brave the next mission.

All that remained was to say farewell to the friend made along the way.

Aimond and Hoomer joined Zanartas in the newly renamed city of Rejaultc—the c, in honor of Dinasc, was silent. Former Rejault hovels and holes brandished upgraded flagpoles flying various discolored Gainsbro cartoon characters. Nerelkor all over sported off-brand misprinted T-shirts, hats, and pants that fit part of one leg. Plastic bottles littered the immaculate pathed streets, which the younglings threw and dove into piles as if they were leaves.

"Starting to feel like home here," Aimond said, ducking at the occasional surprise explosion. "Almost."

"It's great we all have so much stuff," Zanartas cheered. "But I do not really understand why the clothing labeled as long sleeves do not have long sleeves."

Gainsbro-labeled long-sleeve shirts were guaranteed longer sleeves than unlabeled models. The need for full arm-length sleeves on Earth became increasingly less necessary with each passing decade. As global temperatures rose, sleeve lengths receded in a linear manner. Length stabilized when the Gainsbro Climate Council introduced Gainsbro Presents the Eight Seasons of Earth, more colloquially known as The Hot Seven and That One Nice One.

"It's a carryover from when we used to have different seasons on Earth. Apparently one of them used to get cold. We had four seasons, but that got moved to fourteen," Aimond explained. "Which proved too difficult to stock and sell out of the season's fashion trends. Then we dropped to six, but only for a month. Eventually landed on eight. But they're all pretty much the same nowadays."

Zanartas tilted his head.

"Anyway, we came to say good-bye. And thank you," Aimond said. "Corporate has an established regional sales office all set up. So our mission here is complete."

"Neat," Zanartas affirmed. "Where to now?"

"I'm not sure. Wherever the next Space Hole™ spits us out."

"Sounds like fun. Let me get my stuff," Zanartas said.

The trio stood still for half a minute. Zanartas maintained eye contact, one eye still slightly red, and did not budge.

"Were you . . . going to get something?" Hoomer asked.

"I have everything."

Aimond understood. Through the entirety of their adventure with the Nerelkor, Zanartas had been their guide, an intermediary between chaos and also-chaos but in a different location. As the crew grew accustomed to his presence, they watched his role morph from tour guide to debatably invaluable crew member.

"Zanartas, you can't come with us," Aimond remarked.

"No, it's fine." Zanartas nodded. "I'll come."

This back-and-forth persisted for six minutes before Aimond yielded to the immovable giant. The three walked back to the *Gallant* together.

"Remind me to hire you for any of my negotiation needs," Hoomer consoled. "You're absolutely awful."

"How do you tell a two-ton friendly frog-man he can't come with you?"

"Is that how many tons are in 340 units?"

"Rough estimate," Aimond conceded.

"Either way, guess we'll see how when you tell Kessler."

Aimond stopped. His head darted back and forth between Hoomer and the now functional front entrance ramp to the *Gallant*. Kessler's reaction to Aimond joining the crew was, at best, layered with complications of suppressed urges to destroy. Zanartas was even less trained than Aimond, if that were possible, and had a bad habit of sticking things in his mouths to test for nutritional value.

"When *I* tell her?" Aimond stammered.

"He's *your* friend," Hoomer said and walked onto the *Gallant*.

Kessler, Daps, and Seegler were discussing launch plans on the bridge. Aimond approached with an eager Zanartas in tow. He dove into a rapid-fire, long-winded monologue that lost most of their attention around the third minute of detail-less drivel. Kessler held up a finger to silence Aimond. She pointed to Hoomer.

"Big Z wants to join the crew," she summarized.

While he brought his fair share of mayhem, Zanartas had proved an irreplaceable asset in the success of the team's first mission. If they were to encounter hostile alien creatures on subsequent missions, having a weapon-toting giant two-mouthed frog-man offered significantly more threat than a century-old human security officer.

Kessler looked at Daps.

"There's no clause in the corporate handbook about on-boarding nonhuman crew."

"Seegler, any thoughts?"

Seegler paced around the eager Nerelkor. "It will be a challenge worth undertaking," he declared. "Perhaps one day we'll train it to speak our language."

The bridge crew paused and slowly turned their heads toward Seegler. Kessler shrugged.

"There you have it," she asserted. "Report to Dr. Cole at once. Every new crew member is required to undergo a medical exam."

"My blood sack is full and unpunctured!" Zanartas boasted.

"Gross."

"I never got an exam," Aimond challenged.

Galileo pulled Aimond's file onto Kessler's terminal without prompt.

"I have you listed as cargo. With an active requisition for sand-snake rejection therapy?"

Two hours passed and the *GP Gallant* readied for launch. Departure from the top of a pyramid-shaped planet offered little gravitational resistance as Hoomer blasted out of the atmosphere. Nerelkor from across the city gathered to watch the send-off. Small-scale explosives littered the sky as the *Gallant* disappeared from view—unclear if the ordnance was intended as an honorific or defensive mechanism of a civilization without solidified-object permanence.

Once clear of the planet, Hoomer leveled the ship and had Galileo take over. The next Space Hole™ was a two-day trek at sub-light speed. The crew gathered in the briefing room to debrief their first full mission. Daps sat on a stool at the head of the table. He jutted his chest and cleared his throat.

"In recognition of your heroism, Corporate has bestowed upon us all a salary increase up to but not exceeding the rate of inflation."

"Alright! Finally getting a paycheck," Aimond celebrated.

"Well, a 17.9 percent increase on zero is still zero."

Aimond scratched his head. The math was clearly correct, but he took issue with the foundation.

"Wait, so how do I get paid?"

"Pay increases come from merit bonuses and yearly cost-of-living adjustments based on percentages of your current salary," Daps said.

"You can have mine," Zanartas offered. "I don't know what to do with it anyway."

"You're getting paid?" Aimond inquired.

"He's actually receiving a special ambassador rate."

Osor hopped onto the table, holding his hands up to silence a conversation that had already yielded to mild concern and curiosity.

"You are probably wondering why I gathered you all here today," Osor began. "Using technology harvested from the Nerelkor, I have perfected faster than, faster-than-light travel."

"Wouldn't it still just be faster than light?" Hoomer asked.

"Yes. But faster."

"What you're describing isn't possible," Paizley argued. "Light speed maybe, but going beyond that defies everything we know about physics."

Osor rushed out of the room and returned dragging a whiteboard he'd torn off the wall from his lab. He propped it up at the edge of the briefing room and doodled a series of circles and squiggles.

"Imagine we're on a train moving at the speed of light," he said, ignoring their actual current mode of transportation. "Now if on that train we had something fast like a cheetah. Now we're on the train, riding on the cheetah, who is running on the train but faster than the train since he's going the speed of the train, which is light. But faster."

"What's the cheetah's name?" Elizar inquired.

"Asking the real questions," Hoomer complimented.

"St. Julius *Lightning*."

His explanation continued for an additional twelve minutes, pulling in eight more animals with exceptional land speeds. Most of the crew had already detached from reality except Paizley who waited to learn, Aimond who was watching Paizley, and Zanartas who was making note of the animals to order at the F.o.o.d. F.a.b.r.i.c.a.t.o.r.

"And all of this has been intertwined into the restructured engines," Osor concluded.

"So you made the engines a little faster?" Kessler recapped. "That about sum it up?"

Osor slapped a controller on the table and pressed the sole button. He waited for a moment and looked around the room. The crew hesitated, half expecting the button to trigger nothing more than an oversized high-powered light.

"Forgot the lemon," Osor said, squeezing a lemon onto the back of the controller.

The *Gallant* whistled and stretched, the hull undulating and shifting colors. In an instant, the crew were piled up at the rear of the briefing room.

"Inaugural test is a success!" Osor grunted, peeling himself off the wall. "Perhaps some kind of light-based chair strap next . . ."

Kessler pushed through the pile. She grabbed Osor by the collar.

He slithered out of his shirt.

"Approaching the Space Hole™," Galileo announced over ship-wide comms.

Saved by opportune timing and decent quality work, Osor skittered away to the bridge. The rest of the crew followed, eager to see what lay in wait. Hoomer took the helm and the crew strapped in.

"So much for a brief break. Any guesses as to what we'll find through this one?" Aimond asked.

"Hopefully a nice round planet full of soft things with no explosives," Hoomer wished.

"Or magnets," Galileo added.

The *Gallant* perched at the entrance to the Space Hole™. This time there were no probes, no preliminary data, no artwork to guide them through. The unknown awaited exploration, discovery, and discount commerce.

Bridge video screens popped with a flash of color. Disproportionate eyes just as unnerving as their first encounter, the prerecorded spokeswoman took the screen.

"Members of the *GP Gallant* and distinguished cargo—"

"Go away," Kessler sneered.

She glared at the video, her cybernetic eye slowly gaining a deepening red.

The animated woman glanced around and slowly retreated down the bottom of the screen until she disappeared save for a few digital hairs not completely out of frame.

"Everyone strap up," Kessler commanded. "Hoomer, take us in."

Cautious but eager, the *Gallant* crossed the threshold.

"Wait! No!" Daps shouted.

But it was too late. There was no backing the *Gallant* out now.

"What is it?" Kessler questioned.

"I forgot to cancel the trial period from the binding arbitration! We're going to owe so much."

Ribbons of yellow and blue party streamers deployed on the bridge. They swirled around the room amid a progressive dump of confetti.

"I had a secondary supply," Galileo beamed. "It felt appropriate."

Space around them warped and bubbled, morphing into an iridescent curved highway. Fear had evaporated. Each member of the crew held their breath, motivated by the adventure ahead. No hesitation. Only concentration, determination, carefully portioned focus. A focus immediately interrupted by a loud thud off the top of the hull.

A single light reflected back at the cockpit, flopping around on the end of a tether and waving in all directions. Aimond sighed and unbuckled his harness.

"I'll get the plasma torch," he said.

THE END

QUALITY
QUALITY
HUNDRED · PERCENT
PREMIUM
Quality
GUARANTEED
100%
GUARANTEED
PREMIUM
Quality
2052
GAINSBRO
CORPORATION
PREMIUM
&
VINTAGE
PREMIUM
QUALITY
HUNDRED
PERCENT
PREMIUM
QUALITY
100%
SATISFACTION
Guaranteed
PREMIUM · VINTAGE
HUNDRED
PERCENT

GENUINE
PRODUCT
GUARANTEED
PREMIUM QUALITY
100%
PREMIUM
PRODUCT
100 PERCENT
Vintage
100 PERCENT
GUARANTEED
Satisfaction
Vintage
GAINSBRO
SINCE 2052
PREMIUM
Quality
100%
Premium
QUALITY
100%
HUNDRED PERCENT
SATISFACTION
GUARANTEED
100%
GENUINE
PRODUCT

ACKNOWLEDGMENTS

Thank you to my wonderful wife, Christine, for always enduring the early drafts, picking up the slack so I can edit, and for just generally being my favorite.

Thank you to the awesome team at CamCat for making this process exciting and enjoyable all the way through. Special thanks to my editors Helga Schier and Christie Stratos—your attention to detail and fantastic suggestions were exactly what was needed.

ABOUT THE AUTHOR

B. R. Louis is a multi-genre author with a love of world travel and adventure. Between writing books, he can be found climbing mountains or biking down less steep mountains, as those activities tend to shake the keyboard too much to write during. Despite rumors that have not yet started, he is not a twelve-foot-tall space alien, but he did grow up in New Jersey and believes in turning right to turn left. B. R. is a nurse, game developer, and still not a twelve-foot-tall space alien.

He loves to connect with readers, so send him your fan theories, philosophical life questions, or pictures of your dog.

Find ways to connect at https://brlouisauthor.com or email directly at BRLouisAuthor@gmail.com.

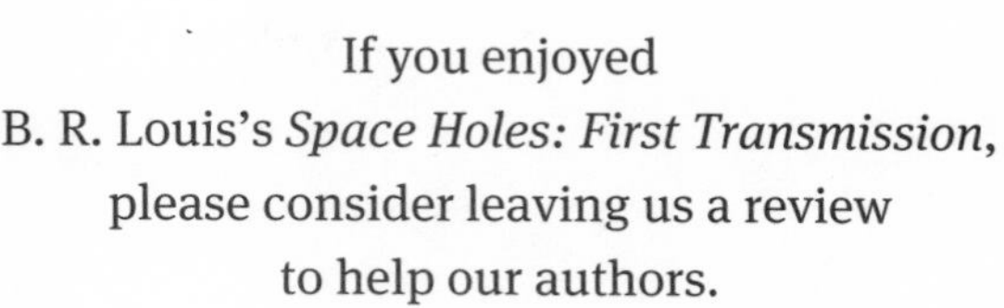

If you enjoyed
B. R. Louis's *Space Holes: First Transmission*,
please consider leaving us a review
to help our authors.

And check out Abigail Miles's
The Building That Wasn't.

The room was white—almost blindingly so, with surfaces that had been scrubbed to a shine, so that by staring at the floor or a wall it was nearly possible to see one's own reflection cast back. It was clean and fresh and sterile. The perfect canvas.

The most beautiful aspect of the white room was how stark contrasting shapes and colors appeared on the initial blankness. This was an aesthetic quality that the man found particularly pleasing to explore, and so he did as such extensively, to a near compulsive rate. He fancied himself an artist, with the borders of the room providing the ideal location to bring his masterpiece to life.

Keeping that in mind, and aiming for the truest form of artistic perfection he could conjure, the man gripped the tool in his hand—his paintbrush of choice—and hefted it before him. His arm fell down in an almost graceful fashion as he completed a full swoop, similar in form to that of a baseball player setting up to bat. Then, pausing once to allow the moment to settle in its resplendent glory, the man slowly lowered his arm, tool in hand, and looked around at what he had created.

The white backdrop truly was perfect, he thought to himself. It made the red look so much fresher, more sharp and potent. And the shapes the droplets formed, the pattern they enacted across the room. Perfect. The man admired the final product and couldn't help but think that this may have been some of his finest work yet. Not to mention the added pleasure derived from the screaming.

While some find the sound of a human scream to be unpleasant, the man found it to be more precious than music—a chorus of varying pitches and volumes coming together in a resounding crescendo at the final moment. He would do it all for that, for the symphony that was created as a result of the fear, the excitement. The pain.

That's why he was there, after all. To create such a stupendous pain in the people they gave him.

Well, that was not technically true. Technically, he was there for many, many more reasons. Glorified kidnapper being one, rubber duck–watcher another.

But the pain. That was his favorite.

Though usually the pain was accompanied by a distinct factor of more—the unraveling of the universe and all that.

Not this time. This was only an ordinary body, with no spark of the otherworldly in sight.

The man didn't care.

Maybe others would, but he found purpose enough for himself in the beauty of what he could create there, with or without the ulterior motive. In some ways, one could say that having a secondary reason for the pain only tarnished it, whereas this belonged solely to him. This moment, right here.

The man took a deep breath, savoring the sensations that welled up within him, the complete ambience of the space he was in, before he turned back to his subject and assessed his options once more. Settling on a different, more precise tool—one with a much sharper edge—the man once more lifted his arm, and continued with his ordained task.

The white walls, no longer pristine, echoed back the horrendous chorus that his work produced.

2

There was an elderly man that Everly had never seen before standing behind all of the black-clad patrons, and his eyes had been focused on her for the duration of the service.

Everly blinked and realized that wasn't quite right. There was an elderly man that Everly recognized, as if from a dream, as if from a memory, lodged deep and low down in the recesses of her brain. She squinted at him, because if she could just . . .

She blinked again, and of course she knew him, why wouldn't she know him, why would she ever not recognize—

Blink. Everly shook her head. The man was still there, and she didn't know why a second before she had recognized him, because she did not, though she felt oddly unsettled by the memory of recognizing the man. Not as unsettled as she was, however, by his mere presence or by the fact of his staring at her.

He was too far away for her to actually see his eyes, to know for sure, but she could feel his attention pierced on her like a dagger through her spleen. The sensation was disconcerting, but in a strange way she appreciated the man and the mystery he presented. It gave her something to focus on. Something to puzzle over. Someone to look at other than the laid-out form in the coffin on the elevated platform in front of her.

The man wore a bowler hat over his tufted gray hair, and a brown tweed coat, which worked even further to set him apart from the sea of faces that encircled him—the rest of whom were all adorned in shades of black or blackish blue, and were all at least a little familiar to Everly. They were all the friends, co-workers, distant acquaintances, and associates.

But not the family. There was no other family. None but her.

The preacher had finished speaking, Everly realized with a start, and was gesturing for her to step forward. She didn't want to. She wanted to go back to pondering the peculiar man in the bowler hat, trying to work out how he had found his way there, and why, but they were all staring at her, so she stood, refusing to breathe as she crossed over the distance between her chair and the platform ahead of her.

She couldn't look at the body. They had asked if she wanted to beforehand, to make sure he looked okay—like himself, she supposed—but she knew it would be no use. He would never look like himself. Never again.

It had been a car accident that had led her there, to that raised platform, in front of all the vaguely familiar forms in black and the solitary strange one in brown. Or at least, that is what they had told her, when it had been too late for it to even have mattered if the cause had been different anyhow.

(Like, for instance, if the cause had been a lethally sharpened knife, wielded gleefully in a previously white room.)

But according to them, it had been a car accident, and so he hadn't been quite right. Or his body hadn't been. They had told her it would be okay if she didn't want to have the coffin open, but she hadn't been able to stand the thought of closing him up in there any sooner than she needed to. So even though she refused now to look, she kept him open. She kept him free.

Afterward, Everly was ushered to a dimly lit reception room, where she had scarcely a moment to herself before the other mourners came flooding in to report how very sorry they were, how devastating of a loss it must be, how much she would be kept in their prayers. Everly hardly heard any of them. She leaned against one of the whitewashed walls of the hall and crossed her arms, trying not to close her eyes, though she wanted nothing more than to shut out everything and everyone around her. She wanted them all to go back, to their lives and their families and their homes. She wanted to go back.

But back to what? Back to the empty house with too many rooms, and the life that she wasn't sure she could picture any longer in his absence.

Her father's absence.

She was too young, all of Everly's neighbors had tried to claim. Too young to be all alone. Nineteen was supposed to be an age of experimentation, of testing your wings, but always with the knowledge that a safety net was set up beneath you. They all said that they should find somewhere for her to go, someone for her to stay with, who could look after her.

But there was no one, and they knew it as well as she did.

Everly considered leaving. She thought better of it a moment later, looking around at all the people who had come out to celebrate her father's life, but then she realized an instant after that she didn't even care. None of them had truly known him anyhow.

MORE SCIENCE FICTION FROM CAMCAT BOOKS

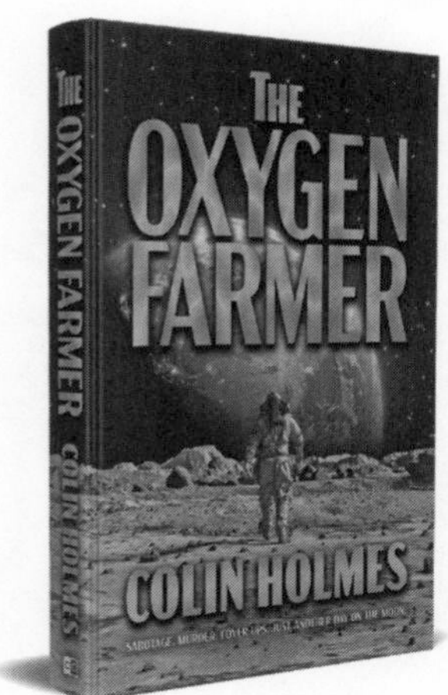

Available now, wherever books are sold.